Show Me

By

Gill Burnett

Other Books by Gill Burnett

Take Note
Note Taken
Last Note

Cushie Butterfield
Who Said That???
Mack Book

By Gill Burnett & Freddie Jones

Eddie the Elf

Copyright © Gill Burnett 2023
This book is sold subject to the condition that it shall not, by way of trade or otherwise, be lent, resold, hired out, or otherwise circulated without the publisher's prior consent in any form of binding or cover other than that in which it is published and without similar condition including this condition being imposed on the subsequent publisher.
The moral right of Gill Burnett has been asserted.

The Final Countdown

'Bye, all the best to you too!' I said to the back of Jan and Peter as they ran over to the opening door. I don't think they heard me, the windows were closed and to be honest I don't think that they were that bothered about me, they had both had a few drinks and had been in a hurry to get from Jan's mam's house, where they had left their kids, to their friends house; where by the looks of it, the party was in full swing. They were nice. I was sure that they would have dragged me in for a drink if they knew where I was going next.

Not to worry, the crowds were getting rowdier; I could hear them all shouting and screaming. It was almost midnight – a new year was dawning. I moved myself into a space and then waited. I strained my ears for Big Ben to toll its first chimes of midnight, but it was so noisy. And then the crowd started – 10. As always in these situations I put my own spin on it, word association; well in this case number association!

10	-	Years since I last got married
9	-	Points on my licence – not good
8	-	Dress size (in my dreams)
7	-	Miles to next destination
6	-	Hours I've been at work
5	-	Best friends
4	-	Sisters
3	-	Ex-husbands
2	-	Daughters
1	-	Just over one month until my 50th birthday

Big Ben chimed and the shouting and singing began. 'Happy New Year….. Happy New Year …….. Should Auld Acquaintance be forgot and never brought to mind …. Should Auld Acquaintance be ………….
'Happy New Year Val!' I said to myself out loud.
Looking around the street was deserted. If there had been 'first footers' kicked out with their piece of coal and their tot of whisky; they had obviously already been welcomed into whatever house they had stood

shivering outside of. There wasn't a soul about; the houses twinkled with their hundreds of fairy lights; it looked like a Vegas strip, but there were no revellers to be seen.

New Year 2013 was very different to the New Years of my youth. In my day we would have been conguring up the street. God I was starting to sound like my mam – 'in my day!' When had that started to happen?? If truth be known, probably when I became a mam, I could remember telling myself off when I found myself saying to one of my girls 'You'll be a mam yourself one day and then woe betide you!' Just like my mam had said to me. What did that even mean??? 'Woe betide' was it another relic left by the Romans along with their wall?

I still had a few minutes to kill. I checked my mobile, no new messages. But in the spirit of New Year I quickly drafted a quick Happy New Year love u XX and sent it off to my nearest and dearest. 'Now what??' It was pointless moving on, I'd be too early, so helping myself to one of the Roses I had with me, I continued to sit.

Already there weren't as many twinkly lights, obviously some people had stayed up long enough to welcome the New Year in, but had scuttled off to bed as soon as the chimes had stopped ringing. I didn't blame them, bed seemed like an awfully nice place. I didn't think I would even be catching a glimpse of mine until early morning. Never mind, it went with the job and what else would I be doing tonight if I wasn't sitting there?

I couldn't answer that. I really didn't know. I had had some brilliant New Years in the past, but for the past 7 years I had chosen to work them. I looked around me, still nothing and nothing sprang to mind to what else I would really want to be doing. The chocolate had been an orange centre and had left a horrible taste in my mouth; that was the thing about picking chocolates in the dark; you just never knew what you were going to get. 'Argh well, best have another go' I said to myself as my hand rummaged around the shiny papers hoping to find the elusive purple one which had long been my favourite.

What else could I be doing??? I never felt like I was missing out on anything by choosing to work New Year, to be honest in my line of work you had to work when it was on offer, God knew what the next hour would bring never mind days weeks or months. So that was my philosophy; I worked when I could and when I had no work I caught up with all of the people and things I had missed out on by working. It made for an erratic lifestyle, but no two days were ever the same so boredom didn't really get a look in.

Next year, I thought to myself. Next year I might actually take the Festive Period off, after all 2013 is a big year for me. I'll have hit the big 5-0; seems like as good a time as any to let my hair down. Maybe!! I'll just have to wait and see what the year brings. That was the thing with me, I wasn't very good at long-term planning. My mobile started ringing. 'Hi Val with a Vehicle!' For the next few minutes I chatted to one of my regular customers, after the customaries were over she said she wanted picking up from work in the morning if I could; it seemed her better half was a little worse the wear with drink and she didn't want him getting caught driving in the morning whilst he was still over the limit. Always happy to oblige, I agreed, writing a little star on my hand to remind me that I would have to write it into my diary when I got home.

And that's who I am. Val with a Vehicle. Not the catchiest of business names, but when I chose it there was method behind my madness. It was all to do with the 'v's. I had got it into my head that if my car carried the name 'Val with a Vehicle' then underneath that I could put 'Va Va Vroom', so that's what it says 'Val with a Vehicle – Va Va Voom' and it's like Thierry Henry speaks to me. The thing is though, unless you know who I am and what I do, the name makes me sound like a removal company. I've lost count of the number of times people have rang me up asking me to move three piece suites and beds, but it always makes for an interesting conversation when I tell them I'm actually a taxi. Not your usual bog standard taxi, I'm female friendly; I like to say that I guarantee women a safe journey home or to where ever it is they want to go. Not that I don't carry men mind, I just like to know who they belong to. I don't do random men; not at my age anyway!!!

But that's my job. Sometimes I love it, sometimes it drives me mad. I'm good at it though, I like to think I mean more to my customers than being just a taxi driver, I think I do, on Christmas morning there were bundles of gifts under the tree, mostly chocolates but there was the odd bottle of wine or two; which I inevitably pour into glasses for other people as since starting the business I also seem to have taken the pledge!

It's tying yes. But the advantages certainly outweigh the disadvantages. I have lovely customers. Hand on heart, there isn't a single customer who I could say that I didn't want. I have learned so much over the years, I could write a book. Everyone has a story to tell, old and young alike. I mean I work in the town I was brought up in, my customers are the people I have seen all my life, but until I started my business I didn't even pass the time of day with most of them, now they are my friends.

It can be lonely mind, for every customer I take or collect from somewhere, one of the journey's I make will be alone.   I don't get scared, I won't let myself be, but there is only so many CD's you can listen to or radio stations to tune into, sometimes it can be very quiet and that's when it's my thinking time. Good things, worrying things, or just things – over the years I've learned to appreciate these times, I'm lucky having a chance to think when I'm out and about means that most nights I'm asleep as soon as my head hits the pillow or sprawled out on my settee, I don't have all the thoughts crowding my head at bedtime, I'll usually had a chance to sort them into some sort of semblance through the day.

The whole taxi thing has made me a bit quirky mind. Not that I wasn't quirky before but my superstitions seem to travel around in the taxi with me. I'm always counting magpies – one for sorrow, two for joy, three for a girl etc etc and I'm surprised I haven't been arrested for dangerous driving after I've seen a funeral. I don't even know where that superstition came from, it's just something I have always done. If I see a funeral cortege I have to hold onto my collar until I see a dog. Some days I have driven miles; especially in the winter when the dog walkers all rush out when the weather fairs up; I'm buggered if it's raining or snowing. But I've grown wise over the years, I know where the window licker pooches are and if all else fails I'll make a special trip to see them. See quirky, but not weird, I just don't like to jinx myself.

But then there's the sign thing…... maybe I do spend too much time by myself. Lots of people look for signs, that isn't particularly weird. If I want to make a decision about something I ask the heaven's above for a sign. Sometimes it happens as clear as a bell, more often than not they are more subtle. I don't do it all of the time, just when I'm in a dilemma, not even sure if it gives me the right answers. On reflection two of my ex-husbands became new husbands because of my tried and trusted method, maybe I should have given it up after the first one ended in disaster! Even taking all the ill-judged advice I have received in the past, I still throw my life to the lap of the God's; three blue cars in a row; a long since forgotten song on the radio; a name, all these things I take of signs that I'm on the right road.

'It's a good job I just do all this stuff for myself' I thought as I eased the taxi away from the kerb, it was 12.10am; plenty of time to make the 7 miles to the hotel where I was picking up my next fare at 12.30am. 'This is going to be my year! This is going to be my story! This is the year that Val with her Vehicle Va Va Vrooms…………

8

Sisters are Doing it for Themselves

I'm Val Collins, or to give me my formal title I am Mrs Valerie Mary Collins nee Mills nee Craig nee James. I was born on 14th February 1963 which makes me 50 on my next birthday. Half a century…. 50 years I've been in existence and what a 50 years they have been. I'm a middle child; two older and two younger. And all girls. In the space of the ten years that my mam and dad had had their family, they had produced five bouncing baby girls. My poor dad, a houseful of women for over twenty years; even when we all started to flee the nest one by one, both my grannies had come to live with us, it had really only been the past 15 years or so that there had been just the two of them. If he was disappointed he never had a son; he never said. In fact if anything he thought that having almost half a dozen little girls was a sign he was a 'real man'. 'Anyone can make a baby' he would say, 'but only a real man could make girls!' And how he reaped the benefits of all us girls now, we all fussed around him, well both of them, like mother hens. I had lost count how many foreign holidays they had been on, it seemed that as soon as any of us thought of dusting off our passports, we'd be on the phone to them asking if they wanted to go too. They say that a 'son's a son until he meets a wife, but a daughters a daughter and you have her for life' and that's very true, most of us hadn't ventured too far away from them and had a habit of popping in all of the time along with our assortment of families. But back to me.

There's a lot of 'nees' but it all started with Valerie James. Born in the early hours of Valentine's Day, my mam had wanted to call me Valentine. But like my sisters before me, Avril born in April, Julie born in June and the next youngest one to me Janet; born in January; she had bottled out of calling us names associated with the times of our birth. It was only our youngest sister, born on Christmas Eve Eve; that had aptly been named Carol.

Considering mam now has an assortment of Great-grandchildren named Sky, India, Phoenix, Jet and Rocky, I think she actually kicks herself at not having the courage to have daughters April, June, Valentine,

January and Holly, obviously the Holly is my spin on a Christmas baby name and one I'm sure my mam would never have considered.

Our house was always noisy; well with five girls in it was never going to be quiet and serene, there was always a disagreement going on, especially with us middle three. Avril and Carol seemed to me to have more privileged positions in the household; Avril oldest and quietest had an authoritarian air about her, what she said went whether she was right or wrong. She is still like that today, we can't make any decisions as a family without having Avril's stamp of approval on it. The upside of this is she is very organised and great to have around in a crisis, she looks at things with her managerial eye and more often than not takes over the situation, whether you want her to or not. But all in all she is nice. Never really getting to know her when we were growing up, it had been Avril I had turned to when my first marriage had gone pear shaped, she was the one who said that I could cope as a single parent, that I didn't need David and his ways, that I could survive the break-up and come out of the other side smiling; and she was right I did and I didn't need him. But hand on heart; I couldn't have done it without her. So when the others all twist and moan about her being bossy; I'm her ally, it's just her way and I love her for it and will defend her until my end.

Carol on the other hand, being the youngest was spoilt. And like Avril; even as a woman she hasn't lost her traits. 45 now, she sometimes goes on like a 13 year old with her stroppy tantrums. My mam and dad still pander to her, her husband spoils her rotten, even her kids seem to go out of their way to keep her happy. Is it because she is the youngest? Or is it just her nature?? Nature or nurture??? She isn't bad, far from it, she has a gentle soul. But it's her way or no way, always has been. So growing up, while the three middle girls fought and scrapped their way to adult hood, Avril and Carol were left alone to develop their own distinct personalities.

The three of us in the middle were like triplets. There is only four years separating us and looks wise, when we were little we looked the same, especially if we were separate. Together, we were different heights and

I inherited my dad's nose whereas Julie and Janet have my mam's. But we were often mistaken for each other; that was until we hit our teens and we changed our looks to suit our tastes in music. Janet was a big Adam Ant fan and breezed around the house in a flurry of feathers and war paint, something me and Julie would never have considered, she looked ridiculous. We were far too sophisticated for all of that and were more into the 'new romantics' look; frills and 3 inches of make-up. When we all discovered boys, our squabbles turned vicious. There's nothing like a good looking boy to throw a proverbial spanner into the works. And it was Janet's first boyfriend who caused the most trouble. Adam Ant wannabe – Stephen Richardson was in my year at school. He was so handsome and even though Janet had first dibs on him and they were to all intense and purposes 'boyfriend and girlfriend', he flirted constantly with me and Julie, especially me when we were at school. The Adam Ant thing did nothing for me, but he was so pretty and a proper 'Prince Charming!' Who wouldn't be flattered, but it caused mayhem. Jealousy between sisters is an intense emotion, Stephen would call to pick Janet up and would stand in the kitchen waiting for her, me and Julie would swoon around giving him drinks and crisps; how I wanted him to 'Stand and Deliver', but as much as he flirted back; he only had eyes for Janet. I hated her. I did everything I could to jeopardise their relationship. I hid her eye make-up so that she would be running around the house frantically looking for it with her little piggy eyes on show for all to see; I would spread rumours about him kissing other girls and watch with glee as Janet sobbed on her bed, I was awful.

Even when I got a boyfriend of my own, I still tried to sabotage Janet's relationship. In short I was a cow. But then all three of us were. Whatever one of the others had, I wanted and they did likewise; for about three years we spat and fought and sniped at each other constantly. My poor mam; she must have been sick of us all. It wasn't just boyfriends it was clothes, friends, make-up, books, records, bathroom time; in short it was any excuse for a fight. We wouldn't even talk to each other in school unless we had to, we had our own little gangs of friends and woe betide any of our friends who might strike up a conversation with one of the other sisters.

But then Julie left school and somehow the dynamics of us sisters changed. All of a sudden Janet and me became friends. In fact the three of us got on so much better. None of us were particularly academic; Avril had left school and had got a job working at the bakery where our mam worked, when Julie left she went to work in the local Presto supermarket packing shelves, but she had money and even though we had fought and sniped at each other for years; now Julie always made sure that she gave me and Janet a bit of pocket money each week. When we could we would walk along and meet her at work when she finished her shift. We would go into Newcastle on Saturday afternoons and buy the latest record we liked at Callers or some make-up or a new top and then we would come home and share it. We actually loved each other and instead of fighting and bickering constantly; we became best friends.

There had been no major dramas in our childhood. We had a mam and dad who cared for each other, they both worked hard and although there wasn't loads of money, we didn't go without. Every year we had a caravan holiday somewhere in the UK, there just wasn't the money for holidays abroad. But I don't think we missed out, the holiday was the highlight of our year. No matter what the weather was like we made sure that for those two weeks we had fun; even traipsing around old castles or some other relic was bearable; there would always be something better to do after it.

So all in all my childhood was a happy one. I knew who I was, I knew where I belonged and who with. I had family support and I had been brought up with morals and a good work ethic. Then I met David and within a few months I was bobbing about on the vast ocean of life; totally out of my depth and drowning in a sea of unrequited devotion. I fell in love. David Craig……….

Queen of the Gas Station

I left school with a handful of O' Levels and a headful of dreams. I wanted to be a paramedic; well that's not strictly true, there was no such thing as paramedics in my day – I wanted to be an ambulance woman. I knew that was what I wanted to do, but to be honest had no idea how to go about doing it. Careers advice at school was no help; they suggested college, but that was as far as it went; they were keen to promote hairdressing or shorthand typing; neither of these appealed. But the biggest stumbling block was that to drive an ambulance, you actually need to be able to drive. And there was the first hurdle I would need to climb; I was only 16. So not wanting to waste time going to college and with the mind-set that I would 'go later', I got myself a job.

I worked on the forecourt of my local petrol station and I loved it. I spent my days filling people's cars up with petrol or running into the shop to bring cigarettes or sweets to the waiting motorists. It was all go go go, as soon as one car pulled away there would be another waiting. I loved the smell of petrol that constantly wafted around me and I loved meeting all the people. My boss, Mr and Mrs McCabe, looked after me like a daughter, they showed me how to work the tills, to reorder stock and how to dip the tanks and re-order fuel. I couldn't see myself working anywhere else and before I knew it, the only ambulances I thought about were the ones that came in for their petrol. Go to college??? Not a chance, I had a job I loved and money in my pocket. There was no way I was going to give it all up to go back to school.

By the time I started having nights out with my friends or sisters, I knew almost everyone in our little town; and the ones I didn't know one of my sisters would. Avril was still in the bakery, Julie at Presto and when Janet left school she started working in the local pet shop. So between us a 'James sisters' night out was a cheap one; we got so many drinks bought for us.

Boys came and went for all of us, but there was never anyone serious. Avril had an on off thing going on with one of our neighbours, Alan. He was lovely, but Avril would boss him around constantly, he would take the huff and they would split up for a few weeks, but eventually she would win him back round again and so it would continue. I truly couldn't see Avril with anyone else, but he would have to learn to stand up to her or he would have a dog's life. Julie just wasn't interested in lads, she didn't have time; she had so many friends and when she wasn't at work she was out with them, the only time she stayed in was when she was saving up to go on one of her many holidays. Me and Janet moved around in a gang, mainly made up of people we went to school with. Boyfriends came and went, but there was never anyone serious for either of us. But then one day there he was in my petrol station in his bright orange Ford Fiesta.

I hadn't seen him before, which was strange because normally I knew most of the people that came in or if I didn't know them I knew of them. Anyway I spotted his car in my queue, you couldn't really miss It; it was such a gaudy colour. When it was his turn, he pulled up, wound his window down and as for £2 worth of four star. I hadn't looked at him until I had finished putting petrol in and went to collect his money. He was draw dropping gorgeous and I found myself blushing as he handed over his money. Then he was gone. But a few days later he was back, I put in his petrol, took his money, blushed and then he was off again.

And so it continued.

I asked Mr and Mrs McCabe about him, but they had no idea who he was. I drew a blank with my friend's as well, they didn't know anyone that drove a bright orange Fiesta. It was while I was talking to Avril about my 'mystery man' that my mam shed a bit of light on him. 'Doesn't Tony next door son's drive an orange car??' she said to Avril. Tony was the local barber and his shop was next to the baker's where my mam and Avril worked. Still unsure, both were given a description and told to find out as soon as they could. Blonde, blue eyes, tallish, gorgeous; within a day they confirmed that my bloke was indeed Tony the barber's son.

David Craig, under my radar because he was three years older than me and didn't go to my school and to be honest, if my memory served me right I could remember seeing him in the past when I had gone to the bakery, but he had been a swotty looking kid; glasses and spots, not my type at all. But what a difference a few years makes.

Now I knew who he was, I wasn't quite as shy. I started striking up conversations with him, nothing interesting just "how are you?' or 'isn't it a lovely day?' and then he was gone again and I didn't see him for weeks. Out of sight but never quite out of mind, I watched for his car pulling on to the forecourt, but for months there was no sign. I asked Avril if she knew anything, but she wasn't interested, she was too wrapped up in her own relationship with Alan and I didn't want to push it with my mam, she would be mortified if she thought I was chasing around after a lad. So I waited. Surely he couldn't have just disappeared into thin air. I kicked myself on a daily basis for not having the confidence to talk to him properly when I had the chance. And just when I thought that he had actually disappeared into thin air, he was back.

This time I wasn't going to let him slip through my fingers without at least trying to strike up some sort friendship with him. So that's what I did. I set my cap at David Craig. And to a certain degree it worked. He called me by my name, he was all smiles whenever he saw me. I dropped hints about where I would be on certain nights in the hope that he would pick up on them and turn up, but he didn't and within a matter of weeks he was gone again.

He wasn't interested in me. So this time I didn't particularly give him a second thought; as if. Plenty more fish in the sea and all that, so I worked hard and partied. I had couple of casual boyfriends, but no one really caught my attention and within weeks they were history.

I looked for him constantly, I couldn't help myself. I looked for signs that he would be back. 'If I have three red cars pull up in front of me, he'll be back!!! If I have a bus and an ambulance, he'll be back! If I have four silver cars in the next hour, he'll be back ….. 'But it never happened, the cars didn't materialise and neither did he. It got me through the days.

Then one Friday just before Christmas I set myself the mammoth test of having two each of red, blue, green and black cars. Not a lot you might think, but the weather was atrocious and the forecourt was quiet. I stood most of the day in front of the little calor gas heater in the shop, mainly thinking about what I was going to wear that night. Me and my friends were off to the local social club, it was the annual Christmas party and this was the first year we were all old enough to go. It was a big thing, it was the party of party in our area, my mam had actually got it together with my dad there, so it had lots of history and always sounded like the place to be on the run up to Christmas. I still hadn't decided on what I was going to wear; it was a horrible day and the dress I thought I might wear had no sleeves and was on the short side and I had some new sandals I wanted to put on; wearing a coat was totally a no-no, the other outfit was pants and a fluffy jumper, much more appropriate but not half as sassy.

For the remainder of the day I made my way in and out of the little shop on to the forecourt; I was wearing my mam's Derry boots and a snorkel coat; not attractive but very practical and how I looked was not that important to me until I realised that my 'sign counter' – the little slip of paper that I kept next to the till that I put little matchstick marks against as the relevant vehicle made an appearance – was only one car short of completion. Usually I would be frantically marking the cars off, but I had been so wrapped up in my forthcoming night out, that I hadn't paid that much attention to it. But there it was, in black and white, I was only waiting for one car. My heart was pounding, this was it, one car and then he would be here….

A red car, how hard was that going to be and I still had three hours left of my shift. Easy peasy. I scoured the dull day watching for a glimpse of his bright orange car; I stood at the window, constantly wiping the condensation off the windows so I could see the cars arriving. I knew I looked a clip, but I didn't care. All these months I had been looking for signs and I had never come this close, not with so many cars in play and here I was on the brink of a perfect score. But it wasn't happening. There were only a few customers and none of them had red cars. By the time my shift was ending I was furious with myself for building my hopes up. I was an idiot, he was never coming back; obviously the thought that counting cars was an idiotic pursuit never crossed my mind. I trusted my methods.

But as I started to tidy the shop and cash up for the day, I was miserable. Some headlights flashed across the shop windows, I didn't even bother to check, just pulled up my hood and stomped out onto the forecourt. And there it was. A beautiful red car. I beamed my biggest smile as the driver wound his window down and asked for £10 of petrol. If he thought I was simple he didn't say and to be honest I didn't care. I had my sign. David Craig was coming to get me.

18

Waiting for a Girl Like You

By the time we actually got to the club, the place was heaving. I'd been late in from work, due to the fact I had dawdled around locking up, thinking that David Craig would pull up wanting filling up the instant the red car had gone. But he didn't and as I made my way home my heart was in the bottom of my mam's Derry boots. 'As if a few cars can predict my life' I thought to myself as I ran my bath. It really was very stupid.

The dress ended up being a no-no. As I twirled around in front of the mirror I thought it looked great, I did. But it was my feet. In the delicate sandals I had bought to wear with my dress, they looked like lumps of corned beef, even under the disguise of my tights you could see they were motley. After raiding my wardrobe and those of my sisters, there wasn't a single pair of shoes in the house that did my dress justice. All the cold days in and out of the cold were taking its toll on my beautiful feet, maybe they hadn't been beautiful but I had never been conscious of them before. Janet thought they were hysterical; she said they looked like my Granny's!!!! Cheeky bugger, but I could see where she was coming from, so it was into the jeans, on with the sweater and my hippopotamus feet safely tucked away out of sight in a pair of suede pixie boots.

Job done.

There wasn't a seat to be had when we got inside the function room, as me and Julie jostled our way to the bar for our halves of cider and blacks, we spotted a table where a group of our mates were sitting. The disco was in full swing and the dance floor was bouncing with people dancing to Blondie; I squashed myself between the seats of my best friend; Lynne and another of my friend's; Lorraine, and they did that little shuffle thing so I could rest a bum cheek on each of their chairs. Shouting into Lynne's ear, I told her about my sign and how I was sure David Craig was somewhere in the room. But scouring the faces and the dance floor there was no sign of him. He was like Scotch mist.

Determined not to waste another thought on David Craig and my signs, I spent the rest of the night drinking, dancing and gossiping with my friends. There were loads of lads there I knew, both from school and work and I had a few dances with two or three of them. I really was having a good night. Me and Lynne were on our way back from the loos when someone got hold of my arm. Turning and smiling, I nearly passed out when I saw that it was David Craig. I stopped dead stock still; letting Lynne hold on without me back to the table.

'Hello', he smiled. 'You're the lass from the garage aren't you?' 'Yes, Val' I beamed back at him. Oh my God I thought to myself, my signs ….. 'David!' The music was so loud I could hardly make out what he was saying, but standing on my tip toes I leant into him 'I haven't seen you around for a while!!' I shouted. But before he had chance to answer a little blonde girl came from behind me, grabbed his hand and pulled him towards he dance floor. Looking at me apologetically, he disappeared into the crowd.

'Bloody; bloody; bloody hell' I said to myself as I made my way to the bar where Lynne was queuing. 'I should have known he had a girlfriend!' I was gutted. Seeing my face Lynne was confused about what had happened to me in the three minutes it had taken for me to get back from the loos. 'He's here, David Craig. I spoke to him for a couple of minutes on the way back. He seemed dead interested in me, then his girlfriend turned up and he went off!' 'Where is he??' Lynne asked. Shrugging my shoulders, I nodded towards the dance floor.

Back at the table, I did my best not to crane my neck and look for him. Lynne did though, silly bugger; she didn't even know who she was looking for. But after a few minutes she shouted in my ear. 'Is that him???' Looking to where she was looking, I stretched my neck so I could see above the heads of the people on the tables in front of us. There he was, tall blonde and wearing a bright blue shirt; and there she was, his girlfriend; jigging around in front of him. 'Yes' I shouted to Lynne. 'Very nice!!! I've never seen him before, but I think I know her, not sure from where mind!!!'

I sat, trying not to look. 'Come on, let's dance, let's have a proper look at her!' Lynne said standing up from her seat. She was going on her own so I had no choice but to go with her. Catching up with her on the dance floor, she really couldn't have picked a spot closer to him if she had tried, to be fair it was packed and it did seem like the obvious place to go. But even so!!! I deliberately danced with my back to him, but I was still conscious he was there. Still I enjoyed myself, song after song me and Lynne danced our hearts out through them; other friends came and joined in, some left some stayed. But when the tempo changed and it was time for the 'smoochies', we all filed off the dance floor.

I hadn't taken two steps, then David was standing in front of me. 'Dance??' I was so shocked and confused I followed him back on to the floor. Foreigner 'Waiting for a Girl like You', started to boom out of the speakers. I was like a rabbit caught in the headlights. 'What's going on??? Where has his girlfriend gone??' I couldn't think straight, he opened his arms and I walked into them, wrapping my arms around his neck as he put his around my waist. It was all so weird. But as we started moving, I rested my head against his shoulder; it felt so right. And there we stayed, swaying against each other until the record finished and the next one began and the next and the next. It wasn't until the first bars of Slade's Merry Christmas Everyone started playing did we pull apart. All of a sudden everyone was on the dance floor, holding hands and bouncing around; and David was gone.

Walking home with Julie and Lynne; I told them about how confused I was about what had happened. But as confused as I was, I was walking home on air in my little pixie boots that hid my hideous feet; they both kept saying how good we looked together. It just kept getting better and better. Apart from the fact that I hadn't spoken to him since we danced or even during the dances, or had any idea why he hadn't just danced with his girlfriend. It was such a muddle. A wonderful; blissful; lovely muddle. He was like Cinderella; he disappeared after the ball…. It was a good job that it was him that was Cinderella and not me; the thought of him trying to fit a shoe on my feet made me shudder. Every cloud had a silver lining.

Merry Xmas Everyone

I don't know if I thought I would see him again anytime soon. I really hoped that he would be sitting on the forecourt the next morning when I got to work, but there was no sign of him. It was ok; I was still glowing after my half a dozen dances with him. I could still smell him and I was sure there was an imprint of his hands on my back. It would do. If that was it, then Merry Christmas to me.

It wasn't a day for signs; I was a little bit hung over and I couldn't be bothered. I just wanted to get myself to the end of the day and get myself home. But the weather was better and it seemed like everyone was taking the opportunity of the break to fill up their cars; fearing they wouldn't be able to in the coming days.

A week away from Christmas; most of the customers seemed fraught, cars full of hyped up kids pushed people to their limits. It was a good time for me though, the tips came in fast and furious. I was saving them for the January sales; I had my eye on a really nice coat in C & A's in Newcastle; it was way out of my usual price range, but using my tips and the hope that it would be in the sale on New Year's Day, I kept stashing the tips in my snorkel coat pocket.

It was such a busy day, I didn't realise that David had pulled onto the forecourt until I was standing in front of his window and watching in awe as he wound it down and smiled at me.

'Hi ya, I didn't get chance to say bye to you last night!' he said handing me over a five crispy pound notes. 'Do you want £5 in??' I mumbled back. 'Of course he wants £5 in, if he wanted £4 he would just have given me £4; he ll think I'm an idiot!' I thought to myself. After putting petrol in I made my way back to his window; there was a car waiting patiently behind his, but it didn't look like David was going to pull away until he had another word with me.

'What time do you finish here?' He asked. I was blushing bright red, I could feel the heat burning through from the top of my head to the tips of my horrible rotten toes. 'I finish at 5,' I answered, but it will be about quarter past by the time I cash up the till and lock up!' 'Ok, I'll be back to pick you up then, you don't have plans for tonight do you?' he asked. 'No, no, but I'm not dressed to go anywhere!!!' I blushed even more. 'See you at quarter past five then.' He said and once again he was gone.
The garage was so busy the rest of the day I didn't really have time to panic. I was in my snorkel coat and mam's Derry boots again. The rest of my clothes were even worse, corduroy jeans and an old jumper. I did think about telling Mr McCabe I wasn't feeling well and I would have to go home early, but then thought better of it; how would I explain being back at the garage for closing time done up like a dogs dinner. So as we were closing I nipped into the loo with the tiny mirror and brushed my hair, re-did my eyeliner, mascara and lipstick, then sprayed myself in Charlie.

By the time I had balanced the till it was almost twenty past five, I just couldn't seem to add up. The windows were steamed up again, so I had no idea if he was outside waiting for me or not. 'if he isn't there, I'll just go home, I'm not hanging around the garage in the dark if he hasn't the good manners to turn up for me on time' I said to myself as I took a big deep breath; shouted a cheery goodnight to Mr McCabe and opened the door. But he was there, engine running and door open waiting for me to slide into the passenger seat.

I Can't Help Falling in Love with You

The night went ok. No that's not true. The night was fantastic. After my initial shyness, self-consciousness about what I was wearing and the fact that I could only smell petrol; the Charlie had lost its fight for supremacy over the four-star petrol; we chatted away as he headed the car into the city centre. Panicking a bit about where we were actually going; I sighed with relief when he pulled up in a parking bay outside a Wimpy restaurant. Over a cheeseburger and a chocolate milkshake; I got to know David.

David George Craig. Age 21. 6 foot 1 inch. Slim build. Libra. Student. Likes football and tennis. Dislikes smokers and dogs.

As I sat nibbling demurely on my burger; really I wanted to wolf it down and order another, but decided he would most certainly be put off me if he knew I had the appetite of a horse; I fell in love with him. He was perfect. He had good looks, ambition and he was funny. The mystery aura he had held by me disappeared when he explained that he was actually at Leeds University; hence the long spells of absence. The 'so called girlfriend' was actually a fellow student at Leeds who he travelled up and down in the holidays with. Apparently she was just a friend and had a boyfriend at Uni who lived in the South; he said that was the reason she was out with him at the Club; she was missing her boyfriend, he had a feeling that I would be at the party and he had persuaded her to go with him in the hope I would be there. I was so flattered. Silly me. No wonder she didn't come and tear my hair out when I had all those 'smoochies' with him.

By the time he dropped me off at home, I had the feeling we were on to something. Something big. And we were. When he returned to University in January we were 'girlfriend and boyfriend.' I couldn't have been happier; he was everything I wanted. He had the looks; the personality and he knew what he wanted out of life. And it seemed he wanted me!!!

I had taken him to meet my family; being an only child himself at first he was a bit overwhelmed by us all. But he got over it, my mam and dad thought he had blue eyes, he did but he also had the sun shining out of his backside. My sisters were gobsmacked; they thought he was way out of my league, none of them had ever had a boyfriend at University, so in our house, he was some sort of demi-God!!

David's family were a different kettle of fish. He was their only child; they had their own business and lived in a very 'exclusive' part of the town. I could sense they were disappointed. The first time he took me to meet them I had dressed carefully, I had bought the coat from C & A, still paying more than I would have liked, but it looked good and I wore it especially to meet David's parents. But I could sense that I wasn't what they had been expecting. Too young; not academic enough, worked in a garage and I probably lived in the wrong part of the town. Tony, David's dad put a brave face on, he welcomed me and fussed about asking me about work, family, where I went to school. But his mam, Sandra, didn't even bother hiding her feelings to spare mine. She looked down her nose at me; sighed as I chatted away with Tony and generally made me feel unworthy of even sitting in her 'lounge' as she liked to call it.

But I liked David, loved him even and I was going nowhere. She could do her worst; I had been brought up with a load of squabbling siblings so if it was a fight she wanted that was what she would get. Not that I said anything; I was polite and courteous, timid even; I wouldn't let her spoil what me and David had.

It was early days though, we hit it off straight away; he seemed so much more independent than me. He was living away from home, he was training to be a teacher, played loads of sports and had friends from all over the country. I was no duck egg; but I hadn't really been anywhere, apart from the odd night staying with one of my grannies or friends; I had never been away from my family. All thoughts I had had about being an ambulance women had well and truly gone and I was happy doing my job at the garage. We were chalk and cheese. But it worked. Even when he was away at Uni we were in touch all of the time. We wrote and twice a week I would be sitting on the bottom step of our staircase waiting for him to ring me.

I missed him so much and I was constantly counting down the days until he came home. He didn't ask me to go to Leeds; I wasn't bothered. Sharron; the blonde from the Christmas party, annoyed me so much; she was so big headed, so by my thinking if all of David's Uni friends were like her, I didn't want to know them.

We were an item and I was happy with that. I knew when he left University he would be coming home for good. I had the man of my dreams, so I could put up with the absences. When he was home we made the most of the time we had together. I would work extra shifts on the run-up to his arrival and then take the time off to spend with him. We were inseparable, much to his mother's annoyance. But I didn't let her bother me, she was a tuppence halfpenny snob; David was going to be a teacher not a brain surgeon. She would have to either like me or lump me. She chose to lump me and made no secret of the fact.

A year and a half after we go together he told me he loved me for the first time. We did 'love you's' at the bottom of letters and on cards; but it had never been spoken out loud. It was in the summer and we were at Avril and Alan's wedding. I had been press ganged into being a bridesmaid, 'all of the rest of your sister's are Val, and you'll have to be one as well!' My mam said. I wasn't keen. It was a summer wedding. That could only mean one thing.

Sandals.

I didn't think my feet were any worse than they had been, in fact if anything they were better. Since getting a boyfriend I creamed and talced them daily. In the winter I wore extra socks and under someone or other's recommendation I wore carrier bags under my boots. So all in all; I thought there was an improvement. But they still seemed to get a lot of attention off my sisters. They were my 'Achilles heel or feet', so whenever they were on show; there were comments.

Obviously I had told David all about them, he had seen them often enough. But whereas my sisters had lovely petite feet; mine always looked huge and puffy in comparison. The fact that I was self-conscious about them probably made it worse, they never got air to them; they were always smothercated in socks, even in bed. And now I had the added embarrassment of them being a bit smelly. You could bet your life whenever there was a pongy smell in the house, someone or other would shout and tell me to put my shoes back on….. they just never let up.

But I wasn't going to let a little thing like having my granny's feet spoil the day. Once I got used to the idea of being a bridesmaid, I joined in the preparations with relish. And best of all was that David would be home in the summer – for good. So by the time the big day came I could hardly contain my excitement.

Avril looked beautiful. Never a 'showy' type, her dress was subtle and elegant. She looked like a princess; we all did. As we all sat in our sitting room waiting for the cars to arrive to take us the two minute journey to the church; I could see that my dad was struggling to keep his emotions under control. But I had to admit; together we were a sight for sore eyes.

Smooching with David at the club later that night; he whispered into my ear. 'I love you Val, I promise as soon as I have a job, we'll get engaged and have a wedding of our own!' I was over the moon. 'I love you too' I whispered back. And I meant it.

From this Moment

The declaration turned out to be bitter sweet. I believed him; I knew he loved me. But when the arrangements were made for his graduation in Leeds; I wasn't on the guest list. I knew that it was Sandra's doing, but the fact that David hadn't insisted that I go irked me. I got the horrible feeling that he was in agreement with his mam and I wasn't quite good enough.

All the signs were there that he loved me. When I say 'signs', I mean the red cars and the blue cars. I asked them daily. 'Does he love me? Does he really want to marry me?' The signs said yes. But they were simple signs. One red car and one blue car – signs that were confirmed in my first hour of work. But I consoled myself with the fact that I asked and they appeared.

So off David and his family went to Leeds. I bought him a lovely leather briefcase with his initials on which he would be able to use for work when he got a job, he was visibly touched. It was a rite of passage; a one that if I was going to be his wife, I thought I should be there. I was really upset, but I was buggered if I was going to let it show.

By the time he came back I was over it. We had booked a few days away in Scarborough and I concentrated on getting packed while he was away. My mam did voice her concerns; but I brushed them away, 'not my type of thing!' I said, trying not to let her see that I was hurt by the snub. She didn't push me.

Scarborough was great. We had had the odd night away, but four nights and five days away from everyone was bliss. Just waking up with him was enough for me, we never got chance to do that at home. There was no way my mam and dad would ever allow David to spend the night at our house; it just wasn't the done thing. So the odd snatched night away was all we had managed to have. Neither were each other's 'first' but we were good and it was so nice to go out in Scarborough; have food and a few drinks, go back to the hotel and in the words of one of my favourite films; Mama Mia and then do dot dot dot.

Then things got even better when we got back, David had an interview to be a primary school teacher in a town five miles away. The news that he had been successful completed our summer; and off he went in September to begin his new career. I was so proud of him.
By Christmas we had more reasons to celebrate. Avril was pregnant, David and me got engaged and Julie announced that she was off around the world with one of her work colleagues the following summer. Everything was changing. It was going to be a short engagement, we decided on an Easter wedding. We didn't have a house to find; the flat above the barbers shop was empty and as soon as we told Sandra and Tony we were getting married, Tony suggested that we move in there; at least until we managed to save a deposit for a place of our own. And I wanted Julie there; I didn't just want a telegram from so far flung country; I wanted her there in a flouncy dress along with the rest of my sisters.

Once again the house was all hustle and bustle. My poor dad; I think he must have started saving for each of our weddings the minute we were born. But he handed over the money for the dressmaker, cars and cakes with a smile on his face. He liked David and thought that we would have a good life together. Even though my wedding wasn't going to be as big as Avril's had been, there was still loads to do.

As a wedding present; Sandra and Tony had arranged for the flat to be redecorated; it was something that David and Sandra arranged together. Once again I was left out, whether they thought they were doing me a favour, I wasn't sure. But viewing it for the first time after the decorators had left, it was clear it was Sandra taste and not mine. But I couldn't look a gift horse in the mouth; so I said I loved it and thanked them over and over, but made a mental note to myself to change it when I moved in.

Our wedding day was perfect; I felt like a movie star in my dress. I had known what I wanted and Edith, the dressmaker; hadn't disappointed me. My whole look had a very Victorian feel about it. Off white, it didn't quite reach my ankles and I was able to hide my sore points in lace up boots. A flower garland and short veil completed the look. My bridesmaids; my four sisters, my best friend Lynne and David's two small cousins were all in identical calf length pale green dresses. Avril's growing bump was hidden by her bouquet and all the men in the wedding party wore morning suits with pale green cravats.

We stood at the front of the Church and made our vows to each other. Within a few minutes I was Mrs Valerie Craig; it had been as simple as that. I glowed with happiness; I was married, and a gorgeous husband who had a good job as a teacher, had a home and even when I caught the look of disappointment on Sandra's face as we made our way back up the aisle, I wouldn't let her spoil my day. I had won, David loved me and now I had the respectability of being his wife.

We moved into the flat and started our new lives together. But it was harder than I thought. David was useless and even though he had been living away from home for years, he must have lived on baked beans on toast. He was useless. No, he wasn't useless, he was lazy. I still worked full-time at the garage, but I was also chief cook and bottle washer as well. Cooking, cleaning, shopping; everything seemed to be my job. The only time someone made me even a cup of coffee was when I nipped downstairs into the shop and spent half an hour with David's dad.

David always seemed to have books to mark or lessons to prepare. I didn't twist, his job was far more important than mine and we were managing to save up a fair bit of money; but even so, at 20 years old I seemed to have turned into his mother.

I was really house proud though and loved to show the flat off to my friends and sisters. When Julie was about to leave on her travels I had everyone at the flat for drinks and nibbles. Avril was enormous by that time and we virtually had to stand behind her and push her up the stairs. But it was a bitter sweet night; we were all going to miss Julie so much but she promised she would write and telephone and two days later we were all at Newcastle Airport to see her and her friend Nicola off. It would be years and years before we saw her again.

We visited both our mam's and dad's often, usually for Sunday dinner. My mam and dad's house seemed empty; three of us girls had gone now, there was only Janet and Carol left living at home. Despite scattering, the five of us were close; we were all excited about Avril's baby coming in the autumn and clucked around her like mother hens. Julie always rang on a Sunday afternoon; even if it was the middle of the night for her; she never failed and we all took turns in having a quick word with her, she was having a ball, they were working their way around the world, literally working, they did bar jobs, cleaning; anything really to help them on their journey. I loved Sunday's at my mam and dad's.

Sandra and Tony's wasn't so welcoming. On the surface Sandra was all smiles and lovey dovey. But she was quick to cut me out of conversations; sitting around the dining room table all the talk would be about David and school. What he was doing? Who was he teaching? Colleagues? She talked in such a way that there was never an opportune moment for me to have an input. Tony seemed oblivious; he would have usually rushed in ten minutes before the meal was dished out from playing badminton with friends and would be quite happy just to sit and eat his dinner. By the time we were in the car going home; I'd be seething. But I would say nothing; what was the point.

All in all, we settled into married life well. David taught and I worked and did everything else. But we were happy. Avril's baby arrived; a little boy who they named Russell, he was beautiful and all of a sudden I was broody. I'd never thought much about babies before, I wasn't even overly fond of them. The few babysitting experiences I had had were with snotty toddlers who wouldn't go to bed and screamed most of the night. Russell was different; he was all pink and sweet and smelled of Johnston's talcum powder. Even the constant puking didn't put me off him, it was amazing how one little 7lb 4oz baby could change someone's mind set.

But we had to be sensible. David was a new teacher and still in some sort of probationary period; we lived in a little two bedroomed flat that wasn't even ours and at the end of the day I was still only twenty. Food for thought though and I entered 'have a baby' on my to do list for future reference.

The months trundled on. David came out of probation and was given a permanent teaching post; the headteacher seemed to think a lot of him. Now he was a permanent member of staff they seemed to expect more of him. He would be late home from work most nights because there was this meeting to go to or that meeting. He would come in from work, have his tea and then doze the rest of the night in front of the telly. Not much fun for me, but I was happy enough pottering around the flat. We still had our weekends and we made sure we made the most of them.

There was a most definite subtle change in our relationship. David seemed to be working later and later, most nights it was after 8 when he got home. And for some reason I seemed to irritate him. I didn't know why this was; I was the same as always, but I didn't seem to be able to please him, everything I did was wrong. He wasn't nasty, just a bit whingey; why had I bought that make of toothpaste? Why did I move his paperwork off the dining room table? Just little things, but I noticed and it unnerved me.

I spoke to my friend Lynne about it, she had married John about six months after me and David had got wed. She put it down to his work, extra responsibility that brought extra pressures with it. She was right. It had changed when he came out of his probation, so I tolerated the snapping and the snide remarks, he'd get over it. And barring that life was treating us good.

I loved my job, even in the winter when the elements treat my poor feet so badly. Mr and Mrs McCabe were good to me and over time they gave me more and more responsibility as they headed towards retirement. They showed me how to balance the books and re-order stock; I found myself running the place alone two or three days a week, but I loved them and I was grateful for them for the extra bit they put in my pay packet every week.

But David's snapping continued. Even on our precious weekends together he seemed to find something to find fault with me about. Making his excuses, Sunday dinner to my mam and dad's was something I did on my own. I wasn't bothered, it gave me a chance to have a gossip with Carol and Janet; and most weekends Avril was here with Alan and baby Russell. David would stay at the flat, mostly doing paperwork, sometimes doing nothing; if he didn't go to his mam's then she would be over with a plated Sunday dinner for him at some point during the day. I never knew what he really did, or what time Sandra actually came. I just knew she had been because there would be a plate and a Tupperware dish that David left in the sink when he had warmed his dinner through. Of course I would wash them and then leave them out for Sandra the following Sunday morning before I left for my mam's.

I didn't know what was wrong. We were still loving where we needed to be. He told me he loved me all of the time and I did my best not only just to look after him properly, but to make sure I always looked good for him. For my 21st birthday he surprised me with a lovely weekend away to the Lake District. He spoilt me rotten; lovely hotel, lovely meals out, he was like the old David. Funny, complimentary, full of fun, but then we came home and within days he was back into 'crocodile' mode.

I tried to talk to him. 'Is it work? Is it me?' but he assured me all was well, so I did what I always did when I was looking for an answer I couldn't fathom for myself; I asked for signs. This time it didn't matter how simple the question was or how easy the sequence should have been; it didn't happen. 'We are okay if a red car comes in this morning!' I would say to myself as I started work. But it wouldn't appear and by the time I left work I'd be miserable. Surely we should have still been in our honeymoon period; we'd only been married a year… I just couldn't put my finger on it.

I kept busy; I spent time with Lynne, John worked away during the week, so I would call and see her on my way home from work; she was my confidant and we would sit over a cup of coffee and try to make sense of David and his moods. I made excuses for him; he worked hard, he was tired, we were still new to this married life thing. I felt like I was slagging him off constantly and would rush home eaten up with guilt about betraying him. Not that Lynne would say anything to anyone. She was a good friend.

We had met on our first day at nursery school and even though I had no recollection; apparently we were inseparable. And that's the way we stayed throughout our school days. Lynne only lived around the corner from us, she had a little sister who was the same age as my youngest sister Carol, her mam and dad always welcomed me into their home and sometimes I would take refuge there when me and my sisters were fighting.

Then something ridiculous happened and I found out exactly why David was like what he was with me.

Cold Cold Christmas

It was another winter and this one was especially cold and fierce. I constantly had the snivels and even though I had taken possession of my mam's Derry boots when I left home; my feet were getting a freezing every day. By January they were a mess; as soon as I got in from work I would unwrap and soak my feet in a bowl of hot water, but my hands, face and especially my feet got so itchy that I would be constantly rubbing cream on them.

Anyway, the whole thing seemed to irritate the life out of David. The first couple of times he saw me 'creaming' he asked me not to do it in front of him. Bloody hell, we lived in a tiny flat, what was I supposed to do? But I did what I could so I didn't offend him and most nights my hands and face would have stopped itching and my feet would be safely hidden away under a pair of socks before his key even went in the door.

But one night I had stayed at Lynne's a little bit longer than I usually did, so by the time I had jumped in the bath and put my jarmies on, I didn't have a chance to put my cream on before he came home. Thinking it wouldn't upset him just this once; I mean I hadn't done it for weeks in front of him, surely he couldn't complain. How wrong I was!

I don't know if it was because his tea wasn't in the oven keeping warm, or that my weather beaten body really did offend him, which ever it was, he went light. I had never seen him like it before. He was shouting and screaming at me, leaving me in no uncertain terms what the problem was between us.

I wasn't good enough for him. I had no ambition; I was happy enough working in the garage for the rest of my life. Can you imagine how embarrassing it was for him; his work colleagues would be horrified if they knew what I did; filling cars up with petrol day in and day out. And look at the state of me; I was covered in chilblains!!! It went on and on and on....

His tirade was relentless and cruel; he not only went at me because of my job, but also my family. Carol didn't get the lickings of a dog; she had just announced she was moving in with her boyfriend; ok they had no plans to marry; but we weren't living in the dark ages. But it appeared none of my family had anything about them. My dad, happy enough working in the office of a local factory where he had been since leaving school, my mam and Avril in the bakery, Janet working in a bookmakers, Carol a hairdressers. It seemed that there was only Julie travelling around the world had anything about her.

I sat stunned. I had no idea. I didn't know he thought we were all such losers, but most of all I didn't know he felt that way about me. It wasn't as if I had pulled the wool over his eyes; he met me at the garage. But I didn't know he was ashamed of me and of what I did. I was too shocked even to cry, the best I could do was sit, my face burning with shame and my hands and feet throbbing with the need to scratch.

He finished. I heard him stomp down the stairs and the door slam. Then the tears came. The tears turned into great big massive sobs and I crumpled into a heap. Even when the crying stopped, I lay huddled up in a ball. I didn't know what to do. 'Should I go??? Has David gone??' I couldn't think straight. All I could do was lie on the floor, scratching away and wondering why he had even bothered to marry me in the first place.

I must have fallen asleep because the glare of the living room light brought me out of my stupor. David was back. He looked devastated. 'Val, please, I'm so sorry!!!' Then he was in front of me, uncurling me and pulling me into his arms. I let him; I was too exhausted to speak, he just kept saying over and over how sorry he was. It all seemed like a bizarre dream; but I knew it was no dream, this was reality. This was what had been bothering him all of these months. This was why he snapped at me. This was why I couldn't do anything right despite all of my best efforts. He was his mother's son. He thought the same we as she did. I wasn't good enough for him. The signs had been right; I was in trouble. He was a teacher and I worked in a petrol station. He had made a mistake by marrying me. He knew it; Sandra knew it and now so did I.

And that became the elephant in the room. As much as we tried to put it behind us, it was always there; sitting in the corner of the room like the grim reaper; sentencing our marriage to death. We tried. If I felt like I tip toed around him before, now I was walking on glass.

We spent a very strange Christmas together. My mam's on Christmas Day and his on Boxing Day. But on both occasions I couldn't shake off what he thought of my family and what his, well his mam thought of me. I over compensated on Christmas cheer because I was so miserable, even baby Russell didn't help, though I pretended he did. I was trying to be perfect. I even surprised him with the news I was going to enrol at college on a Business course; he seemed impressed but I couldn't really tell.

We were drifting further and further apart. Poor Lynne got it all, warts and all. She was shocked at the malice he had shown towards me, he was Prince Charming when anyone was about, and there hadn't been any repeats of his outburst, but he seemed to have a resigned air about him. It was like someone had said 'David you've made your bed, you have to lie in it!' So that's what he was doing. All the energy had gone from us. We were going through the motions and I didn't know how much longer we could keep it up.

Then something extraordinary happened. Rushing into work one morning, the smell of petrol brought a horrible bile taste into my mouth. Thinking it was because I had made a curry the night before and I hadn't cooked the chicken properly, I stuffed some chewing gum into my mouth and tried to forget about it. But the smell of petrol was making me feel really sick and it continued all week. Mrs McCabe noticed that I kept reeling and suggested maybe we would be hearing the sound of pitter patter of tiny feet sometime soon.

Surely not. We were always so careful. Me and David had decided that we wouldn't even consider starting a family until we had a place of our own; somewhere with decent sized bedrooms and a garden. You couldn't swing a cat in the flat. But most of all; we weren't in a good place together. If I was pregnant; then it was from before our meltdown. We hadn't been that intimate since then; so that would make me about two months gone. How hadn't I noticed?

Lynne was my first port of call on the way home. Once again I took her into my confidence, I was keeping well and truly 'mum' about things until I was sure. But I couldn't keep it all to myself; under normal circumstances it would have been David I told, but I couldn't face his disapproval, because that's what it would be; another reason for him to think I had let him down.

So it was Lynne I told. Lynne who said I would have to get myself to the doctors. It was Lynne chatting away in front of me that stirred something inside. Excitement. There was a chance I could be pregnant. A good chance. This was life changing, but underneath the little bubble of excitement I had a knot of dread; this really wasn't what David would want. It wasn't on his agenda; it was a spanner in the works and I wasn't naïve enough to think that this was going to be anything but bad news. But I had to be sure first. I wasn't going to say anything until I was really really really sure and that was a bit away. I knew Lynne would be there for me no matter what happened; she told me as much and I clung on to her as I was leaving.

Back at work the signs were there in abundance. No matter how obscure I made them; they just kept on coming in. So all that was needed was for me to wait for the result of the little pot of wee that I had dropped into the doctors. I was sure though; the petrol thing was still there and I was sucking on Kola-Kubes like there was no tomorrow; I ate so many of them I think I pulled the skin off the inside of my mouth, but I couldn't stop.

At the doctors my pregnancy was confirmed. In a daze I made an appointment to see the surgery mid-wife later in the month. It was all so surreal and I was terrified. I knew now so that could only mean one thing. David.

Lynne tried to assure me that he would take the news well; I think she was trying to convince herself as much as me. But I knew there was only one way I was going to find out for sure and that was by telling him. I was dreading it and for the next week or so I put it off. If he thought I was looking peaky he never said. I don't think he really noticed me; unless it was to ask where something was or what we were having for tea. We were in our own orbits, but they were about to collide and I wasn't sure how much damage limitation I could manage.

42

Say Hello, Wave Goodbye

The long and short of it was that it was over. My pregnancy was the final straw in our fragile marriage. If I thought David would have warmed to the idea; I couldn't have been more wrong. He said it was too soon; we couldn't afford it; that we weren't living in the right place; his career wasn't established enough. But I knew these were all feeble excuses. I had asked the signs – asked them if he loved me and they came back loud and clear. No!

I didn't want to be that didn't love me as much as I loved them. And I didn't want to be with someone who didn't want me to have their child. The timing was poor; but it wasn't as if I had planned it. I held on and held on. I tried to live with him, but he was so cold and I was so sickly I couldn't look after him the way I had. He hated it. He said that if this was what it was going to be like and that was just because I was pregnant; then it would be a million times worse when the baby came.

It was such a horrible time. David came home later and later, sometimes I could smell alcohol on him. It was obvious he would rather sit in a pub than come home to his pregnant wife. There was still only Lynne who knew I was pregnant; I was sure that David hadn't told anyone and I felt like I was waiting for his permission before I dare tell anyone else the good news.

But it wasn't good news. Not for David anyway. I had my ante-natal appointment and the midwife gauged that I was about 13 weeks pregnant, over three months. This couldn't go on. So that night when David got in from work I told him that we had to start telling people we were having a baby. For the second time in our short marriage he lost it.

He was of the opinion I had trapped him. How did that work, girls trapped men so they would marry them!! We were already married. He made no sense. This time I argued back with him. He basically said that I knew he didn't want to be with me, but I deliberately got pregnant so he wouldn't leave. 'Was he leaving me??' I argued I didn't know we were in that much trouble. But there was no arguing with him. He didn't want the baby and he didn't want me. 'Where had all of this come from? Where did this go wrong?' I asked myself as I got ready for bed. I was exhausted by it all, I needed his support not this. As I lay alone in the bed that night I knew that it was going to be the last night I lived in the flat. I needed help, I needed my big sister. She would know what to do. Avril and Lynne would help me to go. I couldn't stay with David; he didn't think I was good enough for him and now he was in that mind-set there would be no changing his mind. Sandra had planted the seed and now that seed had grown in to a huge oak tree, the branches were squeezing the life force out of me.

I rang Mr McCabe and told him that I wouldn't be going into work, he seemed fine about it, no doubt Mrs McCabe had told him about my pregnancy; and then I rang Avril and asked her to come to the flat. While I waited for her to come, I started to pack up my stuff. There wasn't that much and there wasn't anything in the flat I wanted to take with me. All in all it amounted to four bags, not a lot for almost two years of marriage. But I didn't want anything; Sandra had decorated and furnished it, it had been for her precious David not me. If I took anything it would feel like I was stealing it. So I just took what was mine.

David hadn't said anything to me before I left. He would no doubt be expecting me to be sitting waiting for him when he returned, his tea keeping warm in the oven and his clean shirt hanging up for the next day. Well he would be in for a shock. The flat would be cold and dark when he got home and for every other night.

I didn't need my signs to tell me what to do. This was the right thing. I was 22 years old. I was pregnant. My marriage was over.

Home

I got the feeling that Avril wasn't too shocked about my predicament. She immediately put on her organising hat and within minutes we had loaded the bottom of Russell's pram up with my bags and we were leaving the flat. Tony was in the barber's shop; he gave me a cheery wave; if I thought it as strange that I was firstly not at work and secondly trundling out with loads of bags; he didn't come out and ask.

Avril talked all of the way to my mam's. She would do the talking, as it happened it was my mam's late start, so we knew she would be home. By the time we got there, although I was feeling nervous, I also felt braver than I had in weeks. Avril said she would help and I believed her. She was annoyed with David, I wouldn't have been surprised if she went to the flat and gave him a piece of her mind, but for now, I had my mam and dad to face; I had to hope that they would let me stay with them, at least for the short term.

They were fine, more than fine they were great. Mam spent the time before she went to work sorting Carol's recently vacated bedroom for me to move into. It was a biggish house; four bedroomed, though the box room was literally that; a very small box. But the other bedrooms were all of a good size. The one that I was going to use was the next smallest, but big enough for me. Ironically I had never had a bedroom to myself. When I lived at home last time I had shared the other bedroom with Julie; Janet and Carol had had this one and Avril had had the luxury of having a room all to herself; even if she did touch both walls when she lay down flat.

And of course then I had shared a room with David. Just the mention of his name made my heart constrict and a lump rise in my throat. I didn't understand any of it. He had loved me, I knew he had. But then it changed. He had flown high into the sky; he was like an eagle; and if he was an eagle then I was a budgie, quite happy sitting on my perch watching the little world I could see from my cage pass me by. No wonder he didn't want me. He was wild; I was tame, even if the cage door was left open, I would remain on my perch, looking in the little mirror and too scared to venture into the outside world beyond my cage in case something horrible happened to me.

With a jolt I remembered something. I wasn't alone; I had a little person growing within me. I had to be brave. I had already been brave enough to leave, now I just needed to keep the bravado going. If I was a budgie then so be it, I was comfortable in my cage for the time being. One day I would poke my head out of the door and see what all the fuss was about. But for now I needed to stay safe; there was more than me to think about. David the eagle could fly as high as he wanted. It would be a lonely journey alone. 'The bigger they are the harder they fall.' I thought to myself as I started unpacking my carrier bags and putting my belongings away. 'Be brave, be brave …' I chanted to myself. I might not be 'academic or smart' but I could do this. I was determined and I would make sure I bloody did.

My family were brilliant, they welcomed me back and asked no questions. There was no sign of David; it was like he had fallen off the face of the earth; my mam said that the flat looked empty so I assumed he had gone back to 'mammy'. I carried on working, only having my board to pay, I quickly saved up a small nest egg. The ever organised Avril had dragged me down to the council offices to put my name down for a house, but the waiting list was enormous and I didn't hold out much hope of getting anything anytime soon, you needed points; and I was nowhere near having enough to put me near the top of the list. The house wasn't overcrowded, I wasn't on any kind of benefit and being pregnant and alone wasn't the same as being a single-parent.

I think my mam and dad were relieved that I wasn't going anywhere in the foreseeable future. The four of us moseyed along just fine. When my Granny; Ada James had a fall in her home, my mam and dad took it in turns to go around and look after her. She had refused point blank to go into hospital; it appeared once you went in you never came out. So it was left to the family to care for her, but unfortunately it seemed that the weeks were more likely to be months and with us all working in some shape or form; it was a difficult task to manage. So she came to stay with us.

What a bloody handful she was. She hadn't broken any bones, but she had bruised herself quite badly and she had given herself a fright and had lost confidence. The box room was made ready for her and on the day of her arrival we were all there to welcome her. But if you had asked me, I would have said that the woman who came to stay was an imposter; it certainly wasn't Granny Ada. My usual smart as a cookie Granny, who enjoyed nothing more than sitting listening to music and doing a crossword was now a diva. It was all me, me, me, me, me. No wonder my mam and dad couldn't leave her in her own house.

My Granddad George had been dead about ten years and to be honest she had seemed to enjoy being a widow. She had had a big circle of friends, mainly made up from other widows from her Church or from the over 60's club she was a part of. But they went on holidays or day trips to various places of interest and they met up several times a week. She didn't seem to mind her own company and when we called there was always a freshly baked cake in the tin and the house was clean and tidy. On top of that she was always beautifully turned out. She enjoyed nothing better than a spending spree in Newcastle; in fact she spent a fortune on clothes, I had been with her lots of times. She would find an item she liked and then bought it in different colours too. She might have only gone into town to get a skirt and jumper, but would come home with three skirts; all identical in style and five jumpers.

And she adored her granddaughters. Eric, my dad; was her only child, something quite unique in my Granny's day and age. Most of her friends had at least three children each, but whether it just didn't happen or there were problems, I didn't know. All I did know was that each of her granddaughters were treat like princesses by her. She would knit us all jumpers, all identical in varying sizes and of course in her trademark variety of colours.

So when she arrived at our house, she looked dishevelled and a little bit confused; I was shocked. I had seen her since her fall, I'd been around to her house to make her tea and stuff. But she would usually be sitting in her chair and I didn't pay much attention to the fact that she was looking less than her usually glamorous self.

Straightaway she hated the little box room, she did nothing to hide her disapproval and even with some of her knick-knacks in, she was having none of it. My mam and dad were frantic, Ada was going on like a toddler having a tantrum. There was only one thing for it, me and Janet were going to have to double up; so whilst I entertained Ada downstairs, the rest of them moved my stuff into Janet's room.

And so it began. It soon became clear that she couldn't be trusted to be on her own. She seemed to have lost all of her commosense and things that were funny when she first did them, soon wore us all down. Every morning she would get up and strip her bed, after dressing in an array of gaudy coloured clothes she would make her way downstairs for her breakfast. Then she would raise merry hell. She didn't want toast or cereal or for that matter anything we had ready for her; no she would want a nice piece of fish or jelly and custard, cauliflower cheese was a great favourite and she had even asked for a chicken curry; she had never had a curry in her life, she always boo booed it as foreign muck. And that set the precedence for the rest of the day. She had control of the telly, the radio, she took over all of our lives. We had to have extra locks on the doors as she had a habit of wandering off. Not that she went far, but the neighbours would be forever bringing her back because she had gone into their houses and plonked herself down in the living room as if she belonged there.

Of course she had dementia and it was soul destroying to watch. Her moments of clarity became fewer and fewer, she was so confused about who we all were and for my dad it was painful. She didn't know who her only child was and more often than not thought he was a neighbour of hers from when she was a girl. Bob became a regular call in our house. 'Can you get me a cup of tea Bob? Bob do you know where my shoes are?' My poor dad. Sometimes, in the middle of the night, Ada would open mine and Janet's bedroom door; she would switch on the light and then come and plonk herself on one of our beds. She would then tell us about her night out with her boyfriend. I assumed she was talking about when her and Granddad were courting; it had been over sixty years earlier, but she talked as if he had just walked her home.

She called me Edna and she called Janet Maude; her sisters names. When she was 'with us' she would get herself upset; 'why was she at Eric and Pat's house?' 'When can she go home?' It was worse when she had her clarity than when she was away with the fairies. The tablets the doctors gave her to keep her calm increased over time and she started to sleep a lot. It was easier when she slept; but it was cruel and I didn't like thinking about her lying in her semi-coma like state.

And all the time my waist line increased as I progressed through my pregnancy. I was well; very well. I walked backwards and forwards to work for exercise. The petrol no longer made me ill; if anything I quite liked the smell. I had regular check-ups with my midwife and everyone seemed happy that I was doing so well, especially under the circumstances.

I still had no word from David. His dad came into the garage for his petrol from time to time. He was always nice and spent a few minutes chatting; but he didn't mention David or Sandra and if he knew I was pregnant; which you would have to be blind not to notice; he never said anything.

At home it was assumed that I would stay living there, at least until, after the baby was born. I was happy to stay. Avril kept bringing babygrows and bits and pieces for the baby; she gave me a blow by blow account about what to expect towards the end of my time; it filled me full of dread, but this baby was coming one way or another and I would dig deep to find my courage.

Red cars for a girl; blue cars for a boy – I kept a running tab. It went backwards and forwards between the two; just when I thought I had my answer; I'd have a run of the opposite car and my 'sign' would be thrown up in the air again. But I was determined, by the time I left work to have the baby; I would have my answer, so the tab rolled on.

The chaos at home continued. Sometimes when Ada was on form she was funny and me and Janet would sit in the living room with her and laugh with her. She liked a laugh; she would sit and watch something on the telly and she would see a face she recognised, straightaway she would think it was someone she went to school with, or lived next to; met on holiday or was in one of her clubs. But of course the face was a 'famous one' and the chances of her knowing them was slim. It was nice to think that she had been on holiday with the Fonz, or Margaret Thatcher was in her Over Sixties club.

But sometimes she would be angry. Those times were scary because she would lash out at whoever was near her. She was just so frustrated with herself; and confused, she didn't know who we were or where she was. Then she would be quiet for the next few days as she readjusted to her new dose of tablets. It was a roller-coaster ride of emotions with her and every week she was getting more confused and less Grandma Ada.

My last day at work was an emotional one. I didn't think I would be so upset, but the customers kept wishing me well and as the day went on I found myself biting my lip to stop myself from crying. I was ready for leaving, it had been a warm summer and I was finding it harder and harder to move my huge body around. The heat made my feet swell; surprise surprise and I was having to wear a pair of shoes two sizes too big; which although I could actually get on, dug in at all the wrong places and I ended up with blisters that I couldn't treat because I couldn't see my feet.

Even sitting behind the little counter was no help, I'd be sitting for twenty minutes when one of my legs would go into a cramp; I was better moving around so the hippo that lumbered around the forecourt became a familiar sight. But the tears did come; Mr and Mrs McCabe surprised me with a beautiful Moses basket. They knew I hadn't bought much for the baby and the Moses basket was filled full of bibs, vests and toiletries along with chocolates and bubble bath for me. I was so grateful. The card they gave me sent me into a complete frenzy; they had been collecting off the customers, there was a bundle of notes and everyone had sent well wishes. I felt very humbled, I was just the girl who filled up their cars with petrol.

Avril picked me up from work that night and as she packed up the car, I collected the piece of paper that I had kept beside the till for weeks. In recent weeks the blue cars and the red cars had been head to head. But today one car had pulled way ahead of the other. Smiling I put the paper into my handbag. I kissed my employers with the promise I would keep in touch and call in when I could and made my way out to Avril waiting in the car for me. The red cars had won. I was having a girl.

Waiting

The weeks before my due date were filled with shopping and sorting. Poor Janet; her bedroom was invaded with baby stuff. She said she was happy enough; but we made the little box room as comfortable as we could in case she needed to escape once the baby was here and screaming its head off through the night.

Sandra, David's mam put in an appearance. She turned up on the doorstep one Saturday morning. All smiles and carrier bags; she made her excuses why she hadn't called to see me before. I didn't like her and I struggled even to be civil with her, as did my mam and Janet who sat with us in the sitting room I was sure our sitting room wouldn't fall into Sandra's lounge category. She was such a snob. I resisted the temptation to ask about David and she didn't offer any news of him. She asked, 'how are you? When is your actual due date? Did I need anything?' I answered her as pleasantly as I could and assured her I needed nothing. Even if I did I wouldn't ask any of the Craig family for help. Promising we would let her know the minute the baby arrived, she left. I made no move to cuddle or kiss her.

Her visit did stir up memories of David though; how could it not. The whys? What ifs? I was twisting myself into knots. I shouldn't have been living at my mam and dad's. I shouldn't have been relying on my sisters for emotional support. I shouldn't have been taking Lynne into hospital with me; it should have been David who was holding my hand and mopping my brow. Then again; childbirth was probably too beneath him even to contemplate being part of.

I seethed for days. It was hot and I was uncomfortable and miserable. The icing on the cake came in the shape of a solicitor's letter on behalf of David Craig. He wanted a divorce. Not only did he want a divorce but it seemed the blame lay with me. As I read through all of the jargon it became clear that David was divorcing me for abandoning him; the fury I felt was like something I had never felt before. I thought I was going to simultaneously combust.

'How dare he?? How did he dare sit in a solicitor's office and blame me for the breakdown of our marriage. As firstly Janet and them my mam read through the letter, I was inconsolable. He hated me.

Not knowing what else to do, my mam rang for Avril. She was there in no time; Russell in her arms. She didn't even bother reading the letter. She just put Russell on the floor with some toys and made her way upstairs to run me a bubble bath.

I was a big red blotch as I lowered my body into the warm bath. As I lay there I could see the top of my bump sticking out of the bubbles, what a sight it was. Mother Nature hadn't been kind to me; I was covered in what looked like angry red lines; stretch marks. But it couldn't be helped, they had come no matter how much baby oil I lavished on my body. I lifted a foot up out of the water and positioned it on one of the taps. It was huge and very swollen, it looked as if someone had blown it up. 'I'll ask one of the girls to paint my toenails when I get out! I thought to myself. I couldn't be seen in hospital with chipped nail polish.

The water soothed me. I had been so upset, angry and most of all disappointed. David's timing was awful, he must have known I was coming to the end of my pregnancy and talk of divorce would upset me. But that was him; I was of such little consequence to him, as was the baby. I truly didn't understand him. Had he always been selfish and I was just too wrapped up and in awe of him to notice? I hadn't seen him for seven months; he hadn't enquired how I was or even where I was. And now he wanted a divorce, our marriage was to be swept under the table as if it had never happened.

I pulled the plug out and sat while the water drained away around me. Still covered in bubbles I eased myself up and stepped out of the bath. Before I even had chance to pull the second leg over I felt a strange plop and there was a rush of water falling out of me. My waters had broken.
'Avril…………………….'

Truly Scrumptious

Eighteen hours later, I was sitting in bed holding my 8lb 2oz daughter. A girl, well it had to be. The signs had said so. Avril had been amazing, she had mopped my brow and held my hand. My early jaunt into labour had thrown a spanner in the works, it was the one weekend a month Lynne's husband didn't come home and she made the journey to see him. So it had been Avril that had encouraged, shouted and had first glimpse of my daughter.

I wanted to call her Truly. She was Truly Scrumptious, all pink and plump and beautiful. But I chose to call her Samantha. Samantha James, I was going to be a divorced woman, so if I was reverting back to my birth name, I wanted my daughter to be called that too.

I spent seven days in hospital, Samantha's pink hue of her birth quickly developed into a putrid shade of yellow, so she spent three days under the sun lamps. I couldn't take my eyes off her, I sat by her little cot under the lamps and gazed at her in wonder. She was so perfect and I found it hard to take in that I had actually given birth to her.

Every visiting time there would be someone come and see Samantha. My mam came as much as she could; but Ada seemed to be in one of her disorientated states so it made it difficult for her and dad; but he managed to come in and see his first granddaughter. Janet, Carol and Avril took it in turns and a huge bouquet arrived the day after Samantha's arrival. At first dreading they had been sent from David; I was delighted when I read the little card and realised they were from Julie. How thoughtful; I think she was somewhere in New Zealand. After a week me and Samantha were given the all clear and we were off home.

It was strange at first. And just a little bit scary. I had had the support of nurses in hospital, back home Samantha was my responsibility; she would be for the rest of my life, just like my mam was with me. We managed. It was chaotic and sometimes I didn't know if I was coming or going. Samantha's arrival into the house seemed to jolt Ada into a long spell of lucidity. She offered advice about feeding and winding and for that time she not only knew who Samantha was and who she belonged to, she knew who we all were.

Mam, as promised let Sandra and Tony know about Samantha. They came to see her on the first weekend we were home, this time they had the good sense to ring before they came. There was only me in the 'lounge' when they arrived and Samantha was tucked up in her Moses basket. After all of the usual pleasantries you ask when visiting someone who had recently had had a baby, Tony asked if he could have a hold of Samantha? I liked Tony, I had a lot of time for him. I would often wonder if Sandra was like what she was now when he met her. Tony had followed his dad into the barber's shop; the Craig's were well known in the town as barbers, so there had always been a bit of money. Not millionaires by anyone's standards, but Tony's parents had a big house and had a car of their own, which wasn't something common back in those days. So had Sandra set her cap at him, or was she actually nice when she was younger? I would probably never know. But I had no hesitation in picking Samantha up and handing her over to Tony. I made my excuses and went off into the kitchen to make some tea, I'd give them a little bit time to get to know their granddaughter, I was sure they wouldn't be seeing too much of her in the years to come.

Sandra was nursing Samantha when I went back into the 'lounge' carrying mugs of teas. I could have given them cups and saucers, but Sandra thought so little of me and my family, I was buggered if I was going to go to any lengths to keep her happy. For once she didn't even look down her nose, she only had eyes for Samantha. Maybe I was wrong and they were going to make an effort to keep in touch with us.

Tea drank, they sat for another half an hour before they asked if they could take some photographs. Picking up the mugs, I agreed and once again went and busied myself in the kitchen. This time when I returned, they stood up to leave. 'She is so beautiful; thank you for letting us see her Val' Sandra said. I told them that it was fine and they could see her whenever they wanted, more for something to say than meaning it. As they were leaving Tony handed me an envelope; inside was a cheque for £500 made payable to me; 'for Samantha' he said. Once again David's name wasn't mentioned. And then they were gone.

I settled into motherhood and Samantha thrived. I had lots of love and support around me and even though Ada was erratic in her behaviour at times, she was no threat to Samantha and I never thought that she could hurt her. The only cloud on the horizon was David and the looming divorce. I felt such a failure sometimes; the grief for my lost marriage would wash over me and I would have no choice but to wallow in it. I struggled to comprehend where it had gone wrong; had he changed? Or was it me?? Was it so bad that I just worked in a filling station? Did I not make up for my lack of qualifications in other ways? The questions just went around and around in my head, especially when I was up through the night seeing to Samantha. I would lie in my little bed waiting for her to settle back to sleep and my thoughts would torment me; laugh at me and mock me. By morning the thoughts would have disappeared and I'd feel better, but then the night would come and the cycle would begin again.

Avril said I needed to see a solicitor of my own, I had to respond to David's accusations. She was right, so I made an appointment and asked her to come with me and hold my hand. It wasn't as bad as I thought it would be. Mr Carter was very nice, very smart and professional with that aura that people who were clever had, but he was on my side. He asked questions and I answered best I could. I think he was a bit shocked that at three months old, David hadn't even attempted to see Samantha.

I assured him that Samantha was David's and it was his name on the birth certificate. It seemed that David should have made some sort of financial provision for Samantha; Avril had said, but I dismissed it because I didn't know how to approach David about it. It appeared that this was what Mr Carter would be doing for me, he would include the request for financial support in the response letter. Of course I would have a copy of this letter to approve before it was sent off to David's solicitor. As Mr Carter put it 'the whole sorry mess could be cleared up in a matter of months'. It all seemed so easy, legally anyway; emotionally it would take a long time for me to get just a little bit of the confidence I had had before I met David….

Lying Eyes

I was divorced before Samantha had her first birthday. David still hadn't seen her. She was such a beautiful, funny, loving little girl; he didn't know what he was missing. I was back to being Valerie James. Still at my mam and dad's; we were happy there. Me and Janet were still doubled up, well trebled up if we counted Samantha. But I slept better now that Samantha slept through, I had defeated my demons and slept soundly.

I had gone back to work when Samantha was about 6 months old. Avril was a stay at home mam and offered to have Samantha for me. Of course I paid her, I think that they found the bit extra income handy; Alan didn't make a huge wage but Avril hadn't been able to go back to the bakery because her job involved early morning starts. It all worked well. Samantha was happy and that was the main thing. I enjoyed being back at work, I liked the routine and I liked having the money. With the money that Tony had given me for Samantha and the monthly allowance David paid, I had a little bit saved up for when I got a place of my own.

As happy as I was at my mam and dad's, I couldn't stay there forever. Avril regularly rang the council on my behalf and I was creeping up the waiting list, so one day it would happen and when it did I needed to be ready.

I couldn't think about meeting anyone. I didn't have the time or the energy. My life was Samantha, work, my family and sleep. But I loved it. I would often think about how it would be if I was with David, I don't think I would have been able to go back to work and I was sure we would be living in a little semi-detached house with little gardens front and rear. But I knew I would have been lonely; even with David there. I had done the right thing leaving when I did, it was beyond repair.

Once in a while Sandra and Tony would come and see Samantha. Sometimes they would take her for a walk in her pushchair; these times my heart would be in my mouth until their return. I used to worry that they would take her away and never bring her back, other times I would wonder if they were taking Samantha to see David. They were never away long, maybe they knew I would worry. Then I would feel guilty; they were her grandparents and they never came without bringing a present for her and a little something for her bank account.

One day Tony came into the garage. I could see straightaway that he wanted to say something but he was jumping from subject to subject not really saying what he wanted to do. In the end I said 'Is everything all right Tony? Is Sandra ok??' He looked relieved. 'It's David!' He must have seen the look of fright on my face. 'No, no Val, he is fine. I just wanted you to know that he is getting married again. It's his deputy head at school, Mrs March. She's having a baby. I just thought that you had a right to know. And I didn't want you to hear it from anyone else!' I could feel the tears pricking my eyes, it didn't bother me that he was getting married. But who he was marrying and the reason why hurt.

I didn't dare think about it until later that night after Samantha was safely tucked up in bed. Mrs March??? Mrs March??? I was trying to remember which one of David's colleagues she was and what he had said about her. Mrs March??? I couldn't remember her….. then I had it Miss Blenkinsopp!!! She had started teaching at David's school not long after him. She got married; we had been invited to her evening wedding reception. It had been at Lumley Castle and David hadn't wanted to go because he said it wasn't our thing. Miss Blenkinsopp. Miss Blenkinsopp who had ironically got married in March and was going to be called Mrs March!!

Had they been having an affair while I was still living with him? Was that the reason for the mood swings? Was that the reason I wasn't good enough for him? Was that the reason he didn't want me or Samantha? The penny was beginning to drop.

I wasn't angry. If anything in a strange way I was relieved. It wasn't because I wasn't good enough, that was an excuse. It was because he fell in love with someone else, pure and simple. He didn't think I was scum of the earth, he just fell out of love with me. I wasn't what he wanted; neither was a baby. Not then, it was probably different for him now. He was more than likely happy with Mrs March soon to be Mrs Craig; she had travelled a similar path to him. I almost felt like smiling about it. We had been too young; I couldn't have kept the 'perfect housekeeper' routine forever. His mam had spoilt him and I carried on where she left off; I had turned into his chief cook and bottle washer. It wasn't Sandra's fault either. It wasn't her snobbery that had split us up. I didn't know Sandra well, we had never really got to know each other, I spent any time I had with her back pedalling; but I did know she had morals and she wouldn't have been happy with how David had treat me. I could see that now; maybe I could cut her and Tony a bit of slack.

For two years I had been tormented by the fact that I wasn't good enough; my confidence had hit rock bottom. And now it was over; I had my answer. It would have been so much kinder if David had been honest with me in the first place. Yes I would have been angry and no doubt devastated that David wanted someone else and not me. But I would have got over it, I would have got over it much much quicker than I had by him saying nothing. He had done a character assassination on me and mine because he didn't have the balls to tell me what was really going on. He had been cruel and it was unforgivable.

A feeling of disappointment hung over me for weeks. Lynne listened to my rants over and over again. She had been my confidant at the time, Avril had come to save me, but I hadn't mentioned the horrible things he had said about my family; I didn't want to hurt them. So it had always been Lynne and it was her who I went to to help me put the pieces of my life back in place.

Slowly the picture began to take shape. I was the winner here, I had Samantha. I also had piece of mind. I had to just put my ill-fated marriage behind me and start again as best I could. I had done enough wallowing. I loved my job, but maybe I did need stretching, so I took the bull by the horns and signed up for a home correspondence course in book-keeping. It would cost me money and take years to complete, but at the end of it I would have a recognised qualification.

And there was the pattern of my life for the next few years. I stayed at my mam and dad's with Samantha, helped with a deteriorating Granny Ada, used the quiet time when Samantha was asleep to study and live. I started to have the odd night out with my sisters and friends.

Janet shocked us all when she brought home her first serious boyfriend. There had been a few in the past but they weren't serious and never stayed around for long. Graham was different, you could see that straightaway. For one he was older than Janet; she had met him when he took over as manager at the bookies where she worked. He was newly divorced, three teenage kids, which meant a boat load of baggage. But they had hit it off instantly. What started off as a quick drink after work turned into something much more serious? He was a lot to take on and Janet knew it was never going to be easy, his kids would always come first, Saturday nights were always a no-no because that was the night they would come to stay and depending on what the kid's had on to do on a Sunday, they would often be there for the whole of Sunday too. Janet said she didn't mind, they had the rest of the week, but Graham didn't want her pushed out and gradually Janet became part of the little group on a Sunday.

He was always attentive, he spoilt her rotten. At first me and Avril had concerns that she was just a 'trophy girlfriend', a nice piece of 'eye candy'. But we needn't have been concerned; he was a keeper. As the months went on they became closer and closer, I never asked what had happened to his marriage; I was the last person to judge on failed relationships. He worked hard and had a lot of responsibility, but he played hard too and it was Janet he spent all his free time with.

When they had been together about a year, he came to the garage one day and asked how we kept in contact with Julie. I told him about the telephone calls on a Sunday and he asked me if I would be kind enough to pass on his number to Julie, all without Janet knowing. I was intrigued but didn't ask. I didn't have long to wait to find out why, Janet came in from work one night beaming. Graham had surprised her with a holiday, they were off to Nairobi, but more than that, she was going to see Julie.

I was impressed. How thoughtful that was. Julie had been gone for three years and apart from the telephone calls, letters and odd postcards, no one had seen her. I didn't know she was in Kenya, she moved around all of the time, sometimes she stayed somewhere for just a few weeks, other times she settled for months. I missed her, we all did, but she was doing what she wanted to do and I was sure one day she would come home, when the wanderlust had been satisfied and she needed to go back to her roots. But none of us knew when that would be, so we all sat around making little packages up for her. Photographs, letters, and little treats she would be missing from home. I was surprised there was any room left in Janet's case for clothes by the time we had all finished. Then they too were gone; only for two weeks, but even when they returned Janet didn't come home, she moved in with Graham. She came back from Nairobi Mrs Janet Cox.

Our House

I was so impressed with what Graham had achieved without Janet finding out. Between him and Julie, they had not only managed to arrange the wedding but bought a wedding dress and a bridesmaid dress for Julie. It was touching that he thought so much of Janet and knew how much she missed her sister. Julie had missed out on so much family stuff whilst she was away. She had a niece and a nephew she had only seen photographs of, so any thoughts we had that Janet and Graham had been selfish for getting married without us were well and truly quashed. Julie was guest of honour and that was enough for us.

So then there was just me left at home. Granny Ada spent more and more time in her room. She slept a lot of the time, her waking moments were filled with confusion; she was easier to handle now. She didn't wander off, she didn't have the energy. The weight was dropping off her, she had hardly any appetite. We would coax and cajole her to eat, she would say she fancied an egg; so an egg she would have, but as soon as it was in front of her she turned her nose up and wouldn't want it. Her diet was beginning to consist of cups and cups of sweet milky tea. Her false teeth started to rattle around her mouth; they hurt her so we had to take them out. The simple act of removing her false teeth aged her fifty years and instead of the feisty 70 year old she had been when she moved in with us a few years earlier, she now looked like a little old lady.

Samantha was growing up fast. She was bright, beautiful, funny and just a little bit old fashioned. She was a joy to spend time with; everything was a question with her. 'Why? How? Who?' She wanted to know everything. She followed my dad around everywhere; she would help him in the garden or washing the car; they had a lovely relationship. And she would often be found sitting with Ada. Even when Ada was talking complete rubbish, Samantha would sit and ask her 'How did that happen? Why did you do that? Who said that?' Ada would answer and so it would go on, complete silly conversations that would make them both laugh and giggle, sometimes for hours.

Carol gave birth to a little girl, the family was steadily expanding. It was lovely having a baby around again. Samantha and Russell were at the tearing around the house or garden stage and by the time Russell went home the house would be a tip and Samantha would either be hyped up or exhausted.

Then something remarkable happened, I came in from work one night to find the Council had left me a message. After all of these years, I had finally collected enough points to take me top of the list and they had a house to offer me. I was Gobsmacked, I was so excited and terrified all at the same time. I had had it easy at my mam and dad's; shared care of Samantha, shared housework, shared money. The thought of being on my own scared the life out of me. As with every other major event in my life; I looked for the signs.

They were there; of course. All the random indicators pointed to the next path my life should take. Straight to the door of 27 Lavender Grove. I resisted the temptation of going for a peep before I was due to meet Mr Johnston from the Council; I didn't want to not like it. But as me; mam and Avril turned into the street at the appointed time, my fears were confirmed. The street looked all right; there were no abandoned cars in the gardens and there weren't hordes of snotty kids running about; but the little cul-de-sac where number 27 sat; looked shabby and unloved. My heart sank. But I was here and it looked like Mr Johnston from the Council was as well; there was a man in a car parked outside the empty property. I heard Avril snort, followed by my mam sighing; seems they didn't think much of 27 Lavender Grove either. We were all here though and Mr Johnston had spotted us and was getting out of his car, so it wasn't as if we could do an about turn and pretend we hadn't seen him.

Mr Johnston turned out to be a nice man. He apologised for the state of the garden, apparently the previous tenant had been quite old and her garden had got too much for her. I could see why!!! It was huge. There was a good sized front garden which had a small lawn and borders with roses, then to the side of the house was another lawn; this one had trees which mam said were apple trees. Then taking a peek around the back, there was yet another huge garden which was so overgrown you couldn't see where it ended. Not much of a gardener, in fact not a gardener at all; I shuddered. I wouldn't have a clue what to do with it, if I wasn't put off before, I certainly was now that I had glimpsed the acres of garden that went with it.

Going into the house, I was pleasantly surprised. Although it was dated, all the rooms were a good size and the layout of it gave it a bit of a cottagey feel. Against all odds; I loved it. I could see what just a lick of paint could do; as I wandered from room to room I had the biggest butterflies in my belly. I could hear Avril asking Mr Johnston about this and that, if they could do this for me or do that. I didn't care; I would do it all myself. This was going to be mine and Sammy's home, not today, but sometime soon. For the first time since the council had got in touch about a house, I was excited. By the time I finished my wanderings around the house and caught up with mam; I knew I was going to take it and so did she. Bless her, she said she had curtains to fit here and some spare carpet to fit the little room. I was just so excited. A place of my own.

Two weeks later I got the keys. Avril must have done a really good job on Mr Johnston because not only had each room been given a couple of licks of paint and the whole place shone like a new pin, but the garden had all been cleared and now instead of looking like it was an acre long; it looked 5 acres. The garden was a worry for another day, for the time being it was to get the house as ship shape and Bristol fashion as soon as possible. It was all hands on deck and like most family's did, everyone mucked in. I took all the help I could get, along with anything furniture wise I was offered. Surprisingly within two weeks, the little house had re-invented itself as our home.

I tried not to think about moving out as I packed up mine and Samantha's things. I couldn't bear the thought of leaving my mam and dad; and Ada. But Samantha was almost five; I couldn't stay there forever. And they were only five minutes away from my house and they would be helping out with Samantha still so it wasn't like I wasn't going to be seeing them all of the time still.

There was a funny thing about my house maybe that was why the signs had been so adamant that this was the right place for me. It was seven minutes away from everyone. It was a seven minute walk to my mam and dads; to Janet's; Carol's, Avril's; Samantha's school; my work. I had timed each and every one of the journey's more than once. My house was bang in the middle of all of them. If you plotted the journeys to each of the houses; my house would be at the centre of them. If you joined up the dots they would look like a star and I would be the centre of that star. It was meant to be. 7 minutes exactly, not 6 and a half or 7 and a half. 7 minutes. 6 destinations…. now that must mean something!!!

Bag Lady

I was surprised how quickly me and Samantha settled into living on our own. The first few weeks I slept with one eye open; I was just so nervous. There were loads of strange noises; the pipes groaned, the fridge I had been given off Avril's mother-in-law creaked intermittently, an owl hooted or at least I thought it was an owl, my dad said it couldn't be it would just be a wood pigeon or something. So those first few weeks were terrifying. But then the house and its belongings seemed to settle around us, just as we settled into it. I slept better and didn't jump when the pigeon gave out a 'hoot' at two in the morning.

We saw lot of the rest of the family, in fact if anything we seemed to have more quality time with them. Instead of us just 'being there', we tended to actually spend time with everyone and my door was always open for people to call. Ada was deteriorating rapidly, I would go and sit with her one night a week to allow mam and dad to have a bit of a rest. Gran would have moments of pure clarity, but that's all they were – moments. Then she would be back to whatever persona would take over her muddled mind. It was such hard work for my mam and dad, even with all our help. Then there was another mishap which would test not only my mam and dad's marriage, but their sanity.

My mam's mam; my Granny Thora, lost her handbag. Nothing too serious, but she insisted that it had been the Warden of the sheltered accommodation where she had lived for twenty years. Thora insisted that it must have been Mrs Phillip's because she hadn't been out of her flat all that weekend and her only visitor had been the Warden. There hadn't been much in the bag, a few pounds in her purse, a bottle of perfume, a lipstick and her bus pass. But it may as well have been her life savings. Her privacy had been violated and she hadn't taken it well.

Granny Thora had always been a widow. She said that her husband had died when my mam was just two, mam had a baby brother John and older siblings Jeff and Rose. Granny Ada had always told a different story; there had never been a husband, in fact Ada had insisted that there had never even been a boyfriend. 'Thora Barnes was never girlfriend material!' Granny Ada would say. She wasn't been horrible or gossiping, she just told it how it was. Apparently Thora had always been a bit of a girl, never shy with her affections after a drink or two; by the time she was 21 she had 4 children.

My mam didn't talk a lot about her childhood. If it had been miserable she never said, but out of all the children Thora had had; there was only Pat, my mam; who still bothered with her. The other three were long gone. My mam had the odd letter off Rose, but the lads hadn't been in touch for years; either with my mam or Thora. We didn't particularly see a lot of Granny Thora; where Ada was always there for the occasions; birthdays, Christmas, weddings, Thora was always absent. It wasn't that she wasn't invited, she just wasn't interested. She had her friends and she always seemed to prefer their company to that of her family, so with this being the case; I didn't really know her.

There were weekly phone calls off my mam and she dropped in to see her if she was passing, but she didn't go out of her way to see her, so Granny Thora just remained a name in the background, not much known and not much liked. That was until her handbag was stolen. Then she became one of the main players in the family; her and Ada. My poor mam and dad.

The fact that Thora thought that Mrs Philips; the Warden had stolen her handbag turned into a complete farce. At first the police were happy to take a statement from Thora, they were sympathetic and concerned that there may be issues with the sheltered accommodation's long serving Warden. They interviewed Mrs Phillips at length; yes she had been in Thora's flat, but she said that Thora had pulled her emergency cord and she had gone into the flat thinking that Thora was in some sort of trouble. But it had been a false alarm; Thora had pulled it in error; the light switch in the bathroom and the emergency cord were right next to each other. Mrs Phillip's had said she hadn't been happy with Thora, it hadn't been the first time, and she had been dragged away from an episode of Colombo on the telly and knew she was going to miss the end because of Thora. Mrs Phillip's told the police that Thora was annoyed to have been scolded, but there had been no mention of a missing handbag and until the police had turned up at her door, she hadn't known it was missing.

And so the saga began. Thora dialled 999 constantly. Every time she caught glimpse of Mrs Phillip's she would ring the emergency service saying that she was going to be attacked, or broken in to, or she was being abused. Every time she rang the police had a duty to call and see Thora and it didn't take long for them to get fed up with her; she was wasting police time and generating needless paperwork. It quickly came to a head; the police got in touch with the Council who rang the home and in turn they got in touch with mam. At 75 years old; Thora was being evicted. Mrs Phillip's had an impeccable record working for the Council and it was thought that Thora was becoming a nuisance. There were no warning, just a letter stating that she had 28 days to vacate her flat. My mam and dad were at their wits end. They rang other homes and landlords, but as soon as they knew that it was a Council eviction, they weren't interested. There was nothing else for it. Thora had to go and live at mam and dads!!

So Granny Thora's flat was packed up, some of the furniture was sold, there just wasn't room and Thora moved into my recently vacated bedroom. Ada was furious. She had never been a big fan of Thora; she knew her of old, but what made it worse was that Thora didn't recognise Ada. The lack of teeth, thin body and the now lily white hair made Ada look so far removed from what she used to look like Thora didn't know who she was. She would be heard say 'Who is that woman in that bedroom? Who is that woman you are talking to Pat?' Ada didn't have many moments of clarity and most of her days were spent in her bedroom, but every now and then she would be Ada and on these occasions she wanted to be downstairs with the rest of the family. Of course she knew who Thora was and she would spit and snarl at her like an alley cat. The words 'slut; floozy and disgrace' would be shouted across the room. Thora would retaliate and the two of them would be sitting in the arm chairs in the living room hissing at each other. Then just as soon as Ada had been herself; she would be gone again and she would be taken back to her bedroom to rest. Thora would be left seething; she had always had a reputation for her 'mouth like a fishwife', the sudden disappearance of 'that woman' would cause her hours of frustration; she had all this anger and no one to vent it at.

For months mam and dad lived with these two elderly warring women; they were exhausted. They went from one to another, each one's needs as much as the other ones. Ada couldn't go out and Thora wouldn't, so the care was constant. We all helped out as much as we could; mam was only working on a Saturday morning at the bakery, it was really the only day she could ; dad worked full time and the Granny's' couldn't be left to their own devices. Saturday was mam's favourite day of the week; the day she escaped for a few hours.

Thora turned out to be a hoarder; things disappeared out of the living room; magazines, newspapers, letters; anything that could be stacked. Within no time there were piles and piles of rubbish in Thora's bedroom. If mam or dad tried to tidy it there would be hell on, so it was just as easy to leave it. Even when the window of the bedroom was hidden behind piles and the room was dark, dingy and worst of all smelly; there was nothing they could do about it. Mam and dad were distraught with it all.

Then Ada took a turn for the worse and the doctor had to be called. She had pneumonia and even though hospital would have been the best place for her, it was decided that she would be kept at home because that was the place she knew and was comfortable in. A hospital ward might do more damage than good. So Ada took to her bed and never came out of it again. The antibiotics and other concoctions the doctor's prescribed had no effect. Ada's frail body couldn't handle it, the pneumonia was too strong and within a month Ada had gone.

She had died in her sleep. Mam and dad knew it was imminent and had sat with her long into the night. They hadn't rang any of us, they said it was too late at night and it would have been too sad for us. But something strange did happen as mam and dad sat at Ada's bedside. Around midnight Thora had come in Ada's room, she had never been into it since she had moved in. But mam said she came in in her wyncette nightie; climbed into the bed with Ada, cuddled in and went to sleep next to her. Mam and dad thought about moving her out, but decided that she might have one of her 'to dos' so they let her be. When Ada drew her last breathe, Thora woke, kissed Ada on the cheek, got out of the bed and trundled along to her own bedroom.

The Undertaker

Even before dad rang me that morning I knew something was different. As I stood washing the breakfast dishes at the sink; a white feather wafted itself down in front of the window. An angel was calling. I don't know who had told me about feathers; maybe Ada, but I knew that if a white feather floated down around me, an angel was watching out for me. So when the phone rang and my dad told me the sad news, I was sort of ready for it. I had had a sign.

Later, when we were all at my mam and dad's; we all agreed it was a blessing, she hadn't been happy. But it didn't make it any easier. As a family we had been lucky, we hadn't lost anyone for years; Granddad years ago, but it had been Ada who had sorted all the arrangements out, so we were all at a bit of a loss.

Ada was still upstairs; the doctor had been and we were waiting for the undertakers to arrive. I wasn't sure if I wanted to go up and see her; Avril and Janet had, Carol was adamant she wasn't and I wasn't sure. Then the undertakers arrived and the opportunity passed, as we waited in the living room for Ada to make her journey to the Chapel of Rest, I kicked myself; I should have gone up and seen her and said my goodbyes.

The undertakers were coming back to see us, funeral arrangements needed to be made. While we waited we drank more tea, we hadn't all been together for a while, the atmosphere gradually lightened as we remembered stories about Ada. Mam and Avril went up to Ada's room and tidied it around, my mam seemed to need to be kept busy. Thora stayed in her room, there was a lot of banging and shouting going on, but we left her to her own devices, no one liked to go into her dank bedroom; she knew where we were if she needed us.

By the time the undertakers arrived, we were all in a bit better place. Edward Mills of Mills and Boone Funeral Directors introduced himself. I tried not to laugh; they were never called Mills and Boone; were they real people??? Or had they made the name up for affect. Edward Mills seemed a very serious man, not the type to have a tongue in cheek name for his business, so there must have been a Mr Boone somewhere in the picture. He introduced another young man Brian Mills, his son and as they made their way into the living room and sat down, my tummy was doing somersaults.

Brian Mills looked about my age; maybe a bit older. He was tall and dark, not handsome but he had a kind face and in his black overcoat he looked very distinguished. In my head I told myself off, they were here to arrange my Granny Ada's funeral, not for me to eye up. In my head I heard Ada laughing. They were very professional and within no time everything was sorted and they were standing up to leave. Somehow Brian and me had eye contact and the somersaults in my tummy started to resemble a washing machine on fast spin. I blushed. Not knowing what to do I made a hasty exit into the kitchen.

I'd never thought about meeting someone new. I hadn't had a relationship for over six years, I'd had offers; the garage was full of blokes chancing their arm. But there had been no one that had caught my eye. Until now; all of a sudden Brian Mills of Mills and Boone Funeral Director was making my lonely heart soar. I knew nothing about him, it was just a physical attraction, he might have been married for all I knew and I had already done the love at first sight thing and look where that had got me. Samantha was my life, but I had never imagined for one minute that I when I fell in love with David he would have left me pregnant and alone.

That was a long time ago, I now had a place of my own, a job I loved doing and I was well on my way to becoming a qualified book-keeper; I had my family and I had my best friend. Lynne and me had remained friends in the intervening years; she had had a little boy a year earlier; Duncan and was now half way through her second pregnancy. We didn't manage to get many nights out together, but we went to each other house's and sometimes we would have a shopping day in Newcastle or a trip to the coast with the kids. But I was only 27 and the thought of never meeting anyone else filled me with terror. The thought of meeting someone else filled me with terror too mind. It was just a case of which of the terrors would win.

I knew I would see Brian Mills again. Not the signs this time. No, he was conducting Ada's funeral so chances were I would see him on the day of the funeral. It gave the impending day a mixed feel to it, I dreaded saying goodbye to my Granny Ada; but the thought of seeing Brian Mills made my tummy lurch.

The days leading up to the funeral were a mixed bag. We had decided that we would just have something at my mam and dad's after the funeral, so in between work, school runs and looking after Samantha, I would be at their house helping spring clean and prepare enough food for the five thousand. We all mucked in. Thora was a concern; she had hardly been out of her room since Ada had died, she hardly ate the food prepared for her and if we shouted through the door if she wanted anything she would grunt a reply. My dad decided that she was best left to her own devices; at least she wasn't getting under our feet.

My dad must have known I had regretted not going up to see Ada in her bedroom when I had chance. In his own clumsy way he asked me if I would go and keep him company at the Chapel of Rest when he went to pay his last respects to his mam. Unsure; I saw my dad's face fall as I dithered about my answer. My poor dad, he hadn't really had a life of his own these past few years, so on the spur of the moment I said yes. Kicking myself the minute I said it, I didn't have the heart to say I didn't want to go when I saw my dad lolloping to the phone to tell the undertakers we were going to call.

All the way into town I wanted to turn around and run. My dad said that if we got there and I didn't feel like I could go in then that was fine; he was just happy I was accompanying him. I visibly relaxed. It hadn't been set in stone that I had to go in and see Granny Ada. By the time we arrived at Mills and Boone Funeral Directors, I had decided that I would, it was the least I could do.

The funeral directors itself was nothing like I had expected. Whether I had seen too many murder mysteries on the telly where the funeral directors was always a dark creepy place, Mills and Boone Funeral Directors was a total surprise. It was a 1950's detached house. Two beautiful bay windows gave the building a lovely symmetrical look to it. There was a long drive up towards the centre of the house and here it branched off into two where they wound their way to the back of the house. The whole building looked cheery and inviting; I was so pleased Ada was here; she would have liked the cherry blossom trees in the garden.

Inside there was a nice reception area with comfortable armchairs, the lady who came out to greet us ushered us to these chairs while we waited to be taken to see Ada. I was no longer frightened; there was nothing sinister about this place. Even so I held on to my dad's hand and as Mr Mills Senior came to take us into the Chapel; I gripped on even tighter.

Ada looked happy; could that be right? A deceased person could look happy?? Anyway she did. Her teeth must have been back in because the furrowed wrinkles now appeared to be smoother than they had been for months; she had her make-up on and who ever had dressed her had put on one of her famous Marks and Spencer blouses; this one was in fuchsia and she had a string of pearls around her neck. She looked like Granny Ada before she lost her marbles.

And I was so pleased I had gone to see her. I didn't have the courage to touch her never mind kiss her, but I told her I loved her and how much I was going to miss her; I wasn't even afraid to ask her to watch over Samantha and then got myself upset and apologised for even asking her that; she would do anyway. I left my dad to say his goodbyes to his mam in private and made my way back to the reception area to wait for him.

The lady who had first greeted us was back, obviously used to seeing people in distress, she asked if I would like a cup of tea or coffee while I waited. Declining both but asking for a glass of water, I sat and looked out into the garden where the wind was blowing the blossom off the trees. It really was a lovely place. Dad was back and as it was with men of his generation; any tears he had had were well and truly wiped away by the time he got to me.

The walk home was a quiet one, but I linked him and we ambled along in a comfortable silence. If I had hoped to see Brian Mills I didn't feel too disappointed; it really hadn't been the place for swooning after some bloke or other. If I was meant to meet him again, then it would happen.

By the time we got home there was a rumpus going on. There were black bin bags outside the front door, loads and loads of them. Thinking that Avril had got her own way and had got into Thora's bedroom to sort out the rubbish, we rushed in through the front door. But it wasn't Avril on a mission. It was Thora herself. She was throwing bag after bag down the stairs into the hallway; mam and Janet were picking them up and throwing them outside. Neither of them had a clue what was happening; but had said this had been going on for about an hour, they had lost count of how many bags had come out of the room.

Another hour passed and we all took turns in collecting the heaps of bags from the bottom of the stairs and stacking them into some kind of order outside. Then they stopped coming and Thora was shouting down for some dusters and the hoover. My mam took them up; but the bedroom door had been kept shut and Thora had asked her to leave them outside. Thora was behaving really funny and I could see the panic crossing both my mam's and my dad's faces. Oh dear.

It wasn't until I had called after work the next night to pick Samantha up did I get an update on the situation. It seemed that the banging that had been going on since Ada had died had been Thora packing up her rubbish; all of a sudden the piles and piles of papers, magazines and junk mail were being stacked neatly into black bags and flung down the stairs. The bed was stripped; the floor was hoovered and the dust eliminated from every surface. Thora herself had been bathed; clean clothes were now being worn and where her hair had looked like a raggy mat; she was now wearing it neatly in a bun. The woman sitting in the living room resembled nothing of the woman who had resided at my mam and dad's for the past year or so. The most remarkable thing was that she was pleasant.

The sour face had gone and as I popped my head in the living room; she shouted a cheery 'hi Val, are you ok??' I was so taken aback by the gentle voice and her whole attire of Thora, I don't even think I answered her. Where had Thora gone? My mam and dad were as much of a loss as we were. The Thora that had emerged from the bedroom was so far removed from the Thora that went in; if we didn't know different we would have thought that aliens had landed and took the old Thora away and replaced her with a completely new model.

It all beggared belief. And that was Thora; whether Ada's death had some bearing on it; maybe now she didn't have to vie for her position in the house or was it because she looked at her own mortality and thought life was too short. Whatever it was the new Thora was a pleasure to have around. New bonds were formed from then on in; Thora and mam; Thora and dad; Thora and her granddaughters; Thora and her great-grandchildren; Thora and her friends. She was a new person and whereas before we all gave her a wide berth; now we would seek her out, she was, surprisingly; a pleasure.

But as the day of Ada's funeral dawned, a sadness fell on the house. Everyone kept themselves busy but it felt like our lives were in some kind of limbo. Julie rang us all the night before the funeral, it was impossible for her to get back, but she rang each one of us in turn and told us she loved us. Lynne was going to keep Samantha with her after school and then return her to school the next morning; Sammy was delighted she loved helping look after Duncan, so I had no worries about leaving her for the night.

As we all waited in my mam and dad's living room for the funeral cortege to arrive, the thought that I would see Brian Mills that day shot through my head and my tummy did it's strange lunge again. Once again I scolded myself for my atrocious timing of fancying a bloke and once again I heard Ada's laugh in my head. Avril fussed around sorting everyone out; she had a list of who was in which car, I couldn't see what the fuss was about; there were only ten of us going in the car and there was seating for sixteen; but Avril's list was Avril's list and as Ada pulled up in front of the house, we all filed out and went to our nominated car.

The funeral had been lovely well as lovely as a funeral could be and I think Ada would have enjoyed it. She was there, I know she was, she had often talked about it over the years, how she wondered if such and such would go and how Mrs Body from along her street better not show her face; she had had the audacity to throw herself at my Granddad a hundred years ago. So I was in little doubt that she wouldn't be there.

As we filed out of the Church; I spotted Brian Mills. He was standing next to one of the cars waiting to take us to the little service at the crematorium; our eyes locked again and once again the flush crept up my body.

My dad had handled the whole ceremony well; his stiff upper lip was is evidence and I had the feeling that if he could he would have slid away and had a bit of time for himself. But he had a wake to host and for the rest of the day, he made sure everyone had had food and the drinks flowed. It was mainly relatives and a couple of old friends of Ada who came back to the house. Everyone had a memory of her, some from years and years ago, but mainly they were recent and very funny. People weren't being disrespectful, they all loved Ada, but she said some really silly stuff and I hoped that if she was there listening; she would be there laughing at her own antics too.

I spent time with my brother-in-laws; to be honest I didn't really get a chance to see them much but I liked each of them very much. Alan had been with Avril forever and where she was bossy and organised, Alan was laidback. He didn't take Avril too seriously and I knew of old this led to Avril throwing tantrums at him; all of which he just laughed off. I didn't know Ian and Graham as well as Alan, but I liked them both and hoped that they were there for keeps. Brian Mills kept popping into my head and every time he did I got the somersaults in the tummy. I hadn't seen anything more of him after the Crem; he had disappeared like mist, the eye lock thing had disturbed me but even though I had the feeling that I would be seeing a lot more of him; I didn't know how and that irked me.

Then Ada's day was over and we all went back to our normal lives, or as nearly to normal as we could manage. We all re-adjusted. My mam and dad seemed to get some sort of quality of life back. Thora was now an independent elderly person living with them. She re-entered her own world with her own friends and associates; she went to her clubs, bingo and even had a few holidays with friends. She was no longer a burden to them and in return they enjoyed having her there. Just as Ada had been good with Samantha, now Thora and Samantha were great friends. Thora spent ages teaching Samantha how to play cards and knit, they had a similar sense of humour and would sit on the settee in stitches at some corny programme on the telly.

Even though Samantha didn't have a dad around, she didn't appear to be missing out. My dad and her were as close as ever and she had strong bonds with Avril and Lynne; relationships she probably wouldn't have had if I had stayed with David. Sandra and Tony saw a lot of her too. David had two boys now and Samantha knew who both of them were. My nerves about Sandra and Tony kidnapping Samantha had long gone and every school holiday Samantha would pack up her little suitcase and go and spend a few days with them at their house. Simon and Toby; David's boys were sometimes there, Samantha would come back saying that they had all been here; or Simon had done this or Toby had done that. She never mentioned if she had seen David; I presumed that the boys got picked up when Samantha did and just as I wasn't there, the absence of Simon and Toby's parents was probably thought of as the norm.

86

Up the Junction

When Sammy was away I took the opportunity to have nights out with friends. Lynne was off limits for night time socialising; she was either pregnant or nursing a new baby, little William had arrived not long after we lost Ada. But I had a couple of other school friends I had kept in touch with and although both of them had young families; they were always up for the occasional night out.

Judy had always been more Janet's friend than mine. I could only vaguely remember her from school, but I had bumped into her often over the years and she would come into the petrol station and we would have a catch up. When she suggested that I have a night out with her at the local, I jumped at the opportunity. The first time I had arranged to meet her I thought it was just going to be the two of us, but I was over the moon when Adele George arrived to join us. She had been in my class all of the way through school, she had lived at the bottom of my street and when I had been pregnant with Samantha, she had been expecting her first one too.

Our nights out were always a good laugh. Sometimes we would go for food, sometimes just a drink, more often than not we would go and watch a band playing. We would sing, dance and drink too much. Every time I vowed I wouldn't have as many vodkas and coke; the next day was always a wasted day because of my fragile head, but as soon as we got together again, the drinks would flow and the next day I would be a fragile mess.

But I wouldn't change them. We tended to meet up once a month or so. There was always plenty to talk about and the three of us got on really well. We regularly went to a pub on the outskirts of town which showcased local bands. Some of the bands were naff but the house band always finished the night off and they were pretty good. Anyway it was at one of these nights that I crossed paths with THE Brian Mills again. Of course I knew it was going to happen. I had been asking the signs since Ada's funeral three months earlier and they had been positive that he was going to come back into my life…. It had just been a case of how and when.

So one Friday night; at the Fox and Feather; there he was. I didn't recognise him at first. The band that were playing on the little stage when we arrived were all right. As we made our way to a table, drinks in hand, I glanced up at the band that were playing their own rendition of Squeeze's Up the Junction quite nicely. There were four blokes in the band; the signage of the front of drum said 'The Diggers', I couldn't remember ever seeing them there playing. Catching a glimpse of the piano player, my tummy somersaulted in the now familiar fashion it did when I saw Brian Mills of Mills and Boone Funeral Directors.

A piano player???? I sat down but turned my head so I could get a better look. He looked different out of his work clothes. He was wearing a black and red rugby style top and jeans. From the side view he looked very handsome; the spin cycle washing machine was back. Not wanting to be caught gawping at him, I turned my attention to what Adele and Judy were talking about. But the pull was too great and I found myself stealing glances at him until The Diggers finished their set and the band made their way to the bar. Unsure if I should go and make myself known to him, I watched out of the corner of my eye where they were going and who they were with. But there just seemed to be the four of them; no girlfriends appeared and they seemed happy enough propping up the end of the bar.

Thinking it was now or never; I volunteered to go and get the next round of drinks in. Taking a de tour into the loos to touch up my hair and make-up I made my way to the bar; not too close to The Diggers, but near enough for Brian Mills to see me when it was my turn to get served. But it didn't work; if he had saw me, he had made no attempt to come and say hello. I was forlorn as I made my way back to Judy and Adele with the drinks.

As the next band started to play, I was adamant I wasn't going to let Brian Mills spoil my night out. The music was more upbeat and I dragged Adele and Judy up onto the tiny dance floor with me. In the end it turned out to be a really good night. If Brian Mills wasn't interested then that was his loss and I wasn't wasting another minute mooning over him. For once the signs had been wrong; it wasn't an exact science after all, they couldn't be right all of the time could they?

Closing time came and as the three of us made our way out of the door someone grabbed my arm. Brian Mills!!! 'Hi!' He said. 'I thought it was you earlier but I wasn't sure, you look so different' he smiled. Taken aback that he had actually spoken to me after hours of trying to get his attention in the pub. 'I hardly recognised you either!' I smiled back. He said that he had to help load the equipment onto the van, but if I waited ten minutes he would give me a lift home if I wanted. I mumbled a 'yes that would be great' I caught up with Adele and Judy and told them what was happening. They were both sniggering as they left me outside the pub door. They knew all about Brian Mills; the undertaker; I just hadn't told them that he had been in The Diggers that night. Assuring them that I would be fine and no they wouldn't find me six foot under in the morning, I waved them a night night and sat on a wall and waited for Brian Mills to come back.

He was as good as his word and ten minutes later pulled up in front of the pub to take me home. Somehow thinking that he would be there in one of the 'company cars' I was shocked when he arrived in a shiny new Vauxhall Cavalier. Sitting myself in the passenger seat he said 'I'm sorry I didn't speak to you sooner in the night. I did think that it was you, but you look so different!!!' 'In a good way I hope!' I replied laughing, the vodkas and cokes I had drank earlier giving me a bit of Dutch courage. I gave him my address thinking I would have to direct him to the little cul-de-sac in the middle of my estate, but he assured me he knew it; then of course he would, his job would take him all over the place. But the journey home was comfortable, there were no awkward silences and we seemed to bombard each other with questions.

So he was Brian Mills, aged 28. He had gone into the family business straight from school, starting at the bottom and learning the trade. He had been a fully-fledged Funeral Director for just over a year, but his dad still held on tightly to his reins. Never been married but had been engaged for a couple of years. His fiancée had ended it because she couldn't really hack his job; 'it isn't to everyone's taste.' He stressed. The vodka did the talking again at that point and before I had a chance to cram the words back into my mouth they were out 'it will never be a dying trade though will it?' If he was offended he hid it well, he actually laughed at me!!!

And then we were pulling into my cul-de-sac and the little journey was over. I had so much that I wanted to ask and say and to be honest I just wanted to spend some time with him. His hair was almost black, I could see that even in the dimness of the car; and it was cut very short, but I had this almighty urge just to reach out and touch it; to touch him. So I fidgeted in my set and ended up sitting on my hands. Vodka bravery was a dangerous thing and I didn't want him thinking I had no shame; after all he hadn't actually said he liked me; he had just given someone he vaguely knew, a lift home.

But he turned the engine off and continued to sit. Dilemma time!! Should I invite him in or was that too much?? Samantha was away at Sandra and Tony's so the house was empty, a coffee wouldn't harm would it?? But what if things got out of control!! I had been on a night out, but that had been a girly night, not a date night. I had hairy legs under my jeans!!! I had hairy armpits under my top!!! And oh dear me; as for the other bits, I blushed even at the thought of them. No not a good idea to invite Brian Mills into the house on the off chance we might like each other too much. I blushed at the thought of it. It was the kind of blush that took over your whole body; tip to toes. And there it was, the very reason that I wouldn't be inviting Brian Mills into my house. My bloody feet. The intervening years working in the garage had done little to improve their appearance. I tried to make them feel better about themselves by putting on colourful nail polish, but I hadn't done that for a while and in my memory I had the vision of each of my little toes having only a flake of nail polish left on. I had had a real bad case of chilblains over the winter and the motely hue was still quite visible, not only that but there were still a few weeping cuts and they were mainly very dry. First thing the next morning I was determined that I would go off to the chemist and re-stock my feet emergency kit on the off chance that one day I might just well invite Brian Mills in.

Whether I had gone quiet while I contemplated my bodily hair and feet, I wasn't sure. But I think Brian Mills took it as his cue to leave. I was at sixes and sevens; that really wasn't the impression I wanted to leave him with, that I had only spoken to him for a lift home. So while the vodka courage was still on board I said 'would you like to go for a drink one night? If you aren't too busy?? I mean if you would like to…..?' I had made a right pig's ear of it. 'Yes Val I think I would, thank you!' So polite, thank you! And yes he wanted to see me again. Swapping telephone number he said he would give me a ring at the beginning of the following week.

As I made my way down the path to 27 Lavender Grove I heard Brian Mills pull his car out of the cul-de-sac. Smiling I put my key in the lock, if I wasn't very much mistaken, in the silence that had followed the departing car, I'm sure I heard the house sigh!!! Oh good I thought to myself with my vodka soaked brain, a sign – the house likes Brian Mills!!

Black and Gold

He was as good as his word and rang. And I was as good as my word too and gave myself a massive pamper. I soaked and creamed my feet at every given opportunity, the toe nails were given a lavish coat of red varnish and I shaved away all the unruly hair. If there was any chance that Brian Mills and me became close; then I was going to make sure I was prepared well in advance. Of course there were some things I couldn't do anything about; the stretch marks on my tummy and legs for one, but they were just who I was now and he was either going to have to like them or lump them. But the embarrassment of those things were a long way off.

But we did go out for a drink. He suggested a meal, but for a first date the thought of eating in front of him filled me with terror, I could just see myself with prawn cocktail sauce dribbling down my chin. A drink or two I could handle though, as long as I stuck to cider and didn't let myself be lured by the false bravado of vodka and cokes.

As a first date, it went well. Not that I had any measure of what a first date should be like. But we were as easy in each other company and as we had been when he gave me a lift home and the night flew by without a hitch. And then there was another date and another. It was a slow burn; I had Samantha and he worked funny shifts and was often on call. But I liked him, he was easy to be with. He had a wicked sense of humour; ridiculous when you thought what his 'day job' was, but the surly undertaker was his job, his real personality was full of fun.

The band Brian was in; The Diggers, was made up with other funeral operatives from Mills and Boone Funeral Directors. They had been playing together for a couple of years, set up firstly as a mess around, but when they discovered that they weren't too bad, they stuck at it. They played together whenever they could and I loved going to watch them. Adele and Judy were dragged out to whatever pub they were playing at; if they minded they didn't say and seemed happy enough to go along to the gigs pretending to be their 'groupies.'

So I had myself a boyfriend, well of sorts. We hadn't actually spent any quality time together, but we were close. Brian had already met most of the family through his job, but bit by bit I re-introduced him to them again. They were all full of it mind; me and the undertaker, but I laughed it off; my Brian was so far away from the tall aloof undertaker that they were like two different people.

I had started to meet his family too. Obviously I had already met his dad Edward, he seemed nice enough, but whereas Brian left his job at work; it seemed to hang on Edward and even when he was in his slacks and a jumper at home, he still had the aura of an undertaker around him and I was a little bit if not scared then in awe of him. Brian's mam wasn't around; she had jumped ship when Brian and his sister Laura were just little, probably because of the same reason Brian's ex had left, you could either take the job or not. He had a step-mam; Sally. I thought she was the daughter of the departed Mr Boone of Mills and Boone Funeral Directors, but it turned out she had been his wife.

Mills and Boone Funeral Directors was now into its third generation. It had been established by Edward's grandfather and it was then just plain old Mills Undertakers. Edward's father had joined forces with Boone Funeral Directors during reign strengthening there foothold in the local market with the arrival of the mighty Co-operative Funeral Directors. The partnership had worked and the reputation of Mills and Boone Funeral Directors as a caring and affordable business, who gave their loved ones a dignified send-off; flourished and the business survived. Old Mr Boone had been a bit of a boy by all accounts, taking his third bride when he was well into his sixties, he was the talk of the town when his third bride turned out to be a young mortician who worked for him. Sally!

Obviously Sally had been widowed young and with the departure of Mrs Mills leaving Edward with two young children to care for, a friendship had been forged which over time turned into something else and eventually marriage. Brian didn't say much, but he looked on Sally as his mam, he adored her and in return she loved Brian and Laura like they were her own.

Brian's real mam lived in Edinburgh. He said that they wrote to each other from time to time and twice a year around each of their birthdays; Laura and Brian made the journey up to Edinburgh to see her. From what he said I couldn't work out if they were close or not; he portrayed her like some elderly aunt that him and Laura were duty bound to go and visit and I didn't push the subject so I had no idea why she had gone and what had happened to her when she left.

But his family all seemed very nice. Sally had been the lady I had seen when me and my dad had gone to see Ada in the Chapel of Rest; and Laura worked in the office; it was all very much a family affair. Laura seemed nice. A bit younger than me, she was tall and dark like her brother, but personality wise she was like her dad; even when she was 'off-duty' she had an aura of respectability about her. She was a bit aloof and even though she smiled a lot, her smile never actually reached her eyes and I wondered if I would ever really get to know her; beyond the pleasantries, she didn't really have much to say.

And the time ticked on. Samantha was the last of the family to meet Brian. Obviously he knew all about her, but I didn't want to be one of those mams who introduced all of their boyfriends to their children. So I kept her tucked away until I knew me and Brian were a serious item. She knew her mam had a friend and he was a boy; something she found really funny, she had a boyfriend at school; Nicky, who she chatted about constantly. Her and Nicky did this and her and Nicky did that; so in her little head she associated boyfriends as being 7 year olds and it took some convincing that my boyfriend was actually a grown up.

I liked Brian Mills, I mean really liked him. I checked the signs constantly and they were all in favour of him, my family and friends liked him and after we had been 'stepping out' about four months; I decided it was time to up the game; I was going to introduce him to Samantha and let him stay the night!!

I was ready. It had been a long time since I had been 'close' to anyone, in that way I mean. But if me and Brian were going to have a future together then we had to get on to the next level. Adele and Lynne thought that it was strange he hadn't tried; they had seen us together and we were really tactile with each other, so when I had announced it to them one night when they were at mine sharing a bottle of wine, they were shocked. Oh God, I thought to myself as they looked at me as if I had told them that Brian was actually called Sharon and was a woman; was there something wrong with me??? I hadn't thought about it before, I just assumed that I had been really lucky and Brian was one of the last remaining gentlemen in the world. And what did I know about social intimacy; was there some kind of yard stick I should have been using?? At one month you do this, at two month you do that. Was it even measured in months?? Should it be weeks?? I was panic stricken; I had no idea what the rules were! Then again as I sat looking at Lynne and Adele; both who had been married for years, the penny dropped. 'What did they know??' Probably as much as I did!!

It wasn't as if Brian didn't fancy me. I was sure he did. We kissed and cuddled lots and sometimes we had to hold ourselves back. Pubs and cars weren't the type of places for letting things get out of hand. Whenever he dropped me off at home I always resisted the urge to invite him in and he never asked. He was a gentleman; I was sure he was, he was going at my pace and to prove it I was going to seduce him, well seduce him of sorts. The next weekend that Samantha was at Sandra and Tony's and Brian wasn't on call I was going to go all out; meal, wine and me if he wanted me. But what if he didn't???

When I asked him if he would like to come for a meal at mine he seemed keen; he told me to tell him what colour wine to get to go with the food. Did he think I was Delia Smith??? I told him to bring one of each!! I cleaned the house until it shone, more through nerves than good housekeeping; but I was pleased with the results, at least he wouldn't think I was a slob.

I kept the food simple, not wanting to be stressed out on a soufflé or the like, I did soup, chicken and chips with all the trimmings and a trifle for dessert. I laid the table so it looked like something out of a restaurant and the whole dining room aura was one of intimacy.

Dressing in jeans and a blouse; I was going for the 'casual sexy' look that I had seen in magazines, not too in your face but the promise of something tasty underneath. New underwear had been purchased and I had gone through the whole beauty routine earlier in the afternoon. It was all good. Even the sore points at the end of my legs were in tip top condition. The summer was always much kinder to them, but for months I had been soaking and creaming and all the hard work was paying off; they actually looked somewhere near normal and I would go so far as to say; I was quite proud of them.

And every last aspect of my hard work paid off. The night was a success. We ate; we drank the wine; we talked and laughed and got a little bit tiddly. When we had finished drinking the wine, we loaded the sink with the dishes, switched off the lights and made our way up the stairs. And of course there was dot dot dot!!

Good Morning Starshine

We woke about the same time; it felt strange having Brian there, but oh so right. We had had a lovely night and now in the cold light of morning I had no regrets. Looking at Brian his forehead was furrowed and he looked worried. Oh God he regrets it all I thought to myself. He must have been a bit drunk last night and now wishes he hadn't woken up in my house; in my bed!!! I felt ill; I could feel the flush of shame running through my body; my now perfect feet were on fire!!! Sensing I was awake too, he turned and smiled at me; wrapped his arms around me and nuzzled into my burning neck. 'I've been thinking Val!' He said. 'This isn't really me, I mean I don't just sleep with anyone. I think it's because of the job, from being young my dad always instilled in me and Laura that we had the reputation of the business to up hold at all time. No scandal sort of thing!!' He went on. The heat was sweeping over my body in waves, he was going to ask me to keep all of this quiet!! I was so ashamed. I felt like a floosy! My whole body was on fire and I was sure at any minute Brian was going to recoil from me fearing being burnt. 'So do you think?' He was going on. 'If it is okay with Samantha; and we get her seal of approval, we could get married?' What??? I lay in his arms stock still, my body was burning like a red hot poker; had I heard right?? Had Brian Mills Funeral Director just asked me to marry him? I was shivering which was ridiculous because at any moment I thought I was actually going to explode. 'Do you not think it's a good idea?' He was saying. I tried to pull myself together; it was just the shock I told him laughing; it had been the last thing I had expected. Yes of course it's a good idea, I said. Yes we'll sort time out for him to get to know Samantha.

By the time he left I was walking on air. I was going to be married again. No firm arrangements had been made; Samantha had to like him first before we even considered a date. But sometime; maybe this year, maybe next, I was going to be Mrs Brian Mills. I couldn't wait to tell everyone, but I'd be sensible, I'd leave it until we were sure that we would be okay as a little family. I was certain that Samantha would love him as much as I did; what was there not to love, he was kind and funny and he would make a great dad.

But then something niggled at me. I had just said that Samantha would love him as much as I did. I did love him; it felt right, different from David, me and Brian had a much more balanced relationship and he still made my tummy do somersaults when I saw him. And he had asked me to marry him!!! But he hadn't told me he loved me!!! There had been no mention of love, no I love you and want to marry you! It had just been 'lets get married.' Did he love me? If the night before had been anything to go by then I would say yes, but he hadn't said it. The words 'I love you' had never passed his lips. I tiny little minute doubt crept into my mind. Surely you wouldn't want to marry someone you didn't love??? David had, he had thought he loved me, but he hadn't. The first person who came along and tickled David's fancy had killed our marriage. Brian would tell me, once we had the Samantha situation sorted we would be all love and romance. The sooner I got them introduced the better I thought to myself. In the meantime I would be happy where we were. I was Brian Mills' fiancée.

Marry Me

Samantha adored him. Shy at first he soon won her around, we started out meeting up at the local park or pictures and by the time that he actually got around to coming to the house, she was used to him and took everything in her stride. Brian seemed to like her too. His childish side came out whenever he was around her; they were as happy sitting playing snap together as they were going to the pictures. Samantha didn't take Brian's arrival as an intrusion, more the bonus of having an extra playmate. He knew about David and obviously was aware that Samantha went to spend time with her grandparents and half-brothers, but he was shocked when I told him that as far as I knew; David had never clapped eyes on his daughter. The knowledge of the completely absent father seemed to spur Brian into action, because the following weekend he took me and Samantha into Newcastle and into one of the plushest jewellers where he asked me to choose an engagement ring and Samantha a necklace. We were officially going to be a family and I could shout it from the roof tops.

Everyone seemed to be delighted. Avril saw it as a step up the social ladder and insisted in throwing us a small engagement party. My mam and dad were happy I had someone to look after me and Samantha and even Thora thought it was great to have a funeral director as a grandson-in-law and insisted in giving him a list of things she wanted at her funeral for future reference.

So by the time we went to Avril's for the engagement party; we had a date set. Almost a year to the day; a June wedding in the local registry office. If Brian was disappointed that we couldn't marry in church; he never said. I was a divorced woman so there was no way I would be able to walk up the aisle a blushing bride, but the registry office was nice and Brian had paid a deposit for the Wedding breakfast to be held at the local golf club.

All this news we passed on to the guests at Avril's. She had done a good job; both our families were there along with an assortment of friends. It was embarrassing getting gifts, I already had a house all set up, but I smiled and thanked everyone and spent the night circulating. My sisters were there, along with their better halves, my mam and dad; Thora; Lynne, Adele, Judy and their husbands and because I hadn't wanted Samantha to be left out all of my nieces and nephews were there. Avril being Avril had set up a special table of food for them; so they all thought that they were very important sitting around their own buffet.

Brian's family were there too. Edward and Sally; Laura and her boyfriend Joe; the rest of the Diggers and assortment of work colleagues and friends. Mr and Mrs McCabe from my work had been invited but they didn't go out much on an evening so had declined. It was a funny old mix; but the drinks had flowed, the music had been turned up and it turned into a really good night.

By the time I celebrated my 30th birthday in February; most of the preparations were done. Because of the wedding my birthday came and went with minimum fuss. I didn't mind; I was shocked that I was 30; where had all that time gone? I didn't feel 30; I still felt like a teenager, but for sure I was out of my twenties and into my thirties.

It wasn't just the wedding preparations that were taking up our time. Brian was moving in; he had always lived at home so I think the thought of living with me and Samantha was a novelty. We decorated; not that there was much wrong with what I already had; but I agreed that it needed to have Brian's stamp on the place too. So most weekends we would trundle around DIY stores picking paint and paper. By the time we had finished it looked like a completely different house; even the gardens had been given a face lift. For the last few weeks that me and

Samantha lived in the house before the wedding; it felt like we were camping out in someone else's home; everything was new and shiny and smelt of fresh paint.

And then on the 4th of June I became Mrs Brian Mills. The wedding was everything I hoped for; a day to spend with family and friends. This time I had opted for a smart tailored dress; no frill or flounces; I wore a pair of the highest silver stilettos I had ever owned (the months and months of foot pampering had paid off.) The pale purple of the dress was carried through into my bouquet and I had a small tiara on my head. Samantha's dress was pink and I had co-ordinated the wedding to match her dress. She looked like a little princess and spent the whole day smiling; I was so proud of her. Brian looked completely different in a grey suit; never having seen him in anything but black suits; meeting him outside the registry office, he look my breath away, it wasn't just Samantha who had a huge grin on her face all day.

The day went by hitch free. Far too fast for my liking, apart from Samantha's birth, it was the best day ever. I loved the fact that everyone had dressed up especially for me and Brian and seemed to spend the day telling everyone how lovely they looked. But before I knew it, it was time to say goodbye. Even though we had talked about going away on honeymoon; there just wasn't time. Brian had to be back to work on the Monday morning so we had decided we would delay the honeymoon until later in the year and just go home. Samantha was staying at my mam and dad's for the night, which was just as well because the car was jam packed with gifts. With good cheer ringing in our ears and confetti in our hair; me and Brian made our way home. Mr and Mrs Brian Mills; who would have thought it.

Do You Want to Know a Secret?

It took us a while to settle into married life; well not so much married life; living together. I was used to it just being me and Samantha, now I had someone else to think of. Brian had stayed plenty of time on the run up to the wedding, but never for more than one night and that's when he was off work too. I didn't realise that his 'on-call' shifts would be so disruptive. We would just be sitting down for tea, or snuggling down to watch telly, or going to sleep for the night when the phone would go and he would be upstairs getting changed and out of the door sometimes returning hours later, or not at all until sometime the following day.

Sometimes he would be very quiet, Sally had tipped me off never to ask about the 'job'. In his line of work he saw some very distressing things; accidents, children, murders. So I had taken Sally's advice on board and if he was quiet I would just let him be. If he needed to talk; I was there, but more often than not he would say nothing and eventually return to his old self.

We had a honeymoon of such the following September, two weeks in Tenerife. It was more of a holiday than a honeymoon, we'd been married for 3 months by then and we took Samantha with us as well. But it was my first holiday abroad and my first family holiday and I enjoyed every single minute of it. I thought about Julie a lot when I was there; I could see the attraction of living somewhere that wasn't England; different culture, food and people. She had been away over ten years and by all accounts showed no sign of wanting to come home.

I did a lot of thinking on holiday. Brian and Samantha spent a lot of time doing the hotel activities; they were getting on so much better than I could ever have hoped for. I took the opportunity to lie by the pool on a lounger and read a book; or people watch or just think. There was still a niggle in my head over Brian. We were married now; we were affectionate and he was caring and kind. But there had still been no mention of the L word. Not once had he told me he loved me!!! And because he hadn't I hadn't. Was that not a bit strange?? I suppose I should take it as read that he loved me. David had said it all of the time and obviously hadn't so maybe I should be thankful that Brian didn't say and did love me. It remained a worry though and I started to look for signs that he didn't want to be with me.

There weren't any. So I started on the signs; they were positive too. I was messed up; my first marriage had distorted my view on relationships and I needed to stop or else I would kill the marriage off myself. So as we boarded the plane back to Newcastle, I mentally threw my concerns down the aircraft steps and left them in Spain.

There was bad news waiting for me when I got home. Mr and Mrs McCabe had been made an offer they couldn't refuse for their business. My job was safe, but it was one of the big boys and they didn't have pump attendants, everything was self-service. I had been doing the book-keeping for years and really enjoyed it, but the new bosses centralised everything and there would be no need for my administration skills, if I stayed on I would be on the till all day. Mr and Mrs McCabe were so apologetic; they had been made an offer they couldn't really refuse, both well past their retirement ages; I didn't blame them.

I discussed it with Brian and we both agreed that I would take the redundancy package on offer and look for something else. I had been working there or almost 15 years so on my last day there both Mrs McCabe and me were inconsolable; it was the end of an era. But times were changing and people would gladly serve themselves if the price of their fuel was going to be cheaper. And that was that. I was unemployed.

Deciding I would have a little bit time off before I rushed into another job, I initially liked the fact that I could pop and see my mam and dad, or sisters when I wanted. But the novelty wore off and within weeks I started to get twitchy. I missed the McCabe's and I missed meeting customers. There was only so much housework I could do and even though I hated gardening I started to potter around doing bits and bobs. Brian liked me being off though, it suited him better me being at home when he was on split shifts and such and of course Samantha liked me taking her to and from school. But I didn't want to stay at home, I had worked hard for my book-keeping qualification and wanted to use it. But I didn't get a chance even to look. I was pregnant again; I knew it the minute it had happened; I felt different. My beautiful feet came out in a hideous rash and I had a horrible whooshy feeling nearly all the time. I didn't feel sick; I just felt spaced. I resisted the urge to tell Brian until I was sure; I'd been there before and wasn't looking forward to telling him.

Confirmed a month later, I continued to put it off. We had talked about adding to the family, but hadn't actually said when and we hadn't been trying. My mind became cram packed with thoughts of the last time I was pregnant and David's reaction; I couldn't face going through all of that again. So I kept putting it off; even though when I asked the signs they said for certain Brian would be happy. I counted birds landing in the garden; I predicted which friend Samantha would come out of school with; I scoured the credits at the end of television programme – if there were three people called Brian there then it would be all right. They were. But I still put off. The weeks went by; when Brian asked why I wasn't looking for a job like I said I was going to do, I just said there was plenty of time…

It went on for weeks and weeks. I told no one, I just had a head full of thoughts that went around and around my already whooshy head. Then one night when I was out with Judy and Adele watching The Diggers, it all came to a head; or should I say that I actually fell onto my head. The pub we were at was packed; it had a roaring open fire and we were sitting at our usual table that we sat at when we had been to that pub other times. But it was too busy and too packed; feigning that I was on antibiotics so not drinking, I sipped on lemonades all night. This obviously had a damming effected on my bladder and it was whilst I stood up to make my umpteenth trip to the loo that the whoosh came and took me off my feet. Going down like a sack of potatoes I banged my head on the fireplace and split it open. Pandemonium followed and before I knew what was happening Brian and Judy had me in the local hospital's Accident and Emergency department.

And it was during the consultation with the nurse, who wanted not only my medical history but what I'd had for breakfast; that the fact I was actually pregnant came to light. Brian; sitting in the chair next to the bed looked at me in total shock; I was almost four months pregnant and hadn't uttered a word. He was furious; I could see it written all over his face. I had made him look like an idiot in front of the young nurse!!!

By the time I had had my head stitched up and made my way out of the hospital, Brian had told Judy to go home. Any hope of a reprieve while we dropped Judy off was gone. I had some explaining to do and there was no way I was going to be able to put off a minute longer. So as he drove; I talked. I tried the best I could to explain why I had been scared to say anything; he kept interrupting me saying the same thing. 'I'm not David!' And so it went on all the way home and all that night and most of the next day until he went off to work. He was so disappointed in me, his words not mine; I didn't know how he felt. Not that there was anything I could do about it now; I was 15 and a bit weeks. The worst he could do was leave me and I'd already done all of that and I had the tee-shirt to prove it.

It didn't stop me fretting though. All day I worried about him coming home, my head was throbbing off where I had had it stitched and I spent most of the day flat out on the settee. The hospital had advised me to go and see my own doctor about what I called the whooshy head and what they called light-headedness, but the nurse seemed to think it would pass shortly; it probably would now that Brian knew; if only I knew what he was thinking.

By the time he got home, Samantha had arrived from her grandparents aswell. She was all chatty chatty about what her and her brothers had been up to, so it wasn't until she was safely tucked into bed and I was making some supper; did we get a chance to talk. He asked how my day was; I asked him how his had gone. Inept chatter; but the elephant was most definitely in the room.

'I wish you had just told me Val!' The flush blush was back. It started on my face and I could feel it creeping down my body until my feet started to throb. 'I know, I'm sorry. I know you aren't David, but I'm just so scared you will leave me, us; me and Samantha and the new baby! It isn't something we planned is it?' I sat with my crimson face down as I said all of this. 'But the difference is, I'm going nowhere Val! I'm over the moon, to be honest I never thought I'd be a dad; I was happy enough being a step-dad; even that took me by surprise, I've not had much to do with kids and I'm surprised how much I've got out of my relationship with Sammie!' He said, reverting to his pet name for his step-daughter. It was fine; it was going to be fine. He wasn't going to leave me; he was happy!! The flush blushed harder. How could I have even thought that he would leave me??

And when we told Samantha in the morning that she was going to have a baby brother or sister; I thought she was going to burst. There were so many questions! When would it be here? What would it be called? When could it go to school with her? Now that Samantha knew it was a case of letting the rest of the family know before someone from Samantha's school said something; there was no way at 9 years old she wasn't going to keep this news to herself.

So I had myself a mission to call and see whoever I could or if not see them in person then I would ring them. Sally rang me before I even got out of the house to take Samantha to school; she was ecstatic; she said Edward was too. Somehow the thought of Edward Mills being excited about anything eluded me, but Sally's excitement was contagious and I enjoyed the rest of the day meeting up with my mam and dad and telling them our news. Thora said she would knit! I forgot that she was quite accomplished with a pair of needles and agreed to pick some patterns out of her collection the next time I was over. My sisters were all over the moon. I was never sure about Janet; I didn't know if they were trying for a baby or if she was happy being a step-mam; I didn't ask. Even though she was my sister I thought it was far too personal a question. She knew I would listen if she wanted to talk, but to date she had remained tight lipped about not expanding Graham's family.

Adele's reaction was the strangest. I had decided I would call and see her on my way home. It was just before lunchtime and I knew that she would be in because she usually started work at the care home at 2pm – her shifts were 2-10 or 6-2. I remembered that she had been on earlies the week before because she had made a point when we went out on Saturday night about how she was looking forward to having a lie in on the Sunday morning.

Anyway she answered her door in her dressing gown. I did think it was a bit strange because she must have already been up and out taking Luke to school. But she had no doubt been in the bath ready for work so I shrugged it off. Making my way straight into the kitchen I switched on the kettle and made coffees; all the time jabbering on about news I had picked up throughout the morning. A bit of gossip off my mam; something Lynne told me about the school; who I saw in the bookies when I went in to see Janet. But she wasn't listening. She looked nervous. 'You okay??' I asked her. Pulling out the kitchen seat she lit up a cigarette; 'yes, of course I am!! What were you saying??' I couldn't be bothered to go through the whole gossip rigmarole again so I told her why I had went there. That's great!' She said puffing on her cigarette. But it was like she was just saying what was expected of her; it was like the news hadn't actually filtered into her brain.

She definitely wasn't listening to me; so I drained my coffee and promising to call her in a day or two, I left. It wasn't until I had turned the corner and was making my way home that I noticed the van. I would know it anywhere; I had seen it often enough. It was a red transit van; it was the red transit van that The Diggers used when they were gigging….

Is She Really Going Out with Him?

It was the red transit van that Clive; the lead singer used when they weren't using it to ferry their equipment around. Clive who was married to Suzy. Clive who had two teenage girls. Clive who was a funeral operative for Mills and Boone Funeral Directors. And Clive who seemed to be having a bit of a thing with one of my best friends!!!

I couldn't get home quick enough. The flush blush was back and I didn't want to be walking along the street when the red transit van trundled past. Clive might see me and try and give me some concocted story about why he was in the area. He didn't even live in town; I was sure he lived about 8 or 9 miles away in one of the pit villages. So it was with relief that I made it home and closed the front door behind all the shenanigans. There had definitely been something going on; Adele was cagey and nervous. Had Clive been upstairs all the time I had been there? I didn't know what to do. Adele would be on her way to work now; was Clive giving her a lift?? My imagination was going into overtime. I didn't know much about Adele's personal life; she had married a lad that had been a few years above me at school; Steven Smith. They had had Luke, but to be honest she never really talked about Steven.

It was none of my business and I certainly didn't want to be the one to let the cat out of the bag. But it had taken the shine off my day. But on the other hand, I was probably on the receiving end of an affair whether I knew it or not. Even though it had turned out to be a relief all those years later when I found out that David had fell in love with someone else; how he had treat me when he had fallen out of love with me had been horrific. Maybe Adele and Clive were just having a fling, maybe today would be the first and last time and their close call with me dropping by unexpectedly had been enough to bring them to their senses. So I would forget about it. I would forget about Adele and her jumpiness; and I would forget about seeing the red transit van parked around the corner. I would forget everything.

And I did, best I could anyway. The next time I saw Adele she was a lot more attentive and more her usually bubbly self. There were no indicators that she was having an affair; not that I would know what they were. But she said her and Steven had booked a holiday and they were buying a new car; neither of these things would point to Adele leaving Steven so maybe it had just been a one night stand or more precisely a one afternoon stand and now it was over.

I did as the nurse at the hospital had said and booked an appointment with my doctor. I wasn't as whooshy now and everything seemed to be progressing nicely, so there were no concerns there. Brian fussed over me and if I had any doubts about how he felt about the baby then they were well and truly quashed; he was so excited. With no work to go to and little exercise to be had, I piled the weight on. I would waddle around to my mam and dad's and munch my way through their biscuit barrel then waddle off to the school or home. I was the size of a house. By the time I was six months gone I was the same weight I had been just before I had Samantha. My feet were enormous; I would tell everyone I was retaining water; but the truth of it I was fat. Far too fat; but I was bored.

The red cars and the blue cars had a race .... And the red cars won. A girl. I kept it to myself though; I had never had the courage to tell Brian about my signs, I had never told anyone really, just Lynne. She just thought I was quirky. But I trusted them. If the red cars had won, then this baby was a girl; I was sure of it. A very hungry little girl.

I would spend my days visiting my friends and family but I couldn't stay out all day, so I would come home, do my housework and then plonk myself down in front of the telly with whatever I fancied out of the kitchen. I ate constantly and was paying the price for it.

On his day off Brian would drag me around the baby shops and I would shuffle around after him helping him fill up the trolley with all and sundry. It was all very different from when I was pregnant with Samantha; it had been my mam and sisters who had helped me then. Having the baby's father was a completely new experience, if I hadn't been so fat and cumbersome I would have really enjoyed it.

But I would be worn out after an hour or so, hungry and light headed, I would twist at Brian until he either took me for something to eat or took me home. I was just so lazy. By the time I reached 37 weeks the midwives were so concerned about my weight that they referred me to hospital where it was decided that the baby was big enough for me to be induced and delivered immediately.

My bag was already packed and ready but my early admittance into hospital sent everyone into turmoil. Samantha went to stay with Avril; she was going to school anyway so it was no hardship to take Samantha along with her. Brian was there when they started the induction, but progress was slow and they sent him home for the night. When nothing had still happened the next morning they decided that they would break my waters. Six hours later I actually went into labour, but it was slow. Brian was there; pacing around the little room; for once his calm demeanour was rattled. When four hours later I still hadn't progressed much; they decided that the best option would be for me to have a caesarean section. By that time I didn't care how the baby came; I was so huge and uncomfortable, but Brian was worried, I could see it in his face. He declined actually coming into the theatre, deciding just to sit in the little waiting room until it was all over. He was so out of his comfort zone. As they wheeled me away; he held onto my hand and squeezed it tightly. Just before I went under the anaesthetic a thought went through my head; that would have been a grand opportunity for him to tell me he loved me but he didn't ……….

King of the Road

Our daughter was born ten minutes later by caesarean section. I didn't see her for the first 12 hours or so, but Brian had and showed me her on a little Polaroid photograph. She was in special care; there was nothing wrong they said, it was just that she had been born so quickly she was in shock. Even at 37 weeks she was a big girl; 9lb 9ozs. It was all those biscuits I had scoffed. We didn't have a name picked. We had short listed about five for each sex; but until I saw her I wouldn't commit to any of them.

But she was as pretty as a picture. Shock over, she was with me the following morning. Whereas Samantha had been very fair when she was born, the new baby was dark. She was beautiful; Belle. I wanted to call her Belle because she was so beautiful. But Brian wouldn't hear of it, he thought it sounded like a surname. But until we came up with something we both liked, I called her my Belle.

The families arrived laden with gifts for the new arrival. Sally cried and cried; having had no babies of her own and Brian and Laura having being older when she became their mam; the sight of her new born granddaughter turned her into a quivering wreck. Edward was much more restrained, he made all of the right noises but he seemed to struggle to show his emotions; this was his first granddaughter after all. Perhaps that's why Brian was a bit aloof; or was it just the job? But there was no holding Brian back with his affection for the baby. Bringing Samantha in to see her new baby sister; they were both so excited. In fact Samantha was beyond excited; she was fit to burst. She kept stroking the baby's face and when she eventually got to have a hold of her, I cried; she was just so lovely, they were both just so lovely.

Brian took a week off for when I got out of hospital; I had had a major operation so I was limited to what I could and couldn't do. The baby still remained unnamed 10 days after her birth. We couldn't agree on anything. Even though I still called her my Belle; Brian was having none of it. Everyone that visited came up with name suggestions, but nothing stuck. Brian liked Ella, but I was thinking Sam and Ella and that just didn't sound right. Obviously I wasn't going to get my Belle; it was far too contemporary, but I did like Hannah. Brian didn't, he suggested Sophie; Samantha and Sophie – too many ss. I said Jessica; he said no, he said Hayley; oh that was a maybe. But Hayley Mills??? Was that not an actress's name? But I did like it. Samantha and Hayley went well together. Hayley Mills!!!! Did it even matter that someone famous had that name, after all her dad had the same name as a mail order catalogue!!

So Hayley Mills joined the family. She was a very noisy member of the family as well. She like the sound of her own voice and those first weeks were testing. My mobility wasn't fantastic what with my wound and my weight. I couldn't believe how fat I actually was. Leaving the hospital, I felt stick thin, but later trying to get into some of my normal clothes I was mortified, they wouldn't go anywhere near me. Back into the maternity clothes I went, unhappy that I had let myself go and because I felt like that, I ate and ate.

Brian went back to work, but the help kept coming. My mam, Sally, Thora with her plastic bag full of beautiful hand knitted cardigans in a rainbow of different colours. Lynne; pregnant with her third came to get back in the swing of having a new born to care for. With each visitor the biscuits would come out and I'd spend the time dunking the biscuits in endless cups of coffee. I was in a vicious circle.

Hayley was at her worst through the night, she would scream and scream for her bottle and guzzle it so fast that she would get terrible wind that would take ages to get up. I would end up falling asleep on the settee with her, well for a couple of hours and she woke up for her next feed. I was exhausted. Brian helped where he could, but Edward hadn't been feeling very well, so Brian had stepped up and took more 'on call' nights so he was always tired as well and so if he did stir to see to her, I would tell him to go back to sleep and I would go.

It was a miserable time. Hayley was thriving though, Samantha adored her and proudly showed her off to everyone; we even made an appearance in her class at a 'show and tell' day. I must have been doing something right, even if it didn't feel like it.

Then something remarkable happened. Hayley was 3 months old and she slept through the night for the first time. Waking after an undisturbed sleep; I bounded out of bed and over to the cot fearing the worst. But there she was, her little chest moving up and down, fast asleep. And that made all of the difference. After a week of having five hours sleep each night, I was full of energy. My wound had healed and whereas before I had waited for my mam and dad to come and see us or Adele to take Samantha to school, I was there doing it. I pushed Hayley miles and miles in her pram. The weight started to come off little by little. But it made all of the difference. I was no longer looking for the sugary things, I didn't need them. I started cooking and eating healthier food and the first time I got back into my normal clothes I cried. My body was a mess mind. I already had stretch marks from when I was pregnant with Samantha, but the existing ones had been stretched even further and were bright purple and I had new ones, which were not quite as dark; but were still an eyesore. And I had them everywhere. Boobs, tummy, legs, everywhere imaginable. They were there though and there was nothing I could do about them. I couldn't even exercise; the midwife had said nothing too strenuous for at least six months.

My feet too; after all of the months where I hadn't been able to see them, I had neglected them. Out of sight out of mind. They were all dry and flaky again; really not a pretty sight. Out came the bowl and the creams and I was off again trying to make the best of a bad job. For some reason the nails of my big toes had turned a weird yellow colour and if I was honest there was a funny smell, but I started on my daily regime and hid the yellowing toe nails with a shocking pink nail varnish.

My feet weren't the only things that concerned me. Brian and me hadn't been close for months. Mainly my fault; I had felt the size of a whale and I went out of my way to keep my first bloated pregnancy body and recently flabby body under wraps. There had been cuddles but that was as far as it went. As the weight started to come off I started to feel more like my old self and thought that Brian would feel the same. But so far it was just cuddles; had I totally put him off me? Would he ever think about me as a woman again?

All my insecurities were back with vengeance. I would listen to him snore next to me in bed and my head would spin around in circles. Should I make the first move?? Fear of rejection put paid to that idea; so I would analysis. We had a new baby and even though Hayley was easier now, it was still hard work. Whereas before Brian would come in from work to his meal and a few hours peace and quiet before bed; now he came in to chaos. It didn't matter how hard I tried to be organised, I couldn't quite pull it off.

Not a natural homemaker, I would leave everything until the last minute, then have a frantic hour making tea. Obviously this all depended on what sort of mood Hayley was in, but usually Brian would have to help out and sometimes it could be 10 o'clock before we actually got our tea. Edward was struggling with a bad back; one of the drawbacks of the job. For many years he had been a pallbearer and now he was paying the price. So what started out as a temporary step up to senior funeral director, was quickly turning into permanent situation. All in all; our new lifestyle didn't leave much time for me and Brian to be close as we had been pre-Hayley.

By the time Hayley was six months old, I was starting to get itchy feet; literally, my feet were in prime condition due to my daily administrations!! I had always work full-time, up until I had got made redundant just before I got pregnant. Now that Hayley was older and Samantha was more independent, I thought it was time I dipped my toe back into the work market. I was an experienced qualified book-keeper, surely there was someone who could use me, even if it was just part-time. But there was nothing local; I had never had to commute before, the thought of bussing in and out of work didn't appeal. So then I had plan b. I would learn to drive.

Brian was supporting us totally, my redundancy money was still in my savings account so I could easily afford to learn to drive and get myself a little run around. I asked around and there was a local motoring school which seemed to have a good reputation and pass rate. With provisional licence in hand I booked a course of lessons. I thought I would take to it like a duck to water; I had not only watched Brian behind the steering wheel; but I'd worked with motorists for years; how hard could it be. But I was useless.

For a start the gear stick felt like it was on the wrong side; never good with my left hand, I struggled to work my way through the gears. The three pedals at my feet confused me and I stalled constantly. Poor Eric, my instructor was forever having to use his pedals and guide the steering wheel to get me out of trouble. I couldn't understand it; Brian made it look so easy. Even my sisters; none of who I would say were bright – all drove. I just didn't get it. I would sit at the window waiting for Eric to pull the little learner car into the cul-de-sac; and I'd feel sick. I would sweat my way through the lesson; Eric intermittently pulling the car over so he could draw me diagrams of road positions; gear positions or just have himself a cigarette. Surely I shouldn't have been paying for his cigarette breaks. By the time I got to the end of my lesson and we pulled back up outside the house; I would be one big red blotch; the funny thing was; so was Eric.

I refused to give up. I read my highway code from cover to cover over and over again; none of it making any sense but hoping that somewhere in the deepest recess of my brain; some of the jargon was going in. When Hayley was having her naps; I would practice my pedals. For some reason without the luxury of actually watching my feet; I didn't know which pedal was what. So I improvised. I took tins out of the cupboard and placed them beside me on the settee and hiding behind a newspaper I would set myself a little task. Brake and clutch; accelerator; brake. Obviously I had to distinguish one pedal from another, so I used beans for the brake, tinned carrots for the clutch and because I didn't have any tins in my cupboard beginning with the letter 'A', I used a tin of fruit cocktail; sure there would be a piece of apricot in the tin somewhere.

My hard work started to pay off. I started to get it. I had had about 18 lessons by that time and all of a sudden I wasn't stalling as much; Eric didn't need to grab the steering wheel as often and we had no cigarette breaks. I had cracked it. I could drive.

By the time I got to lesson 25; Eric said I was test ready. I was so excited. I asked Brian to take me out for extra practice lessons, but he refused. He said he had loads of bad habits and he didn't want to undo all the hard work Eric had done with me. But I knew the reason why he didn't want to take me out in his car. He was scared. So I persevered with Eric and when test day arrived I was brimming with confidence as a driver. Then I failed.

Ten more lessons to polish me up, back in for my test and I failed again. And then again. I didn't even have the luxury of saying that I failed on the same thing all of the time; I wasn't useless at any one thing; I just wasn't good enough at all of them. I felt sorry for Eric; every time I pulled into the test centre I could see him hopping around waiting to see how I had got on. I so wanted to make him proud of me. I didn't want to stop though; if I did I knew I would never go back to it and it had already cost me the equivalent of a small family car.

I resorted to the signs; they weren't hopeful and I went into my fourth test with little hope of passing. I was right to have no hope and I failed again. It was getting to be embarrassing; I was a standing joke in the family. So I booked another 10 lessons and another test. This was number 5 and I was determined that this time I was not going to fail.

I had resisted the urge to ask the signs; if I was going to fail again, it would be a surprise. Test day arrived on the same day 3" of snow fell. Eric was sure that the test would be cancelled, he even drove down to the test centre concerned that I had never driven in the snow and wouldn't know what to do if I got into a skid…. He had so little confidence in me. But the test centre was open and the test went ahead and I did skid and I did know what to do and I passed my driving test. This time when I drove back into the test centre there was no sign of Eric, it was blowing a blizzard. So I sat and waited for him to come out to the car, already sitting in the passenger seat because I knew he wouldn't trust me to drive home, he had tears in his eyes when I showed him my test paper with the big tick for pass on it. It was one of the happiest days of my life.

I wouldn't miss Eric; he was a constant reminder of what a failure I had been in the past and I certainly wouldn't miss getting out of his car and having to make straight for a bath because I stunk of Woodbines. But for years and years afterwards I would see him out on lessons in the area and I would always give him a cheery wave, certain that he wouldn't be telling his current pupil what a terrible pupil I had been.

Careless Whisper

By the time Hayley turned one year old; Samantha was off to senior school. She was quite the young lady and it seemed strange to think that as far as I was aware; David still hadn't seen her. She still went to see Sandra and Tony regularly; they were even good enough to take her away on a couple of holidays. They adored her, but always asked for my approval before they bought her anything major. She never questioned who Sandra and Tony were; she knew they were her grandparents but she never said if they talked about David and if they did; what explanation they gave about David not seeing her.

Brian and Samantha were close still. She was more like his daughter than she was mine. She liked music and Brian had bought a second hand piano for her when she was about nine and he had taught her how to read music and play it. She was becoming quite accomplished and took extra music lessons after school when she went to the comprehensive.

Mine and Brian's relationship had settled back down, we were close again. I still wasn't working. After the ordeal of my driving lessons, I was exhausted. By the time we had trailed around every garage in the vicinity looking for 'the' car for me, I had lost interest in going out to work and instead took to my new found freedom as a driver.

What a difference it made to my life. I could pop around to my mam and dad's whenever I fancied; I would give Thora a lift to one of her clubs and I would go and see my sisters and nieces and nephews whenever the fancy took me. I didn't have time to go to work. I didn't even mind being a designated driver when I went with Judy and Adele to watch The Diggers play. It didn't happen that often now; Mills and Boone Funeral Directors were really busy, so when they did get chance to all play together somewhere it was a big deal and we all turned up to watch.

Adele hadn't left Steven and Clive and Suzy had just celebrated their silver wedding anniversary so I took it that the afternoon I had stumbled across them had just been a one off. I tried not to watch them when we went to watch The Diggers, but I did. To anyone else, there would be nothing to see. But I saw it all. They might have been fooling everyone else but I saw the looks and I knew that I had been wrong; there was still something going on.

It had nothing to do with me; I saw lots of Adele and she seemed the same as she always did. She lost a bit of weight and her hair was always cut and coloured beautifully, but she was the same old same old and if she was having an affair she was keeping it very close to her chest. I did ask a couple of leading questions, but she didn't bite; she didn't even have the audacity to look embarrassed. Maybe it had just been the once; maybe the looks were just 'what ifs!'

And because we didn't do The Diggers thing as much as we used to; I let sleeping dogs lie. I had plenty on my plate, I had one daughter hurtling towards her teens and the other towards her terrible twos. Then Brian came in late one night from work announcing that his dad was retiring and he would be taking over the family business. Edward's back hadn't improved and it looked like he was going to have to have an operation, Sally had decided that if he needed to be off work for a while, then he may as well retire and they could start to enjoy themselves more. This obviously meant that not only was Brian going to have to step up to the mark, so was Laura. Sally had been an integral part of the business forever; people expected to have a Mills or a Boone handling their loved ones. Sally had made it her job to meet the bereaved families and take on board what it was they wanted and nothing was ever too much trouble. Even afterwards, when the funeral was over and the dust had settled, Sally would go and see if the ones left behind were coping all right; she would help them fill in forms, claim benefits and if she thought she wasn't coping then she would suggest some sort of support. She was going to be a hard act to follow and one I wasn't altogether certain Laura would be able to replace.

For years Laura had shadowed Sally, just as Brian had been with Edward. But where I thought Brian was more than capable of filling his dad's large shoes, I thought Laura was lacking. I didn't see her as a people person, she didn't seem to have any empathy; her aloofness came across as snobby, stuck up or even cold. I knew Brian was concerned, he had sort of said so over the years; 'Laura is more back room than front of house!' He would say. And I had to agree.

The following months were an ordeal for all of us. Brian was overworked and stressed. The usual seasonal influx of business brought on by the cold weather didn't help. He was hardly ever at home and when he was he was either asleep in the chair or snapping at me and the girls. I wanted to help but didn't know how to; I had been married to Brian for over four years, but I was still ignorant about his work so what help I did offer was scoffed at by him. Best I could do was keep the girls happy, the house tidy and meals on the table for whatever time it was he returned.

I knew for certain that Laura wasn't working out. I did think about offering to do it, but I knew he would make an excuse about me not being experienced enough to cope with bereaved families and make me feel stupid. But I did suggest that they advertise for someone to do the job, someone who had experience and would lighten Laura and Brian's load. It was a well-received suggestion and one Brian said he would talk to Laura; Edward and Sally about. But as quickly as I did something right; I seemed to have done something completely wrong. This time it was something I couldn't control or even make a suggestion about. But Brian was furious and it seemed to be my fault!!

This Ole House

Brian was on a late start at work; we were having the luxury of a late breakfast together when he mentioned that Sally and Edward had been looking to buy a bungalow. Edward had had his operation and was making a slow but good recovery. Anyway, Brian said that they had been looking for something more manageable to live in and had seen a few bungalows they had liked. Not really thinking about the consequences of this news; I asked where they had been looking etc etc. It wasn't until Brian said that it would make more sense if we moved into their house when they moved out.

Really!! They had a beautiful home; all the fixtures and fittings were of the best and it was big and airy. But it was also attached to the funeral home. Years and years ago when Grandpa Mills had started to become successful, he had bought the premises where the business was now, with the sole purpose of converting the existing house into the funeral home and using the annexe at the side of the house to extend and convert into a family home. From the driveway you couldn't even see that there was a large family home to the rear. You had to take the sweeping drive to the right of the building to get to it. It was similar in design to the funeral home; double fronted with pillars and post. But it also had an adjoining door that led into the back rooms of Mills and Boone Funeral Directors and even after all these years, it still freaked me out.

The garden at the back had huge hedges so there was no view of the other building; but you could hear the cars pulling up, doors clattering and footsteps on the gravel and from the upper rooms of the house you had a clear view of all the comings and goings around the back; the business side of the funeral directors. And besides Laura lived there. I didn't want to share a home with someone who looked like the grim reaper; because that who she looked like now. The added responsibilities had given her a funny aura; it must have been the added pressures of her job; but she looked like death and had said as much to Brian after I had seen her a few weeks earlier. If I had just lost someone I wouldn't want Laura coming to sort out the arrangements!! She would terrify me. And I certainly didn't want to share my house with her.

Surely Brian wasn't thinking about us going to live there; especially with the girls? I didn't want to live there. As lovely as it was; I liked our house. I was comfortable living where we were; yes it only had two bedrooms and the girls were sharing, but for the minute Samantha liked having Hayley in with her. It wouldn't stay like that; once Samantha started wanting her friends staying and stuff, she wouldn't want her little sister in the room with them earwigging and telling tales. But we had talked about getting an extension, we had room. Now this though and Brian had the look on his face that said that this was what he wanted. The blush flush was back. I sat sipping my coffee burning.

I really didn't want to move to Sally and Edward's house. I was seething that Brian had taken it as read that I would want to go. He had been brought up there so it was second nature for him; but it was an ordeal for me. The phone went and Brian left for work; some crisis or another. I sat thinking longer; over my dead body was I moving there!!

Then he was back and he was fuming. The crisis at work had taken shape in the form of Steven and Clive fighting. Adele's husband had rolled up at the funeral home and thumped Clive. All hell had let loose and by the time Brian had got there; the police were in attendance too. Brian was livid; Mills and Boone Funeral Directors had an implacable reputation and there he was instilled in a brawl between one of his employees and a friend. The long and short of it was that Clive and Steven were carted off to the police station and Brian had to fiddle around with the rotas to get cover for Clive.

Not best pleased when he got home, he gave me an update on what had happened. The flush blush that had abated only an hour or so earlier was back and Brian saw it. He took it as guilt. That I had known all of the time what was going on. Adele was my friend; she must have told me. I feigned my innocence. No she hadn't said anything; and that was the truth, she never had. But he was having none of it. The reputation of the business ….. the inconvenience that the melee had caused ….. he went on and on and on. Hayley started to get upset; she was used to her daddy being quiet, but he wasn't one for losing his temper and shouting and she didn't like it.

I didn't know whether I should ring Adele. Something must have happened because Steven wouldn't have gone off on one for no reason. Hayley was almost four now; so if Adele and Clive had been having affair; they had been getting away with it all of this time. I hoped she was all right. From what Brian had said Steven was livid; I hoped that he hadn't hurt her. Deciding that I needed to get away from the ranting Brian; I took Hayley and went and sought refuge at my mam and dads.

I sat drinking coffee at the kitchen table and updated my mam on what had happened. She didn't like gossip, but she did say that she had heard something in the bakery a couple of weeks earlier about Adele looking at a flat above a shop a few doors down from the bakery. How didn't I know?? Why hadn't she said?? If she was leaving Steven surely she needed support. I had seen her lots of times recently; Samantha and Luke were both going on a skiing trip from school to Austria and there had been a number of meetings at the school for parents. Me and Adele had gone together!! I felt terrible, she didn't trust me enough to tell me how unhappy she was with Steven or even how happy she was with Clive. I felt useless.

My mam assured me that sometimes secrets were so deep it was hard to bring them to the surface and it would usually take something catrostophic to happen to bring it to the fore. I wasn't convinced. While I was having my whinge I told her about Sally and Edward's house and Brian's plans to move us there. My mam had been there lots of times since me and Brian had got married and could see the potential; but was in agreement, it wasn't a place for children and with Laura being a live in lodger there as well; it didn't seem like a good prospect. I was going to dig my heels in over this one.

So I was a sad person returning home. I wasn't a trustworthy friend and I knew that I was going to have a battle on my hands with regard to the house move. Brian was still livid; he didn't lose his temper often but when he did it would go on for days; first the temper and then the sulk. He was still adamant that I knew about Adele and Clive; the flush blush returned and even though I knew little; I looked guilty.

For days and days I stayed out of his way. Both Clive and Steven had been cautioned by the police and Clive had returned to work, but it did little to lighten Brian's mood. Adele rang me; asked if we could talk. Too much too little I thought to myself, but agreed to meet up with her. I didn't mention it to Brian; red rag to bull and all of that.

I met Adele in town; Hayley was at nursery school and it seemed like a good idea to get out of the immediate vicinity; walls had ears and all of that. Plonking myself down next to her in the little coffee shop; she looked awful. I smiled and that was all it took for the tears to start; a friendly face. I didn't know what had been going on but surely it hadn't been so bad that there was only me still talking to her. When the tears dried she started to talk. Apologetic at first; I brushed it off saying it didn't matter; two faced bag that I was; I'd been livid.

And then the story came out. How unhappy she had been with Steven. Clive giving her a lift home the night I bumped my head and had to go to hospital. How she felt about Clive. It just kept on coming. I asked questions; there were blanks that needed to be filled to complete the picture. But the long and the short of it was that she hadn't been happy with Steven for a long long time. He smoked weed; something that had totally gone over my head. I had been to their house loads of times and had never seen Steven smoking anything more sinister than a cigarette. But he had and the habit was a daily one. Not only had Steven's personality changed, but all their money went on keeping him supplied. Looking back; their house, even though it was always clean and tidy, never changed. There had been no decorating done for years, the furniture was the same furniture they had bought when they first moved into the house and even though they both worked full-time; Adele had looked panic stricken when the cost of the skiing break for Luke had been confirmed.

She said it wasn't just the money though. Steven had changed; he had no affection for her not because he didn't want to; he couldn't do it. And they ended up in a vicious circle of highs and lows culminating in Clive showing Adele some kindness and her falling completely in love with him. I didn't say anything about the day I had called; her acting suspicious and the red transit van. She knew I knew and we left it at that. But what had started out a distraction had turned into something else and after all the time of the secret affair; she had plucked up the courage to leave.

Adele and Luke had moved into the little flat above the hairdressers a few doors down from the bakery a week earlier. Clive had had no intention of leaving Suzy, they had decided that long ago. Adele had left Steven because she couldn't live like that anymore; not to have a relationship with Clive. She said she loved him, wholeheartedly; but she wasn't a home wrecker and what they had would never move onto the next level. Telling Steven that her and Luke were going had been terrible she said, he didn't understand and said he would get help. But she said he had said it all before and she couldn't live like that any longer. Luke was a teenager and if she had condoned Steven taking drugs; he could follow suit and she didn't want that.

Adamant that was it, they moved out. Only for some kindly neighbour to tell Steven about her 'gentleman friend' and that's when all hell had let loose. Unable to keep it from Suzy; Clive had to front up. Adele said she told Steven that it made no odds; she hadn't left him for Clive she had left him for herself and more so for Luke. She wasn't going to go back, there would be no reconciliation. The break had been made and even though she said that the flat wasn't up to much; it would do for the time being. Her and Clive were over. It had only ever been an affair; she loved him but she said that from the beginning he had told her he would never leave Suzy. They had been caught and now it was done. Clive was staying put.

I understood. I understood why Adele had done what she had done; she couldn't stay in a loveless marriage and one where her child was at risk. Driving back to pick Hayley up my heart went out to Adele; she was all alone now; she had Luke but he was a teenage boy and she was going to have to handle all the worries that came along with teenage boys on her own. But it was better than living a lie wasn't it? And it made me think of Brian. He thought I knew all about Adele and Clive, I didn't; I just had a suspicion and that wasn't any sort of foundation for making accusations.

But he was still in a mood; the temper had subsided but he was quiet and surly and whereas usually they just lasted a few days; this one was dragging on. With the news that Sally and Edward had found a bungalow that suited them just perfect, the house move row was back. But I fought and I fought; I dug my heels in and point blank refused to go. It wasn't a happy home.

By the time removal day came for Sally and Edward, we were no further forward. If he thought he was going to get his own way with this one he was sadly mistaken. If Adele had the courage to change something she didn't like in her life; I surely wasn't going to bow down and give in to something I knew for sure would make me unhappy and even a little bit scared.

We all went along with Brian to see the new bungalow. Situated on the outskirts of town, it was huge. I had had a vision in my head of a tiny bungalow on an exclusive estate, but what they had bought took my breath away. It had its own private gates, a long drive where at the bottom was the biggest bungalow I had ever seen. It was totally private and to the front a small stream trickled by. It must have cost a fortune; all their years of hard work had certainly paid off. Edward seemed like a new man; still moving around gingerly; he looked what I could only describe as happy, something that I had never seen him like before. Edward took the girls and Brian on a grand tour of the gardens, while Sally showed me the bungalow. It was truly amazing, even though they had only lived there a matter of days, it already had their stamp all over it. As she chatted she kept saying things about their former home. The extra curtains for each of the rooms were stored in the cupboard in the small bedroom. The door into the kitchen would need looking at because it didn't close properly.

Sally took it as read that we were moving in there. Had she presumed or had Brian said?? I was furious. It seemed that my feelings had been totally ignored. The row on the way home blew any row we had ever had before out of the water. The girls sitting in the back of the car had sense not to say anything. I was a ball of fire. Hot from tip to toe, I used the heat to fuel my attack. I was not under no circumstances going to go and live in a funeral home.

By the time we reached home my temper tantrum had died down. It seemed Brian's had too and as I busied around the kitchen sorting out some food, he disappeared into the hall and went straight onto the phone; no doubt checking that his precious business had managed for a day without him, I thought spitefully to myself.

Samantha was picked up straight after her tea to go and stay a few days with Sandra and Tony and by the time Hayley was tucked up and asleep in bed it was almost 9 o'clock. There had been no mention of the row either off me or Brian, in fact we had barely spoken. I plonked myself down and flicked through the channels on the telly looking for something to distract myself. Brian came into the living room wearing his overcoat. I hadn't heard the phone ring which usually heralded his departure so I was shocked he was dressed and ready to go. 'I'm going to stay at the house Val!' He said. 'What do you mean? Your dad's??' I said trying to see the expression on his face; was he going because of the row? 'Yes, Laura can't stay there by herself, I'll ring you tomorrow! Night!' He said walking out the door. And then he was gone.

Don't You Want Me Baby?

I didn't know if he had just gone for the night or what. If he was waiting for me to run after him, he'd have a long wait. There was no way I was going to that house and that was my final decision. Family home or not; it wasn't my family home and Brian was bang out of order expecting me to live somewhere I wasn't happy.

I spent the night tossing and turning in bed. Had he left me? I didn't know. We hadn't been getting on so well lately, but the foundations were still in place. I loved him, I might not have told him, but I did. He was kind and caring and a good provider. He hadn't been so full of fun since Edward had retired, but that was just because of the job. Or was it?? Did he love me? I couldn't answer that; like me, he had never said. We had been having a relationship for 8 years and neither of us had told the other that we loved them.

If he was just making a statement; then it wouldn't work. I would never, under no circumstances move into that house. I might have been ungrateful; it was a beautiful house and it would have made Brian's job a lot easier, but I couldn't do it. By the time morning came, I hadn't closed my eyes. My feet were throbbing and the familiar itch was there, a sure sign that I wasn't happy. But as I sat on my bed and rubbed antiseptic cream on them; I knew that they would get worse before they got better. I wasn't giving in.

But he didn't ask me to. He rang just after lunch asking if I was ok, if Hayley was ok. Had I heard from Samantha? There was no mention of him coming home and he hadn't asked me to go and see him. And so it went on. Used to his absences, the girls didn't ask where he was. It wasn't until Avril called unexpectedly one teatime, did I even tell anyone what was going on.

Poor Avril. It always seemed to be her who got my woes. She sat on my settee while I told her the whole sorry tale. She would have given anything to live in a house like the one I refused to move in to; I could remember clearly on Hayley's 3rd birthday; Avril oohing and arging around the garden and house. But she understood; it wasn't a place to have a teenage girl and a little girl live. Always a one for action rather than pandering; she asked about my finances; the rent and what my immediate plans were.

The house had stayed in my name, every month Brian had put money into my account to cover the rent and any other needs I might have had. He had always been generous to a fault, but if he had left me then this arrangement would probably be coming to an end. He would provide for Hayley, I was sure of that, but whether it was enough to keep a roof over our heads and keep me and Samantha; I didn't know. I still had a monthly maintenance payment off David; but that had been the same since my solicitor had set it up, it barely covered Samantha's bus pass never mind clothe and feed her.

Avril suggested I went back to the solicitors; find out exactly where I stood, what financial provisions could be made and then she said I should think about getting myself a job. By the time she left an hour or so later; I was deflated. I was 36 years old and I was now under no illusions; I had two failed marriages behind me.

I put everything off though. As always I waited weeks and weeks before I did anything. Brian would come and take the girls away, sometimes it would be for their tea or if he had time they would have a run down to the coast or over to see his dad and Sally. He never mentioned coming home. He didn't particularly talk to me. I would ask how work was and he would give me a brief update; Laura was doing better, she was backroom again and they had employed a lady to become a funeral coordinator; she was working out well. Yes, they were busy. No his dad didn't come in to work much now. All mundane talk. We skipped around the real stuff just as we always had.

Avril was right though; I did need to sort things. I was living in some kind of limbo; happy in the fact that the mortgage was being paid and I had a few pounds in my bank. But I wasn't happy; my feet were still red and itchy so even if I thought I was coping; I wasn't. Hayley was at school full time, so I spent my days either at my mam and dad's or lumped in front of the telly at home. I needed to work. And I needed to get back to work as quickly as possible before the rot well and truly set in.

Agonising for hours over my CV; I took the finished product to Janet's work and asked if I could use the computer in the office. She obviously was well aware what was going on; Avril wasn't famed for her discretion, or maybe it had been my mam and dad, either way as soon as she saw me she was around the counter and giving me a cuddle. Giving my CV the once over, she added a few choice phrases in 'take on any duties required of me and references available on request'; I hadn't even thought about references. When I was happy with the finished version; she printed off about 50 copies, how many jobs was I supposed to apply for and more importantly, how many would I get knocked back for.

But it was nice seeing her and three cups of coffee later and sound advice about where I should be applying I made my way home. Still in a positive mood I rang the solicitors that I had used from my divorce from David and made an appointment. Alarmingly, the receptionist said that my appointment was with Mr Carter!! Wasn't it Mr Carter that had dealt with my last divorce, how embarrassing; I was a complete failure in the marriage stakes?

Determined to at least have something positive to tell Mr Carter when I met him a fortnight later. I started my job hunt in earnest. Sitting with the yellow pages; a writing pad, envelopes and stamps, I wrote to all of the companies Janet had suggested, along with some I had found on my own. It was a laborious task; every letter was a replica of the one before but the pile of envelopes grew and by bedtime they all had stamps on and were ready to post in the morning.

Then the waiting game began. The postman was now my most eagerly awaited visitor to my door and the answer machine remained constantly on. But a week passed by and I hadn't received as much as a rejection letter. Maybe I was unemployable; after all I hadn't worked for over 6 years. So I continued to wait and Mr Carter's appointment got closer and closer. Perhaps I had aimed too high. I should have maybe applied for more menial jobs; what is it they say 'it's easier to get a job when you've got one!'

So I continued to wait. I scoured the job page of the local newspaper and made several visits to the Job Centre. Another dozen jobs applied for and still nothing. I cleaned the house; a real proper clean. I threw out clothes belonging to me and the girls and I put Brian's things into black bin bags and put them in the cupboard under the stairs. He wasn't coming back. He hadn't said he wasn't but it had been two months and the only time he had darkened my door was when he came for the girls.

Hayley came back from one of her 'daddy days' very excited. Samantha hadn't gone; she was on a dry slope training trip in preparation for her forthcoming ski trip; so it had just been Hayley. It turned out that her daddy had been busy decorating bedrooms for Hayley and her sister; Auntie Laura had taken her into town and they had picked new curtains and bedding for each of their rooms. I was flabbergasted. It seems that any hope I might have had that Brian would come to his senses sometime soon were over. That was that.

D.I.V.O.R.C.E

A few days later, still unemployed and a little down in the mouth; I once again sat and told Mr Carter my failings. As ever upbeat; he once again said he would do his best for me. As Brian was a prominent businessman he saw no reason for him not to pay adequate maintenance for Hayley; and for me if I so wished to pursue it. I wanted nothing for myself. By hook or by crook I would get a job, even if it was picking rubbish up day after day. The good thing was the house was still in my name and because Brian already had other accommodation, he thought that Brian wouldn't want some sort of compensation for the money he had contributed over the past six years.

The divorce was another matter; I had two grounds, desertion or unreasonable behaviour. Both were relevant, but the desertion seemed like the less likely one for having to 'get the dirty washing out'. So that was the way we were going to go, Mr Carter would draft up a petition and then all I would have to do was sign it and then see what Brian or more likely his solicitor had to say about it. Courage in hand I then asked Mr Carter if he could locate David and maybe get me some extra money. As shocked as he had been the first time that David still hadn't seen Samantha, he made a note and said he would be in touch in due course. How long exactly is due course??? I like dates, but had to be happy that at least something was being done.

I was a single parent again. This time of two daughters; one teenager and the other a precocious 6 year old. I felt guilty when I spent the money that Brian put into my account, but I had no other money, so spent only what I needed and hoped that one day soon one of the many many jobs I had applied for would come good. I was surprised how quickly I had settled into my new life. I had lots of friends; I was seeing a lot of Adele, I think she found my house much more inviting than her little flat. I didn't mind, it was nice to have her around and Luke and Samantha spent hours together listening to music in the girls bedroom.

Adele too was playing a waiting game; she was waiting for the council to house her. Her flat was damp and she had been having a lot of trouble with the bus stop outside her front door, well not the bus stop; the kids that hung around it. The police had had to be called numerous times and now even they were recommending that Adele and Luke be moved before there was any real trouble.

There was no more Adele and Clive anymore. There hadn't been since the incident at the funeral home. Suzy had forgiven Clive; even took some of the responsibility for him having his affair and with Adele being free of Steven she lost interest in Clive. There's a whole wide world of blokes out there she said. Having taken up internet dating, I lost track of the men in her life and the dates and things she had had recently. But she looked well, she wasn't taking the dating thing too seriously and if she did take things further with any of the men; she would do it when Luke wasn't at home.

Adele made it all sound so glamorous; her phone was constantly ringing and she was always out having a meal with this one or a drink with that one. She seemed to have a man for every occasion; a one she would go to the pictures with another she would take a walk on the beach with. Tempting as it was, it wasn't for me, but I loved listening to her antics over a cup of coffee, it all made me feel normal if not a little boring.

My family still played a big part of my life. Avril was turning 40 later in the year and she was trying to plan a family holiday to Majorca. She wanted everyone there; I made excuses about jobs and money but she wouldn't hear any of it and duly paid the deposits for me and the girls. Even Thora was going. She was almost 80 and as fit as someone 20 years younger. Moving into my mam and dad's has been the best move ever for her; after her initial episodes, she was a different person. Independent and feisty, she was forever gadding about, mam and dad hardly knew they had her. She baked beautiful cakes and wasn't shy about making them something delicious for their teas if she had time.

My mam and her now had a lovely relationship; whatever had happened in the past was now well and truly put to bed. Still no sign of her other siblings, my mam now said that it was their loss. The Thora of today was very different to the one that had brought her up.

More pressure, now I had a family holiday to pay for as well as kitting Samantha out for her forthcoming ski trip. I doubled my job seeking efforts; now I was applying for anything, I obviously wasn't wanted in the world of administration. I tried to keep upbeat, but I was nervous, I didn't want to be reliant on my estranged husband, each deposit in my account made me feel sick. I didn't want to be a kept woman.

Mr Carter wrote; Brian wasn't contesting the divorce, didn't want anything out of the house and agreed to the sum that Mr Carter had suggested as maintenance for Hayley as long as he was allowed unlimited access to both of the girls. I couldn't argue with that, he had been the only dad Samantha had ever known. I rang Mr Carter straightaway and told his secretary that I was in agreement with all of Mr Mills's terms.

When the phone rang and Mr Carter's secretary asked if I had a moment to spare so he could have a quick word with me, I was perplexed. He came onto the line and in his impeccable clipped tones asked if I had managed to secure employment. Oh bloody hell I thought to myself, there was obviously something wrong with the letter I had just received. 'No not yet, but I am trying…' I stammered into the phone. 'It's just one of my former colleague's is looking for a girl Friday type for his new practice …….' He was going on and on and I didn't hear what he was saying. I did catch the end though. 'So I'll get Cathy to give you the address and if you can get straight around there, he'll have a look at your Curriculum Vitae. I'll speak to you soon Mrs Mills!' And then he was gone and his secretary, who I took to be Cathy was back on the line and I was scribbling an address down on Hayley's spelling book.

I still had a couple of hours before I had to pick Hayley up from school, so I ran upstairs, showered, changed and was out the door in 30 minutes. Parking in town was mad and even though I didn't have an appointment time, I could feel the flush blush coming on as I sat and waited for a space. The flush made me panic more, I would be a soggy ball of sweat by the time I actually got to the address. The walk settled me down and I didn't feel half as hot by the time I got to the office. Going into the reception, I was a bit embarrassed saying my solicitor had sent me, but the girl seemed nice and took my CV and told me to take a seat. I waited and waited, the girl came back and moved papers around her desk. I waited some more. The phone rang on the desk and the girl agreed, put the phone down and then came around the desk and asked me to follow her along the corridor into an office at the end.

Lifting up off his chair to greet me, Andrew Muir looked to be in his early forties; probably about the same age as Mr Carter. He was wearing a dark grey suit with wide pinstripes and he had a bright yellow shirt and his tie was similar to his suit. He was the most flamboyant man I had ever seen. Introducing himself he asked me to take a seat and then went on to tell me a bit about himself and his new business. It seems that he had been to university with Mark Carter; mmm Mark, I never thought about Mr Carter actually having a first name. Anyway the long and short of it was that Mr Muir was now setting up his own practice specialising in family law and he was looking for someone to be a bit of an all-rounder. Mentioning it in passing to Mark, he had said that one of his clients was looking for a job and that's how I was sitting there now!

Mr Muir had read through my CV and seemed to think it looked promising; he was just about to advertise the job but said if I was prepared to hold off if I was willing to go and do a trial; maybe a week and see how it goes. 'You have been out of the work force for some time, but you do have the experience I'm looking for, but I think for both our sakes, a week try out will determine if we are suited to one another!' He went on. I couldn't believe it. Somehow, I had blagged myself a job; well a week of work unpaid, but it was a start. Thanking Mr Muir probably a bit too much, I left the office promising to return the following Monday morning at 9am.

And that was that. I was re-employed. The week went well, by the Wednesday I felt like I had always worked there. I put little systems in place and soon had the little office in the room next door to Mr Muir running in some sort of fashion. I loved it. I liked Jayne, the receptionist, there was only the three of us working there so I would have been buggered if I hadn't liked her. But from the start she was helpful; she talked me through the procedures and was always there if I got stuck. I wasn't sure how I had done, I hoped that I had proved myself enough in my trial but by the time I left on the Friday afternoon, Mr Muir hadn't surfaced and I left for the weekend not sure if I would ever be going back.

I needn't have worried though, I had barely got through the door at home when the phone rang; Mr Muir. Delighted it had turned out so well he wanted to offer me the position of a full time job, embarrassed that he hadn't been able to see me before I had left, he said he had my wages but hoped that I would collect them myself when I returned on Monday morning, of course I was returning. I would be working in a proper office doing a proper job. I would be independent. I'd see him on Monday.

My job made so much difference to me. I had routine, the girls had routine. It was hard work being a full-time working single mam, but we managed. Samantha was old enough to be able to collect Hayley from her after school club if I was caught up in traffic or anything; and she appreciated the pocket money she got for helping with housework or doing a bit of shopping.

When she came back from her school skiing trip she had got herself her first real boyfriend. Fair like her dad, she was a pretty little thing and I knew sooner or later I was going to have to deal with the boyfriend thing, we had talked about it often, what to do what not to do. She was sensible though and I hoped that she would talk to me before she did anything she might regret, but that was hope; she was almost 16 and her mam would be the last person she would want to have 'boyfriend' chats with. What did surprise me was her boyfriend, sheepishly she told me it was Luke; Adele's Luke! They had been all the way through school together and had spent lots of time out of school together too, what with me and Adele being friends. I hadn't seen that one coming, they were close but I had never thought of them actually being an item. Adele was delighted, I wasn't so sure. Because they always had, they moved between each other's houses and bedrooms with ease. Never having to worry about it before, now that they were girlfriend and boyfriend this threw up a host of problems. Adele said I shouldn't worry they were sensible. When Adele and Luke literally moved around the corner, I gave up. If they were going to do anything they could do it anywhere, they didn't need to have the luxury of their bedrooms. So I accepted that they were now inseparable, I liked Luke and I knew he would look after Samantha, she was happy and as her GCSE's approached, I was pleased to see that she seemed to be continuing to stay focused.

Because I was now a working woman, we got to go on Avril's birthday holiday and had a great time. It was so good to spend time sitting doing nothing with the family. The kids all had a ball; Samantha moped for the first couple of days missing Luke, but a couple of phone calls home later she perked up and enjoyed the holiday as much as Hayley did. I was lucky, I might have had two failed marriages behind me but I had a family that loved me, two amazing daughters and a job I was loving more each day.

I struggled with my job at first; not the work that was all quite straight forward. It was the content of the work. Mr Muir specialised in family law; some of his cases involved children and domestic violence; some of the things I had to transcribe were harrowing and sometimes the incidents would hang on me for days. But I liked working there. Andrew Muir was very thorough and professional; he expected high standards and in the beginning I used to dread returning to my desk to find my latest typing covered in red correction marks. But as time passed I grew in confidence and realised that sometimes it was his handwriting or the way he spoke that led to the mistakes or sometimes he just wanted to change the wording altogether.

Jayne was turning into a very good friend; at 28 she was ten years younger, but if someone had told me she was 18 I would have believed them. She had worked with Andrew at his previous practice and had taken a leap in faith leaving a secure job behind to go and work in a one that was unproved. But business was thriving and Mr Muir was getting a really good name for himself. Within two years another partner had been taken on and I employed a junior as such to help out with the increasing paperwork.

I was doing good. I wasn't sign watching and even though Brian and me hadn't worked at being married, he had become a really good friend. It had seemed ridiculous him standing on the doorstep waiting for the girls to get themselves ready, so I had invited him in and from there it had progressed to coffee and sometimes he would even eat with us. It was so much easier him being a friend than being an enemy. It was nice to be able to ask his advice and if I needed support with either of the girls; he would be there.

Mills and Boone Funeral Directors was doing well. He was still living in the house with Laura, which although I thought was a bit weird; seemed to be working out well. Laura helped out with the girls if Brian was called out; Samantha and her were especially close; they both played the piano competently, as did Brian and would often go off to concerts together.

Samantha left secondary school; her results were ok, apart from music which she had excelled at, thanks to Brian. Thinking that she would want to stay on and do her A Levels; I was surprised when she opted to go to college to do business studies. I thought she would have wanted to do something with her music; like my dad always said 'you should always play to your strengths.' But she said she wanted to do something more practical. So off to college she went. Even more surprisingly was when she started helping out at Mills and Boone Funeral Directors, firstly in the office with Laura, but then she took an interest in all aspects of the business and decided this was the path she wanted to follow.

I was unsure, she was so young and Undertaking was such a serious business. Me and Brian talked at length about it; he describes his journey into it and it seemed that it wasn't something you could just 'do.' It took years and years and even if Samantha started her apprenticeship now, it would more than likely be ten years before she got to be experienced enough to be able to conduct funerals. He seemed to have a plan; office first learning all about the paperwork and legalities; then if she was still wanting to make a career out of it, she would start at the bottom of the operations and work her way up. It was a job; it would be a good job if she had the stomach for it. But I wanted her to finish her college course first and then still attend college in some form; I didn't want her completely isolated, she needed to mix with people her own age.

When Brian next called to pick Hayley up he brought with him a training plan that him and Laura had drafted. Samantha unaware that there was a position being created for her, was over the moon. Agreeing to finish her diploma, apart from working with Laura in the holiday; it would be another 18 months before she would start her apprenticeship, time for her to learn to drive she said. It would be a five mile trip to work for her; she had her bedroom still at Brian's, but sitting at the kitchen table with her and Brian; I vowed that I would teach her to drive, I wasn't going to lose her completely to Brian and his sister.

Samantha and Luke were as close as ever. I liked him very much, I wasn't sure what he thought about having a girlfriend who was going to be a funeral director; he himself was on an apprenticeship as a mechanic, but there was no telling if they would even stay together that long. They were so young.

I still saw lots of Adele. She still hadn't found the 'one,' but was still having fun looking. She certainly got lots of attention on our nights out. Me on the other hand must have had some sort of invisible electric fence around me, because I got very little. It didn't bother me too much; but it would have been nice to get just a little male attention.

I didn't think I was bad looking. The weight I had gained having Hayley had eventually dropped off; the walking/run thing I did to and from my car to work helped. My good friend Lynne kept my hair in check. After finishing having babies, she had taken herself off to college and trained in hairdressing. Now her kids were all up, she had set herself up as a mobile hairdresser and I had been one of her first customers. She would come to the house every four weeks and cut and colour my hair. It had started up just me and the girls, but then Avril, Janet and Carol came and sometime Adele. It was a proper girls night in and it gave us all a chance to have a catch up. It was a lucrative night for Lynne.

So my hair was always nice and whereas I had never had an interest in clothes, working in town had given me more opportunity to shop for clothes. Jayne was a proper clothes horse and whereas in the beginning I would just tag along with her on our lunch breaks, all of a sudden with a little bit more money in the bank, I had started to buy a few things for myself.

After I had been at work about a year. I had my biggest extravagance. I bought the house and I had an extension built. It wasn't practical having the girls in the same bedroom; every day there would be screaming as one of them had moved something belonging to the other. When they started spilling into my bedroom, I knew that we were either going to have to move to something bigger or have the extension built that me and Brian had talked about.

Unsure that I would even be able to get a mortgage, with the discount allowed from the council and taking into account that I needed a lot more money for the extension; the mortgage went through and for some unknown reason, was working out cheaper than the rent.

I was a home owner. The plans for the extension took forever to get through and then the building work itself seemed to take a lifetime, but it was worth the wait. I had an extra bedroom and downstairs the kitchen was moved into the new part and the old kitchen/diner was now a large dining room. I was so proud. The girls were happy, they each had a bedroom of their own and instead of having one of the girls in my bed every night; I now had the full stretch of it all to myself.

The year I was turning 40 was going to be a big year for all of the family. My mam and dad had decided that they were officially retiring; Samantha would be 18 and Julie was coming home, just for a visit but it had been over 20 years since we had seen her. I didn't want any fuss for my birthday; but sisters were sisters and friends were friends and I wasn't going to get away with doing nothing. So it was decided; a big family party when Julie was home and a weekend away for me to celebrate the big four oh!!

Blackpool; we were having a weekend in Blackpool – in February!! But the common consensus on 'haircut' night was that was the place to be. It was all girls of course; sisters, Samantha and one of her friends,

Lynne, Adele, and even poor Jayne had been roped in to going. I couldn't even say I was looking forward to it, I was dreading the fuss and walking around with a big badge proclaiming I was 40 did nothing to excite me. Kiss me quick??? Candy rock?? I hadn't been to Blackpool for years so I wasn't thrilled at the prospect, but everyone else was so excited, especially Samantha and her friend Jenny and by the time we were on our way, their excitement was contagious and I couldn't wait to get there.

As it turned out, it was a life changing weekend. It was the weekend that I met Phil Collins….

Invisible Touch

It wasn't THE Phil Collins, mega superstar; it was my Phil Collins a plumber from Stockton. But he changed my life. In one look across a crowded bar, that was it. Husband number 3 was in my radar.

We had arrived in Blackpool at around lunchtime, having decided that we would bus down, we had spent 4 hours; less a couple of toilet and tea break stops in the comfort of a National Express destination Blackpool. It hadn't been too bad, we had played a quiz and a few games of some sort of bingo all courtesy of Mrs Arrangement herself; Avril. But the journey had flown by and soon we were all checking into Bay View Guest House; which must have meant that it had a view of the bay windows opposite and not of the sea which was what I had assumed, but was sadly disappointed because it was in the midst of rows and rows of identical guest houses.

But it was clean and tidy and the family room I was sharing with Adele, Lynne and Jayne was alright, if a bit cramped with its assortment of beds and furniture. Not that I had chance to enjoy the surroundings, no sooner had we dumped our suitcases then we were back out on a tour of Blackpool's afternoon delights. Firstly we all traipsed around the shops; then had a walk along the front, a tram ride and then a ride up the tower. By the time we returned to the guest house my feet were killing me.

Nevertheless, a quick shower and change of clothing into my killer 40th birthday dress and then the party really started. Everyone landed into our room with an array of various bottles of alcohol and then there it was – the dreaded 40th birthday badge!!! There was no escaping it, Samantha pinned it on to my dress and with a flurry of spray glitter out of a can on my newly washed and styled hair by Lynne we were good to go.

The pubs were packed. It was a head count at every bar to make sure we hadn't lost anyone, but as the drinks flowed I really started to enjoy myself. The only bug bear I had was that my feet felt as if they were three sizes too big for my shoes. Obviously going for the full effect I had bought a pair of four inch stilettos; they had been lovely and comfortable when I had tottered around the house with them on a couple of nights earlier in the week. But I hadn't taken into account I would have walked 20 miles around Blackpool before I would be wearing them next and now the soles of my feet felt like they were on fire. I daren't even take a foot out of them; I knew I would never get them back on and the night was still young and barefoot wasn't really a good look for a woman my age. So I just had to put up with them. As I glanced down I could see that they looked all swollen and puffy; more drink!!! If I was drunk surely I would forget about them. But it really was like walking over hot coals!!!

Nevertheless, we all partied our way around the night spots of Blackpool, finally going into a nightclub on the sea front. We had seen it earlier in the day and one of the girls must have mentioned it to our landlady because we somehow had ended up with complimentary tickets for free entry and a couple of drinks. Result!! The entry price alone was a tenna and I had never paid that in my life to get into a nightclub; even some of the more plush ones in Newcastle. So the rest of the night we all danced together in a big circle, shaking our stuff and generally having a great time. It was when I was walking back from the toilets that I saw him. I looked at him; he looked at me and he literally took my breath away.

For the next hour I forgot all about my feet. I went to the bar; I danced; I sat in the booth with the girls. And all the time I kept an eye out for the object of my affections. From what I could make out he was with a group of lads; they seemed to be partying the same as we were, drinking and having a laugh. Every time I looked for him, he seemed to be looking at me; my stomach was doing the old somersault routine and even though the alcohol was making me much braver than I usually would be; I still didn't have the bottle to go over. And so we played eye ping pong. I looked at him and he looked at me.

Even when I was on the dance floor, I knew instinctively where he was, I would spin around dancing and I was right; there he was at the edge of the dance floor watching. He was smallish; well not small but certainly not as tall as either David or Brian had been, but he was muscly or at least I thought he was, I couldn't really draw my eyes away from his face. My stomach was doing so many somersaults it threatened to bring up all of the alcohol I had consumed.

When the music changed tempo as the night drew to a close, the slow records came on. As I went to make my way back to our table, a hand came out and grabbed my hand; it was him. We didn't say anything, but made our way into the middle of the dance floor and wrapped our arms around each other as if it was something we did every night of the week. He smelt lovely. Aramis?? No it was more subtle, Kurous.

As each new song came on, we stayed where we were, swaying in each other's arms. And that was as far as it went. The music finished, the lights came on and the bouncers came in. It was over. We unwrapped from each other and a big roar went up, my friends and his. Looking at him in the harsh electric lights, he was even better looking than he had been in the disco lights. I so hoped that I wasn't wearing beer goggles!!! Unsure what to do, I made my way back to the girls, the jeers continued and as I approached them I gave a little bow, grinning from ear to ear.

Even though we were all the worse for wear, Avril still managed to do a little head count and a check to make sure everyone had their handbags and shoes and then ushered us all to the exit. A little disappointed that my bloke seemed to have disappeared into thin air, I linked Adele's arm and followed the rest of the girls out of the nightclub. And then there he was. Standing outside the door, well less standing and more loitering. Is he waiting for me??? And he was.

He asked for my name and number; and then he was gone. One of his mates came and picked him up in a great big bear hug and ran along the street with him. As I made my way back to where the girls were huddled around waiting for me to return, I thought that would be it. I had given him two numbers for me, but I doubted I would even hear from him again, even if he did want to get in touch I had written my number in eye liner and the chances of it surviving until the following day were slim. But it had been fun while it had lasted; all in all surprisingly I had had a great night.

Now there was the torturous walk back to Bay View Guest House. All of a sudden my feet were killing me and I had no choice but to ease the shoes off and walk the rest of the way back in my bare feet. By the time I slumped into my lumpy single bed my feet were on fire, not on top of the soreness I was sure they had cuts and bits of grit imbedded into them.

I lay in the bed and listened to the various snores of Lynne, Jayne and Adele. They were all flat out, but I was wide awake and sober as a judge. Thoughts of the bloke in the nightclub went around and around in my head. So my head spun, my stomach did somersaults and my feet throbbed, but somewhere in the middle of it all I managed to fall into a deep dreamful sleep, where I dreamt of nightclub bloke and rollercoasters. When I woke to the smell of toast and bacon I could remember the dream vividly; maybe it was a sign, on reflection it probably was, but I chose to ignore it. It was breakfast, a bit of shopping and then the long, long bus journey home, it seemed to take a week, there were no games and the toilet/tea stops seemed to make the journey even worse. It was a very sorry looking group that got off the bus in Newcastle.

The weekend over, Hayley picked up from Brian's and back to the normality of home and work, I really didn't expect to hear from the nightclub bloke and I was right, there was no phone call that night, or the next week. I was a bit disappointed, if only I had written my number in ink! I thought to myself as another weekend started and I still hadn't heard from him. Not meant to be!! So I threw myself into a 'Hayley' weekend, she had missed out on the whole Blackpool experience so it was her weekend. She needed new school shoes, so it was a day at the Metro Centre, firstly getting shoes and then lunch and a trip to the pictures. Thoughts of the nightclub bloke started to become distinguished from my thoughts, it obviously hadn't been meant to be.

But it made me feel sad. I hadn't met anyone that had made me feel giddy for a long time. The timing was all wrong. I hadn't checked the signs; I didn't need to, it was never going to happen. I had no name, no idea where he even lived. Later that night when Hayley was in bed and I was sitting by myself, I cried. I cried for what might have been. I cried because I was now 40 and I cried because I was so useless at relationships. David had fell in and out of love with me virtually before I was out of my wedding dress, I doubted that Brian had even loved me; no that was wrong he did love me, he just had never been in love with me.

I had two beautiful girls from two men that had left me because I hadn't been 'it'. Bitter sweet. By all accounts David was still happily in love with Miss March and Brian was happy living in that huge house with his sister; there had never been any mention over the years of a new girlfriend, just him and Laura and him and his work. They were very different; David had never made any attempt to see Samantha, I still didn't know if David saw Samantha at her grandparents, she certainly never said so I didn't think she had. As far as I could make out Brian was her dad, the same way he was Hayley's! His devotion to both his daughters was as keen as David's abandonment and I knew if anything ever happened to me; Brian would be there for them both.

Once I started on the self-analysis I couldn't stop. I sat with my feet soaking in a bucket of hot soapy water and a coffee in hand and went through both my marriage in some sort of slow motion. I looked for the things I had done wrong, did I not pay them enough attention? Was I too laidback? Did either of them know that I actually loved them? Were there signs that they actually loved me? The images rolled over and over, in no specific order I danced backwards and forwards. The tears dripped off my chin, until there was no more liquid to drop and the water in the bowl had gone cold.

Drying my feet off I was on my way into the kitchen to empty the bowl, when the telephone started to ring. Who's that ringing at 10 o'clock on a Saturday night I thought dumping the bowl and making my way back into the living room? 'Is that Val?' Said the voice at the other end of the phone. 'Yes' I replied stumped at who it was, I didn't recognised him. 'It's Phillip, we met last week in Blackpool!' Flabbergasted, I plonked myself down on the arm of the settee.

Two hours later, I pushed the end call button on the handset. I couldn't believe it. He had found me. Apparently, one of the numbers had smudged and he had rang four wrong numbers before he actually got me. I was impressed at his determination. Phillip Collins; plumber from Stockton, which is less than 30 miles away from me. We had talked and talked and laughed and flirted and by the end of the call we had arranged to meet the following Tuesday night in Newcastle. I had a date. Someone was interested enough in me to drive 30 miles to take me out for a drink. I was cock-a-hoop. 'Phillip Collins' I thought to myself as I made my way upstairs to bed. I had a date with Phil Collins. Tuesday couldn't come quick enough. I really hoped that I hadn't been wearing beer goggles, all the girls assured me that he had been as gorgeous as I had remembered, but even we were all in a drunken haze and he might be a bit more like the real Phil Collins than I had remembered. Not that there was anything wrong with Phil Collins, but in my mind's eye I was thinking he was more Jonny Depp. I really was stretching it if he was more Jonny Depp; why would anyone that gorgeous be interested in me?? Before I even made it into bed the euphoria was starting to fade and the self-doubt return. Maybe he would like me more if he was more Phil Collins …..

Truly Madly Deeply

Tuesday couldn't come quick enough. I resisted the urge to look for signs and worried more about what I was going to wear. As we were meeting as soon as I finished work, I wondered if I should just go suited and booted in my day wear. Or do I take a change of clothes with me and go for a more casual look. As it turned out a phone call late the night before decided it for me. Mr McCabe, my old boss from the petrol station had passed away earlier in the day. Although he was now in his eighties, it was still a shock and it took the wind right out of my sales. Even though I hadn't worked for them for years and years, I had still called to see them regularly. They were virtually housebound now, but were always over the moon to see me and especially so if I had one or both of the girls with me. They never forgot any of our birthdays and there was always a bundle of presents off them at Christmas. They had been so good to me and Mr McCabe's death really shook me up.

So instead of sorting out what I was going to wear for my date the following night with Phil; I ended up on the phone to various family members telling them about Mr McCabe; my mam and dad were especially upset, they had been good friends with them both over the years and I think it brought home to them how old Thora was and the chance that they would be losing her sometime in the very near future; after all she was now over 90 and although she was still fit as a lop, every day they had with her was a bonus.

And I didn't sleep well that night; I thought about how Mrs McCabe would be feeling. They had been childhood sweethearts, had married young, had had no children, and spent all their working life together and their retirement. In short they had probably spent every day together for over 65 years. She would be lost without him and it worried me.

I tossed and turned. I saw witching hour, then three and four. Somewhere before five o'clock I must have fell asleep, because when the alarm went off at 6.45 I felt like I had only just closed my eyes. I looked dreadful, usually I wouldn't have been bothered but it was date night and I was going to be turning up with black eyes and an ashen face. Nothing I could do about it, I slapped my make-up on and just about had time to iron a new work blouse I had bought at the Metro Centre at the weekend, find a pair of shoes that wouldn't cripple my still tender feet and get in the car and away so I wouldn't be late for work.

The day flew by, the practice had a big case starting at court the following week so it was all hands on deck to make sure that everything that could possibly be needed in the court room was packed up and indexed. Before I knew it; it was 4.45 and I dashed into the loos to re-do my make-up and freshen up. I still looked rough, there was still black shadows under my eyes, but Jayne had given me some greenish concealer that she said would work wonders and she was right. I didn't look like a zombie like I thought I would, it blended in well and the dark shadows vanished. Ten minutes later, with newly sparkly eyes courtesy of my dewy eye drops, I looked almost human and ready to go.

Jayne gave a wolf whistle as I walked through reception, still a bit self-conscious because I was in my suit, I appreciated her seal of approval. She sprayed a dash of Chanel No.5 on my pulse points, hugged me and wished me good luck. All of a sudden I was terrified. What if he didn't turn up? I hadn't spoken to him since Saturday night. What if he had changed his mind and had rang last night to tell me he wouldn't be coming? I had never been off the phone!!! Oh well, I thought to myself. I go to the appointed rendezvous point and if he didn't turn up in 30 minutes, I would slide away and go home.

But as I approached the door way of the City Vaults in the city centre, I saw him straightaway. Hip hip hooray!!! I hadn't been wearing beer goggles; he was as handsome sober as he was when I was drunk. Let's hope he felt the same or I would be back home before I knew it.

I needn't have worried. From the minute we sat down at a cosy table in the corner of the pub, we never stopped talking. He said something, I said something, he said something else, then I did. The night flew by. And all the time I was conscious of just how good looking he was. Very dark, he had a six o'clock shadow that gave him a rough, rugged look. A plumber by trade, he was also a keen footballer and went to the gym a few nights a week. He was fit. And I fancied him.

By the time he walked me back to my car, I was smitten. The good looks, the humour; what wasn't there to love about him. When he pushed me against the car and kissed me, I was altogether at a new level. He was something else. And unbelievably, he seemed to think the same about me. I drove home on cloud nine. This was something else. This was toe curling. This was what a new relationship should be all about. It was fireworks and fire and stars and altogether heavenly. I was seeing him again the next Saturday and I couldn't wait.

When I took a phone call at work the next day from my mam, I couldn't take in what she was saying. Mrs McCabe had died in her sleep. Within 48 hours of her husband dying, Mrs McCabe had gone too. I was distraught, how did that even happen? Was her heart so broken that it just gave up? Was that even a real thing, dying of a broken heart? It was just too sad. I cried my way through the rest of the day, I didn't want to go home because we were so busy, but I may as well have. Everything was blurry with tears, every time I thought of how Mrs McCabe must have felt when her husband had left her, it brought on a new wave of emotion.

So when Saturday came, I was still not feeling my best. Both the girls were upset, but I was proud of Samantha when she said that Mills and

Boone Funeral Directors were taking care of what would be a double funeral; I knew she would make sure that everything was carried out beautifully. I cried buckets when Samantha told me that there had been specific instructions left by the McCabe's for music and readings for their funerals. It was like they knew they would go together.

But I grinned the biggest grin when I saw Phil standing outside the same city centre pub again, he really was very good looking. The stubble was still there, was that what they call designer stubble?? Because it didn't seem to have grown in the intervening days. The pub was much busier and noisier than last time, so after a quick drink, we walked down the Bigg Market to a little Italian restaurant I had heard Andrew from work talk about. The place was packed, but the waiter assured us it would only be about a 30 minute wait if we were happy to sit and have a drink; and we were. This time I didn't have the car with me, Adele had offered to bring me in and to be honest I really needed to have a catch up with her, the journey into town was the perfect opportunity.

After she had whooped at me in my new Next Jeans and top, I settled into the passenger seat. She knew all about the sad news of Mr and Mrs McCabe and said that they had been an institution in the neighbourhood so of course she would be going to the funeral. I updated her on the Phil Collins situation, all the while my tummy was doing its somersaults and could feel my toes curling in the relative safety of my new little black boots. She told me about her latest internet find, Peter the consultant. He apparently worked at the Freeman hospital, relocating to the area because of his new job, he had joined a mutual dating website; Geordie Go-Getters and had met Adele. They had been meeting up for about 3 months and so far everything seemed to be going really well. In fact Adele was glowing with happiness and even when we talked about the kids and their relationship, the glow continued to shine. Maybe this was the one. I hadn't actually met him yet, but Samantha had and I always thought she was a good judge of character and she really liked him. Samantha and Luke were as close as ever, they spent as much time as they could together and even though I thought Luke might have bailed when he realised his lovely, happy, bubbly girlfriend wanted to be an undertaker, to date they seemed even closer. They were having a two week holiday in Spain later in the year and that was always a tell-tale situation for young relationships, so we would have to wait and see.

So when Phil ordered me another glass of wine and himself a pint, I sipped at it gladly as we waited for our table. Once again the conversation was effortlessly, we talked about my former bosses and their recent passing; Phil even thought it was funny that I had been a petrol attendant, after all he had seen me in my snazzy work suit which was as far removed from my old Derry boot and snorkel days; as was possible. He told me about his job, him and his dad ran their own small business, his mam looked after the books. He had a couple of older sisters, both who had left home and had kids. He lived at home with his mam and dad. I wanted to ask if there was a significant ex somewhere in his past. But he had changed the subject and the opportunity had passed.

By the time we were actually seated at our table, two glasses of wine had been consumed and my stomach had thought my throat had been cut. It had been more like an hour and a quarter than 30 minutes; but the wait had been worth it. The food was delicious and so was the company. Usually, under pressure eating in front of strangers; I wolfed every course down like I was never going to be fed again. If Phil thought I was a bit of a pig he never said and devoured his meal and picked at mine too. I liked a man with a healthy appetite. The wine flowed and by the time we were on to our coffees, we were both a little bit worse for wear. We giggled together at nothing, he really was handsome, especially when he laughed; it was just so sexy. Into another pub for another glass of wine, then it hit me; 'how was he getting home? He was as bladdered as I was!!' I felt myself starting to flush up, I didn't know how to even broach the subject. He said he had drove up, I even knew where he had parked the car. The last buses had been and gone and a taxi down to Stockton would cost a fortune. So we had two choices, we booked him into a hotel; or he came back home with me. I blushed up even more.

Hayley was at Brian's and Samantha was staying the night at Luke's dads, so the house was empty. But was that not all a bit too forward. When he arrived back from the bar with another glass of wine, I was squashed into a corner. Taking advantage of the fact that I wouldn't be able to get away from him; he kissed me. The toe curling was back, they curled up so much it hurt. It was the best kissing I had ever done and I didn't want it to stop. Taking a breath and a drink of my wine, the words were out of my mouth before I even thought about it. 'Do you want to stay at mine tonight? I could bring you back into town in the morning for your car!' And the next thing was we were out the door and into a taxi heading back to mine.

And of course there was dot dot dot. Lots of dot dot dot! I had never experienced anything like it. In the morning there was more. I was on cloud nine. I was so happy I even got up and made us a huge breakfast, we sat in my newly decorated kitchen diner and talked and ate. I had a bit of a hangover, but I had no regrets. If I was a one night stand then I was going to enjoy his company before he left. And there was more dot dot dot before we jumped into my car and we headed back into town to retrieve his car and say our goodbyes.

I felt so naughty. My body ached as well as my head, but I didn't regret a minute of it. I had the feeling everyone knew what I had been up to, but I didn't care. My mam and dad both commented on me having a bit of a spark when me and Hayley called on the way back from Brian's. Even Adele said she could tell and I had only spoken to her on the phone, I hadn't actually seen her. I was a one night stand and I didn't care. I had no illusions about hearing from Phil again, but that was fine.

I had experienced something new and even if I never did it again, at least I knew what it felt like.

But I did hear from him. He rang later that night. And he wanted to see me again. It was okay, I was okay, I must have done something right and at that minute I felt like the sexiest woman in the world. Yes, of course I wanted to see him. And that was that, I had myself a new boyfriend and for once I didn't feel insecure or inadequate. I was a sassy 40 year old with a lush boyfriend.

My life was good. Apart from the McCabe's funeral which was one of the saddest things I had ever seen. The two coffins side by side, joined in death as they had been in life made a heart stopping sight. Every attention to detail had been carried through by Mills and Boone Funeral Directors, down to the hymns in the Church and the music played as the curtain went around the coffins. There wasn't a dry eye in the Crem as We'll Meet Again played gently out of the speakers. I was so proud of what Brian and Samantha had done for them.

Phil and I met up a couple of times a week. Sometimes he came to mine or if we were both pushed for time we would meet up half way. The girls met him. Hayley adored him straightaway, he showed her some cheats on a computer game she was obsessed with and he became her hero. But Samantha was a bit harder nut to crack. She thought he was too young for me, that I wasn't looking at the bigger picture. The age thing itself had been a bit of a shock. In Blackpool and again on our first date, I hadn't particularly noticed that he was younger than me. I was so blown away with his puppy dog brown eyes that I hadn't paid much attention. It wasn't until the morning after our second date, when I woke up first in my bed that I actually looked at him. Asleep he looked boyish and I was a bit shocked. As with everything with me, I swept it under the carpet and never mentioned age to him. He obviously knew how old I was; I was wearing a huge badge stating the fact the night he met me.

It wasn't until weeks later when he asked me to go to his sisters birthday party with him did it hit me that he was definitely over 10 years younger. Phil's next oldest sister, Kim was turning 30. This being the case then Phil had to be at least a year younger than that. It was worse. He was almost four years younger. He had just recently celebrated his 26th birthday. How hadn't I seen that?

But by then I had fallen for him hook line and sinker and I couldn't have given him up even if I had wanted to. Samantha was right to be concerned, he was younger and it was a recipe for disaster, but I didn't feel older than him and I don't think he felt too young for me. We were equals in every way. Initially everyone was shocked. My parents, his, my sisters, his, my friends and of course his. The months ticked on and it looked like he was here to stay.

Just like Starting Over

Julie came home. It was strange, she looked so different. The years of living in the sunshine had taken its toll, she looked so much older than her fair skinned sisters. But she was happy living the nomad life but more than that she was happy to be home. She met all her nieces and nephews, her Granny Thora who she hadn't really known at all and then of course all of her brother in laws. She knew Alan and Graham, but she didn't know the rest and if she was shocked that I had a 'toy-boy' she never said and treat him as she did the rest of the lads.

It was a happy family time. The party was great and when the two weeks were up we all went to the airport like we had done 20 years earlier and waved her off. There would be some of us she would see again, but there were others she would only meet on that one visit. Another 10 years would pass before we would see her again, but technology was changing all of the time and whereas we would sit around the phone on a Sunday at my mam and dad's waiting for her call, now we all kept in touch with her in our own way.

There had been no skeletons in Phil's cupboard, as far as I could make out anyway. He told me he loved me all of the time and I did the same. We might have been having a distance and an age-gap relationship, but we were doing fine. I wasn't sign watching, well not initially anyway and I was taking good care of myself, feet included.

When he asked me to marry him after we had been seeing each other four months, I had no misgivings and agreed. Samantha still wasn't convinced, she thought he was not only too young, but a bit selfish and spoilt. I couldn't see it and when Samantha realised that her moaning was falling on deaf ears, she gave up. But telling her we were getting married caused her to have an almighty strop and all but move into Brian's. It was the only fly in my perfect moment. But a fly in the ointment it was and no matter what I said she was having none of it and refused to live in a house with me and Phil.

I don't think my mam and dad were convinced either. But them being them, they kept their own counsel, but I could sense something when I saw them. Not wanting to make trouble when there was no need for any, I ignored them and ploughed on with the wedding arrangements. But it was a whirlwind and if I stopped and thought about it I would start to panic, so I didn't stop. Not for a second, I worked hard at work and when I didn't see Phil I made sure that I was always with someone or doing something and I would fall into bed exhausted. When I was with Phil I had no doubts, we were mad for each other and couldn't keep our hands to ourselves. I had never had such a physical relationship with anyone and the novelty didn't seem to be wearing off.

The wedding was planned for the end of September. It wasn't going to be a grand or lavish affair, it was going to be small and understated. Money was tight so everything was being kept to a minimum, but everyone who was important to us was invited and there was going to be over a hundred at the evening reception. Hayley was going to be a bridesmaid, well the only bridesmaid, Samantha had refused point blank. I don't think it was in dispute, more that she had wanted to spend the day with Luke, their holiday had been a success story and they were closer than ever.

So on 28th September I became Mrs Val Collins. Despite everyone having reservations, they might not have said it to my face, but I could sense them; everyone had a brilliant day. I wore an ivory lace dress, quite wedding for me, but when I had seen it in a bridal shop one day in my lunch break, I had to have it. It was perfect and I felt so beautiful when I wore it, I had lost a bit of weight and the heels I wore accentuated the fact. Phil wore a dark suit, the six o'clock shadow was there and looking back on the wedding photographs if you didn't know, you couldn't tell that he was over a decade younger or was it that I looked 10 years younger. I looked younger in my third wedding day photographs than I did in my wedding to Brian when I was only 30, the difference was I glowed with happiness. Phil was the one, the one I had been waiting for.

Moving in together turned out to be harder than I had thought. Phil still had to go to Stockton every day to work, so this added a couple of hours onto his working day. Hayley didn't seem to mind that someone else had moved into the house, she liked Phil and there was no strain in their relationship. But Samantha hadn't particularly warmed to him. She was pleasant enough, but I could tell that she didn't think much of him. She didn't moan to me about him, she just didn't come to the house much. She would stay at Brian's or Luke's, I missed her. We would talk or text every day, but it wasn't the same. I felt like I had sacrificed Samantha to have Phil and that was the first chink to appear in my new marriage. When a tired an irritable Phil came in from work, had his tea and slumped in front of the telly, I wondered whether it was worth it.

Suddenly I was counting cars. The signs weren't good. The passion of our relationship had started to dwindle, having him there every day soon put paid to the amount of dot dot dot that went on. I would come in from work and have to start tidying up the mess Phil had left behind when he went to work, then it would be tea to sort and after all of that he would come in from work, dump his work stuff, eat his tea, and then the would sit flicking through he telly only stopping when he found something he wanted to watch. I hated TOP Gear with a passion. It was like having another teenager in the house. In the space of a few weeks, everything had changed.

I didn't say anything to anyone. We were still supposed to be in the honeymoon phase so I smiled and said everything was wonderful. But of course it wasn't. I was beginning to get the feeling that I had mistaken lust for love. We didn't really know each other that well, 7 months of a part-time relationship didn't make a good foundation for a sturdy marriage. I had never taken into consideration that Phil was not just the only boy in his family, but also the youngest. He had still been living at home with his mam and dad, with a mam that didn't work so probably spent her days running after both Phil and his dad. Phil didn't have a clue how to do anything for himself, he couldn't even cut the grass.

And because I was having to do everything, he started to annoy me and this had an effect on the whole relationship. I would go to bed in the huff and keep my back turned away when he eventually dragged himself up off the settee and up the stairs to bed. When he bought himself a games console and spent even more time sitting in front of the telly surrounded my crisp packets and cans; it was the final nail in the coffin of our marriage. I didn't need another child; I already had two and I certainly wasn't prepared to let my new husband behave like a one.

So for the first time in my life; I actually spoke up and said I wasn't happy. For days and days I had asked the signs and they had all said the same thing. This has been a huge mistake. The next time we had the house to ourselves I told him we needed to talk. He looked clueless. I told him I thought that he had replaced his mother with me. He didn't understand, he said that he didn't know he was expected to help around the house, his dad didn't. And at that moment I knew I was fighting a losing battle. Phil said he would try and bless him he did. He would spend time in the kitchen with me, watching what I was doing and chatting, he really didn't think he was doing anything wrong and he soon lost interest and went back to his game. Nothing really changed.

After a tiring Christmas and New Year where I entertained the majority of both his family and mine, I had had enough. He had asked for a new game for his console for Christmas and soppy me had bought him it; big mistake. It took over our lives, I ended up having to record the programmes I had wanted to watch over Christmas on the telly because the game was never off. Even when we had company he would sit on the settee and shoot aliens. I couldn't take any more and on 4th January

I told him it was over and I wanted him and his game to move out. He did without a fuss. Promising Hayley he would keep in touch, he packed up his bags and went back to live with his mam and dad. We had been married less than four months and already it was over.

I had been a silly old woman, blinded by what I thought was love. It was embarrassing and I felt like a fool. It was going to take me a long time to bounce back from this fiasco, not because I was broken hearted over Phil, he was a nice bloke and I would miss him. It was just that I didn't trust my instincts, I thought I was right when the signs were telling me I was wrong. I didn't listen and now I had a third failed marriage under my belt, Samantha had seen what was happening, probably everyone had, but I hadn't wanted to know. I was in my bubble with Phil and no one was going to get in with us and spoil the party. But the bubble must have been made of tissue paper, because it had ripped easily and I had fell to the ground with an almighty bump. Lots of humble pie was going to have to be eaten, especially with my smart elder daughter, Samantha.

Cry me a River

People were kind, there was no element of 'I told you so' off Samantha. By the time I celebrated my 41st birthday on Valentine's Day, it was like it had never happened. But I remembered, from my 40th birthday to my 41st birthday, I had met someone, married him and then separated from him. It had been quite a year. But it was nothing like the year that would follow, it just seemed to be one bad thing happening after another.

The sadness started on 9th March. I had gone into work as usual on the Monday morning. The practice was bigger now, Jayne and me now shared an office, she looked after the general administration side of things whereas I looked after the finances. There was a new girl on reception and we had a couple of ladies who worked on a job-share basis in our office. It was a nice place to work. Andrew Muir went out of his way to make sure all of his staff were happy at their work. In return he expected high standards and professionalism at all times. We were all happy to do this and worked as hard as he did.

The cases could still be as harrowing, but they were one offs and I like to think there were a million good people out there for every bad one, but it was the bad ones that stuck in my mind. The abused child, the beaten wife, in some cases much worse.

Andrew Muir's private life had always been that – private. There was no Mrs Muir, but there were lots of women in his life. Girlfriends? Maybe! Whenever we had functions to attend there was always a beauty on his arm, after all he was good looking, clever, funny and very very rich. But the same girl would never appear twice and it made me sometime think he had commitment issues.

Jayne thought it was nothing to do with commitment. She thought that his flamboyant style of dressing meant only one thing, he was batting for the other side. I didn't think so, as well as no regular girlfriend, there was no male partner either. Lots of male colleagues and friends, there was no whiff that he might prefer male company behind closed doors. His private life was very much private.

Until that Monday morning. Often out of the office for long periods of time, alarm bells didn't ring when there was no sign of him by 11 o'clock. When Lucy off reception popped her head around the door and said that two police officers had arrived and asked to speak to one of the partners we still didn't bat an eye lid. There were often cases that brought in the constabulary.

When an hour or so later, Mr Fowler; the junior partner rang through and asked if Jayne would gather all of the staff into our office and he would be along to talk to us in five minutes. Baffled, I sat on my chair and swung it from side to side waiting to see what exactly was going on. Deathly pale, Mr Fowler stood in front of all the anxious staff and delivered us a devastating blow.

Andrew Muir had been found dead that morning by his cleaner. The circumstances around his death were suspicious and until it was proved otherwise, this was being treat as a murder enquiry. The police would be coming to the office later in the day to take statements from us all. I couldn't believe it, he was so young and larger than life. He couldn't be dead.

I was distraught, we all were. We gave up trying to work and instead drank endless cups of tea and coffee as we waited for the police to arrive. There was nothing I could tell them, I hadn't seen him since the previous Friday lunchtime and I genuinely knew nothing about his personal life. We all had basically said the same. Andrew Muir had left the office over the lunch time on the Friday and we had no idea where he was going or who he was going with. None of us knew of anyone who would want to harm him. It was awful.

The next day the other partner, Mr Watts and the junior partner, Mr Fowler asked us to work as normal as we possibly could under the circumstances. We had no choice, us downing tools wasn't going to help anyone, but it was difficult. Mr Muir was all over the paperwork, every time I saw his signature or saw the red ink marks on a document I would feel the tears prick behind my eyes. It was worse for Jayne, she took a lot of instruction via his Dictaphone and the sound of his voice was starting to freak her out.

Newspaper reporters started to bombard the office with calls asking us a story, we were constantly on our guard, when the television cameras set up camp outside we virtually barricaded ourselves into the office and did some kind of commando manoeuvres to get in and out of the building.

The stories flying around were horrific. It is so true when they say that what the media don't know they make up. All and sundry seemed to have something sleazy to say about Mr Muir in the end I couldn't read a newspaper or watch the television. But friends and family kept me updated. My mam would ring me and say 'I didn't know your boss was this …..' Or Adele would call for a coffee and tell me who had come forward selling their story looking for their five minutes of fame. None of the stories seemed like they were about Mr Muir, but then I hardly knew him really.

Because it was a murder enquiry, it took 6 weeks for the body to be released for the funeral. The post-mortem had revealed that he had died by strangulation. What the police couldn't work out was if it was suicide or was there someone else involved. Apparently, because of where the body was, it would have been difficult for Mr Muir to have carried out the act on his own. But so far no one had come forward.

If we had any doubts that Mr Muir preferred men, this was blown out of the water at his funeral. It was like a gay-pride march. And lovely to see. His parents were obviously more in the loop than his employees were and had requested everyone to wear bright colours, the congregation was a rainbow of colours. All the flowers were pink, the hymns in Church were All Things Bright and Beautiful and Love Divine and then at the Crem Mr Muir went out to I'm Every Woman and we left to the sound of Village People singing YMCA. It was so tongue in cheek, but it made me smile. The whole thing was larger than life. Just like he was.

Workwise, we were all in limbo. The partners couldn't sort anything out until the police closed the case and then even though there appeared to be a will which was straight forward, it would have to go to probate. The best we could do was carry on regardless and try and fill the void in the office that Mr Muir had left, a near impossible task.

The good thing was that because of everything that was happening at work, I didn't think too much about my own failings. Phil rang me often, I think he missed me, but we were more mates than anything else. I missed our intimacy, but the price for that was far too high. I had Samantha back, Phil was no sooner out of the door and she was back, now staying home more often than staying out. I think she thought I was going to be on a real downer and wanted to keep an eye on me. But I was more upset with myself for letting myself get swept along with the whole Phil and marriage thing.

Brian had taken to popping in for a coffee with me again. For the whole time I was with Phil he had waited in the car for Hayley when she was off to his. But like Samantha, the minute Phil had gone, he was crossing the threshold again. So I had two of my three exes on speed dial, it was strange to think that they made better friends than they did husbands, but I counted my blessings for the small mercies that made them both friends.

When the police revealed their final findings, we were once again all a bit shocked. A 'friend' of Mr Muir's had eventually come forward and told the police what had really happened that ill-fated night. The man, who the police only referred to as a Mr G; had been having a relationship with Mr Muir for some time. Apparently Mr G was a supposedly happily married man, who also worked within the law business. The relationship had been going on for over three years, but because of the delicate situation that they found themselves in, it had been done in secrecy and that was the reason Mr G hadn't come forward immediately. It had been a sex act gone wrong, as simple as that. Nothing simple about it, because I really couldn't get my head around it. What sort of sex act resulted in death? Nevertheless the police were happy with Mr G's explanation and the coroner eventually returned a verdict of Death by Misadventure.

And then the tricky part began. It took months for everything to be finalised. Months where everyone did their best to keep the business running as smoothly as possible. But in the end it was pointless. All Mr Muir's assets had been left to his parents; they had no interest in the business and even though they advertised for a partner to come in and take over, there was little interest. Even Mr Watts and Mr Fowler tried to raise the funds to buy into the business, but the banks weren't lending money out, not even for a going concern and we weren't surprised when each of us received a letter from Mr and Mrs Muir Senior stating that they were closing the business and we were all being made redundant at the end of the following month.

It was a sad time. One by one everyone left. By the time came for the doors to close, there was only me and Jayne left. We both felt like we owed it to Mr Muir to see it through to the bitter end, we liked to think that he was somewhere in the big courtroom in the sky watching us as we packed and archived, laughed and cried. I was going to miss Jayne so much, we were good friends. She already had a job to go to, she was taking two weeks holiday and then starting work for one of the bigger law firms in Newcastle.

I didn't have a clue what I was going to do. Jayne had revamped my CV and I had a manila envelope full of them at home. But I didn't feel right. My hands and feet were continuously itchy, winter had only just started so I doubted that I had my chilblains back, but they were very painful. When a rash appeared around my tummy, my mam was adamant I had shingles and booked me a doctor's appointment. She was right, I did. All of the stress of the last year or so had taken its toll and for the next six weeks I really felt quite poorly. I wandered around my house in my dressing gown, after Hayley left for school I would take myself back to bed. Emerging an hour or so before she was due back in, I would have a bath, put clean PJ's back on and then make my way downstairs to make her tea. I didn't leave the house. My hands and feet were covered in little scabs which itched and itched and if they weren't itching they were burning hot. The rash around my tummy subsided and faded away, but my hands and feet continued to drive me mad.

Samantha thought I was depressed and set about filling me full of all sorts of vitamins and potions she had read about somewhere which would boost my immune system and jump start my life. But while I waited for this life changing experience, I continued to scratch and burn. It was embarrassing. Whenever anyone came to the house, which was often because people weren't used to not seeing me; friends and family arrived at regular intervals with food and wisdom, I would sit on my hands and hide my feet in socks. Both of which made them feel worse and I would writhe away at them the minute whoever was there had gone.

Then Thora took a real bad turn and was admitted into hospital. My mam said it was quite serious and didn't think she would ever come home again. I was so upset. I had grown to love Thora over the years, whatever she had done when she was younger was forgotten about, we all made mistakes. She was such a character and I knew I would never forgive myself if I didn't go into hospital and see her before it was too late.

Samantha said she would drive me, Hayley was with Brian so all I had to do was have myself a bath, cream my hands and feet and get myself dressed. It seemed to take forever. I was all fingers and thumbs, instead of just having hot hands and feet, now my whole body was on fire. By the time I got out of the front door I was dripping with sweat. I was so nervous, I hadn't been in the fresh air for weeks and my heart was beating at an alarming rate. I needed to go though, so I swallowed great mouthfuls of air and got into the passenger seat of the car.

Samantha chatted away and her radio was playing in the background. When she pulled into a parking space at the hospital, the normality of the car ride had calmed my nerves and I felt better. Even the walk to the ward felt ok. The burning was starting to subside and my heart was beating at a more steady rhythm. Thora was sitting in bed looking a picture of health. I had been expecting her to be asleep or in a coma or something, so I smiled a huge smile at her when I saw that she was actually comptismenstis and looked as pleased to see me as I was to see her.

But my mam was concerned, I could see it in her face. Thora had been having trouble breathing and an oxygen mask lay beside her on the bed for when she needed it. But for the next hour we chatted away just as we always had. She asked me to show her my hands. 'Your great-granddad had the same thing' she said. 'You got trouble with your feet as well?' She went on. Telling her how I had always had bad feet but the hand thing had only happened a couple of times. 'Milk' she said.

Milk?? 'Not to drink, the proper stuff, not that fancy stuff you all drink now. Pasteurised milk, when your hands and feet are at their worst, soak them in milk for as long as you can, let them dry themselves and then do the same again the next day and the next day. It won't cure you altogether because you've got it now and it will always come back. But it will send it away for now!' How strange, I thought and for my great-granddad to have the same thing aswell. I was the only one in the family to have it as far as I knew and all of a sudden I felt special. My inheritance.

Me and Samantha kissed Thora goodbye, she looked so well I had no qualms about leaving her and I promised I would see her again in a day or two. Leaving the hospital we made straight for the supermarket where we bought milk and a new washing up bowl especially for the task along with some bits for the house. I hadn't been shopping for ages and actually quite enjoyed it.

Later, with my feet soaking in the milk, the phone rang. Mam. Thora had passed away half an hour earlier. Barring Julie, I had been the last of her granddaughters to visit. Mam thought she had been waiting to see me before she went. I had left, she closed her eyes and went to sleep. She didn't wake up. She had been 93 years old. The Woodbine smoking, good time girl had lived to a ripe old age.

It was yet another time of sadness. Thora was a huge miss to my mam and dad. For the first time since Avril was born they were on their own. Five daughters and two mothers had lived with them all of their married life. Newly retired, they didn't have a clue what they were supposed to be doing. My heart went out to them.

But Thora's miracle cure had worked. It truly was a miracle. Even before we had had Thora's funeral, the itching and burning had died away, the scabs healed and the redness had gone. Thank God for

Thora. Now I knew what I had to do when it came back, long before it got out of hand I would soak everything in milk; proper milk. I would bath in it if I had to.

Thora's funeral had a very special Funeral Director. Samantha James Mills of Mills and Boone Funeral Directors. Thora's great-granddaughter. When the hearse pulled up in front of my mam and dad's house we all trooped out and into the waiting car. I cried with pride when Samantha got out of the passenger side door of the hearse and dressed in her undertaking attire; a long black coat and her top hat with a little veil billowing at the back of it, she went to the front of the hearse and walked her Great-grandmother to the Crematorium. The walk was over a mile and I knew of old that usually the director would jump back into the car for most of the journey. But Samantha didn't, she walked all of the way. I cried with pride. Samantha really did have a calling. And I cried for Thora.

Whatever Thora might have been once, she really was well thought of. The Crem was packed as was the local pub where we had decided to hold the wake. It seemed everyone had a tale to tell. She really had been quite the character. I found out more about her in that afternoon than I had in all the time she had been my grandma. We laughed, cried and sat open mouthed at some of the things her friends told us. She had been an ace poker player and had often hustled men who thought they would have an easy time taking her money. She could speak French fluently, thanks to a French boyfriend. She once had a fling with a priest. The stories just kept on coming. Avril was mortified, but even she had to admit that at least we could never say she was boring.

And Avril came to the rescue with regard to the lost sheep who were my mam and dad. A holiday. Avril and Alan were going to go to Italy because guess who was living there? Julie had put roots down there and had been living in Tuscany for about 8 months, a long time for her really. Anyway, Avril and Alan were going to rent a villa for three weeks somewhere near where Julie lived and they wondered if my mam and dad would like to go too. Wild horses couldn't have stopped them. And for the first time since Thora had been admitted into hospital; my mam and dad were smiling.

Brian came and sat with me in a recently vacated seat. He was still family and I was pleased he was there. Asking how I was I told him all about Thora and her magic milk. I also told him how proud I was of Samantha and that he had been right to push me to allow her to join the business. I knew for sure that it wasn't just Thora's funeral that she would conduct with care and respect; she would be the same with every single one she carried out. She had a flair for it. Brian shocked me when he told me that for her 21st birthday; Laura and him had each decided to give her a 15% share of the business. She would own 30% of Mills and Boone Funeral Directors. Not for the first time that day I was crying. It was so generous, it would set Samantha up for life. Brian was going on to say that there was no one else to take over the reins when him and Laura retired. Laura still hadn't married and the chances of her having any family were slim. But still, Samantha wasn't even blood. Hayley was showing no interest in the business, she even said now that it 'freaked her out sometimes', so maybe it made good business sense to have Samantha fully on board now.

Brian, as generous as ever asked if I was okay for money. Having not worked for over two months, my redundancy was eeking away. But no I told him, I was good for the minute and hopefully now I was feeling so much better I would find another job soon. He was such a nice man. I just wished things had been different between us, but they weren't and I was happy that he was still in my life. He was a great dad to both the girls and I knew he always would be.

But finding a new job turned out to be an impossible task. Instead of recruiting it seemed most companies were shedding staff. Even the Job Centre said that applications for every job had trebled. I sent off countless applications and waited with eager anticipation for interviews. But there were no letters or emails inviting me to show off my skills and talents. I was starting to get scared. My redundancy money was running out and for the first time in years I was having to start watching what I was spending. I was allowed to claim Job Seekers Allowance, but that was just over £100 a fortnight, it didn't even cover the mortgage.

I applied for more menial jobs, but it was the same old story. I rang family and friends and asked them to keep their ear to the ground for anything. But no one heard of any jobs going anywhere. There were so many other people in the same position. Brian once again offered to help, but I was having none of it. The itch was coming back in my feet. I couldn't see any great change, but there was a definite stir and I knew that the job hunting and lack of funds was starting to get to me.

Six months after having been made redundant, I still hadn't found alternative employment. I was trying all of the time. I bought the basic brands at the shop and kept the heating off unless one of the girls was in. I seemed to spend my days shuffling around the house in layers of jumper and cardigans with a constant red nose. I hadn't fallen behind on any bills but I would in the next few months unless I started to put some money in the bank.

I had been right about my feet, the itching and burning came back. This time I had to recycle the milk. I would soak my feet and hands and then pour the milk in to container with a lid. I'd leave it outside in the shed just in case one of the girls used it on their cornflakes. Samantha would call and do a supermarket shop every couple of weeks; I was embarrassed and ashamed when she did it, but so grateful to her for the help.

I sold my car. There was a good enough bus service if I needed to go anywhere and I really couldn't justify keeping it when everywhere I needed to be could be walked to in less than 10 minutes. Samantha had a car anyway that I could use if need be and it seemed like a luxury having a 2 year old car which was worth 10 grand sitting outside doing nothing. Some of the pressure was off. But there was still no job. I started looking at signs. The birds in the garden whilst I had my morning coffee were my favourite indicator on how the day was going to go. Every day was the same. 'No job for you' the birds would say.

My mam and dad went off to Tuscany, I was lost. Part of my daily routine was to have a walk around to their house for a cuppa. I could feel myself sinking into the depths of despair and I didn't like it. I had to do something. I took myself off for walks. I couldn't believe that there was no job out there waiting for me. I had to try and keep positive or else I would make myself ill again. There was money in the bank again, but it wouldn't last forever.

On hairdressing night Lynne, Adele and Janet turned up. Lynne was doing really well, her client list was growing daily and she rushed about from house to house. People were cutting their cloths accordingly and whereas ladies were happy paying city centre salon prices, they now couldn't justify it and still wanting stylish haircuts and colours, they turned to the one man bands that were mobile hairdressers. I even asked Lynne how long she thought it would take me to learn to cut hair. She thought I was joking and laughed it off, but I really was deadly serious.

It was Janet gossiping about what had been happening in town that sowed a seed in my head. She was telling us about a girl who worked in her shop being attacked by the taxi driver who was bringing her back from her night out in Newcastle. Seemingly he had taken a really dodgy way home and had pulled into an industrial estate and maybe thinking that she was drunker than she appeared; he had sexually attacked her.

It was awful and the thought of anything like that happening to either Hayley or Samantha filled me with rage. How dare someone who should be trusted with our wellbeing and safety take such a liberty? How many other women did it happen to? The only reason we knew about this one was because the girl worked with Janet. There must have been loads that similar things had happened to, maybe worse. Just because someone had had a little too much to drink, they shouldn't be put at risk.

And then I had it. I might not be able to get a job using my administration skills, but I could drive, quite well actually. I could be a taxi driver. No I could be more than that. I could be a taxi driver offering women safe travel. I was so excited I wanted to burst. Before I knew it I was asking the girls what they thought. Janet looked at me as if I had lost my marbles. 'Really??' Adele said. 'You want to be a taxi driver??' I babbled on and on and by the time we were sitting around having a drink of wine, I had convinced them that it was the most brilliant idea in the world.

I hadn't felt this excited about anything since I had married Phil. I didn't even know how to go about doing it, all I knew was that I was going to run my own small business. If no one wanted to give me a job, then I would make one for myself. Names for the business went backwards and forwards, but I knew what I wanted to call it. I just wanted something simple – Val with a Vehicle and I wanted more vs so underneath the Val with a Vehicle I would put Va Va Vroom. Perfect.

Wanna Be Starting Something

I had a purpose now. From the minute the thought entered my head, I knew it was something I had to do. I did some research, there were other female driving taxi firms, but for every success story there were ten more that had failed. I couldn't afford to fail. I had to make sure that whatever it was I was going to do with it; I had to be the best.

It wasn't going to be cheap to set up. I made spreadsheets with the costs as I came across them. Obviously the car was going to be the biggest expense, but then there was insurance and licences and the marketing was going to be pricey. I didn't have anywhere near enough money, but I ploughed on, drafting myself a business plan. Worst of it was, I would have to do a Knowledge test. I thought that only London cabbies had to do it, but a phone call to the council's licensing department clarified that I did indeed need to so a test similar to the Knowledge, they called it a locality test.

More expenses kept piling on. Liability insurance, CRB checks, fire extinguisher and first aid kits; these didn't cost a lot, but the start-up costs just kept on piling up. But I didn't have a lot of choice. There was still no other employment being offered to me, I hadn't even been given an interview anywhere.

The bank weren't very helpful. They thought that it was an interesting enterprise but they weren' prepared to give me a loan and suggested I applied to various organisations for funding. Lots and lots of form filling and even more jumping through hoops, I was declined for any funding apart from one the council were obliged to give for new small businesses in the area, or more precisely new micro businesses. It was only £500 but it was better than nothing.

My mam and dad weren't keen. They had returned from Tuscany like a couple of teenagers, I'd never seen them looking so young and energetic. My dad had loads of ideas about what he wanted to do with the back garden. It had been neglected over the years, now thanks to the beautiful gardens he had seen on his holidays, he was inspired and couldn't wait to get to the garden centre and buy new plants. Julie had been well by all accounts, they had managed to see quite a bit of her and had tales of nights out eating under the Tuscany stars and trips around local landmarks.

When I told them about my business idea they were mortified. Driving around on my own in the middle of the night was a stupid idea they said. What if I was attacked? I showed them my business plan; impressed that I had even managed to prepare such a document they started to get interested. My dad asked him to leave it with him, he said he wanted to check my figures. They were fine, I had checked and double checked them, I'd overestimated on some things but I wanted to err on caution and had used worst case scenarios. My mam really wasn't sure, 'how will you get fares? Who will your customers be?' The questions just kept on coming, but I had answers. I had done my research, I would keep it simple. Most of all I would have a job, something that had alluded me all these months.

I spent my days drafting up marketing ideas, the name I was sure of, but how to word the marketing without causing offence to the hundreds of male taxi drivers in the area was hard. I felt like I was saying all male taxi drivers were sexually predators and I didn't need them hating me before I even got on the road. What I needed to get across was that I was a woman and if any females out there were nervous of travelling in taxis, then I was their woman.

I still didn't have any idea how I was going to fund my business, I had enough money to put the wheels in motion; but I was still short of the vehicle cost and hoping for some sort of miracle. In the meantime I applied for my licence with the council. First thing was to get through my locality test. I studied maps of the area the council had suggested, it covered the whole county, places I had never even been to never mind knew. But needs must and I studied maps and made lots and lots of notes.

I was no good at road numbers. No matter how hard I tried they just didn't stick in my mind. I knew landmarks, an Asda on that road, a Church on another, but the road numbers were alien; I was a woman, we didn't do road numbers. So I went into the test with little hope.

The locality test was only available to sit once a month and as I made my way into the civic offices, I was really scared. I had done a sign check that morning in the garden and had counted cars all the way into town as my dad drove me in; all positive signs but I wasn't convinced. The waiting room was full of men, they looked me up and down and passed knowing looks to each other as if they were saying 'not a chance.' But I was determined.

In the plush council chamber, I gave a huge sigh of relief. The instructions at the top stated clearly. *Explain how you would make the following journeys or locate the places using road numbers or significant landmarks.* Result. I could do this. Question One. From Waverley Street how would you make the quickest journey to Newcastle International Airport? Question Two. On what road is Newcastle Crematorium located? And on the questions went. Two hours later I walked out of the council offices confident that I had done a good job. Smiling I jumped into my dad's car and began the four week wait for the results.

I was right to feel good with myself, I passed with flying colours. Stage One – tick. I carried on with my application, I needed a CRB test done and that was going to take a few weeks, but I still had lots to do anyway.

I searched garages for the perfect car, I didn't particularly want it to look like a taxi but it needed to be practical and a diesel. My poor dad. He drove me from one garage to another, nothing was jumping out. Everyone said I needed a pink car, but I was having none of it, I wanted subtle. And then I found it, my perfect vehicle for a taxi, a PT Cruiser; it was two year old, diesel, roomy and best of all it was quirky. I fell in love with it. But it was a little more expensive than I had wanted to pay, I was devastated. I went home and re-crunched the figures. It was no good, even taking the figures to a more realistic figure, I was still short.

Finance was an option, but my unemployment status wouldn't help. I rang the garage and asked. They could try they said. Nip back in and fill the forms in they said. But would that not be more disappointment? I could ask Brian, he would help in a heartbeat. But I didn't want to. This was my project, my business and I didn't want to be beholden to my ex-husband any more than I was already.

It was my mam and dad who came to my rescue. They turned up one afternoon to tell me that they were going to Spain with Carol and Ian for two weeks. I laughed, they had just got back from Italy. But they were so excited it was infectious. They had been to the library and got themselves a little guide book so they could explore the area properly. Holidays suited them. As we sat drinking tea and chatting, they told me they had eventually got around to clearing out Thora's things, nowhere near the hoarder she once had been it had still turned out to be a mammoth task. They had taken the majority of it to the tip, the better stuff to a local charity shop. But they said I would never believe what they had found. They had found her handbag. THE HANDBAG. The one that she had accused Mrs Phillip's of stealing. The handbag that had got her evicted from her home. My mam said it was definitely the one, there was a few pounds, a bottle of perfume, a lipstick and her bus pass. The bus pass had been issued the year before she had moved in with my mam and dad. It really was the bag. My mam and dad laughed and laughed about it, had she forgotten she had it? Probably not. Had she done it deliberately so she could live with my mam and dad? More than likely. She was a sly old dog. But they had all lived together happily for all those years, my mam had had chance to get to know her mam. It didn't matter anymore, maybe to poor Mrs Phillip's who maybe had a bit of a blot on her copy book, but it wouldn't matter now, she would be long retired. What was Thora like!

My mam and dad asked how things were going and I showed them all the stuff I had done since I had last seen them. They were impressed, I had carefully worded the postcard size business cards I would be putting through letterboxes and leaving at businesses. I only had the proof, but it looked classy. When my dad handed me a cheque I was confused. It was made out to V Collins and the amount was enough to buy the deep mauve Chrysler PT Cruiser outright. I was flabbergasted. My mam and dad weren't wealthy by anyone standards, they couldn't afford to give me money. I voiced my concerns, but they were having none of it. They said they were fine, they wouldn't have offered if they couldn't afford it would they. 'Take it!' My mam said. 'Ada and Thora will be very proud of you having a go on your own!' And then I cried. It was just so generous of them, I didn't even know if I would ever be able to pay them back. The whole business might be a white elephant and then what? I would only be able to give them a fraction back of what they gave me. But they were having none of it.

After they left I couldn't do anything. I didn't rush off to the bank to put the cheque in. I just sat. This was really going to happen, my mam and dad had faith in me. I should have rang the garage and told them I wanted the car, but I couldn't. I just sat. I could feel my feet glowing; but I didn't care, I thought they were glowing with happiness so I could cope with them. I had had them under control for weeks now, as soon as I felt the stirring of the heat, the milk would come out and I would sit soaking them for hours. The whole burning, scabbing thing hadn't happened for months now. So with my warming feet, I spent the rest of the afternoon just sitting, tomorrow I would go at the business with vengeance. But for that moment I was happy enough to just sit. I was happy. For the first time in months and months and months; I was happy. I was still as useless as ever with relationships with the opposite sex. But it didn't matter, I would be ok. I would work hard and make this whole taxi thing a success. I would make my mam and dad proud of me, show them that they were right to have some faith in me and what I was capable of. And I would show my girls that anything was possible if you worked hard at it. Val with a Vehicle – Va Va Vroom…….

Who's Going to Drive You Home, Tonight?

A week after my 44th birthday, I was on the road and ready to go. The taxi looked fantastic, a bit tongue in cheek with the Va Va Vroom, it certainly got lots of attention. I think I had overestimated how many business cards I would need; I had ordered 5000, I wouldn't need to order anymore for a decade. I had my new Blackberry's number printed on the business cards and all over the taxi. Opting to use the mobile as a contact number instead of the landline; I was literally taking my business with me everywhere I went. I encouraged people to text for a taxi; I couldn't always answer the phone and sometimes when there was a poor signal it was hard to hear what people were saying; a text put it into black and white and I hope people would appreciate the fact that I would text them when I arrived to pick them up. The mobile opened up all sorts of possibilities for me; things that main stream taxi firms weren't doing and I intended to utilise it to the best of my ability.

The biggest ace in my pack was that at the end of every journey I would sit and wait until my passenger was safely in to where ever they were going. It would add a few minutes on to the timing of the journey, but I thought that it would be well worth it and people would appreciate it.

The CRB took forever to come back. It was the only thing holding me up. I began to think that the staff at the council thought I had a charge sheet as long as my arm. The day that it arrived I jumped for joy, with no misdemeanours to report, I rushed around to the council and waited for four hours while they 'fast tracked' all of my paperwork.

It was time. I was about to take a huge leap of faith and I was terrified. I rounded up everyone I could think of and asked them if they would do me the biggest favour and post some business cards through letterboxes for me. Of course me being me; I had a map of the area and had broken it down into little sections; everyone had their own specific area, I was leaving nothing to chance. I certainly wasn't going to take the chance of some doors having two and others none. So armed with my list of streets; I dropped off business cards to all of my volunteers, took a bundle for myself and with mobile in pocket, I set off pushing them through doors and dropping them into all the local establishments. Everyone I met thought it was a great idea. But my mobile remained silent.

The next day I had a couple of calls. One wanted to know how much I charged to the airport and the other asking how much to the local supermarket. They didn't make bookings, even though they said they would get back to me. Had I set my prices too high?? I was fraught with anxiety. I had made a huge mistake. My mobile went everywhere with me; I kept it in my pocket, down my bra, but usually I had it in my hand and checked it constantly, just in case I had no signal and that's why the calls weren't coming.

And then I started to get a few texts. Adele; Janet; Samantha; Brian; even Julie, all asking how I was getting on and how many runs I had done. It was embarrassing; 'none' I would text back and they all replied saying the same thing 'early days.' It didn't help, I was beginning to panic. But then on the Thursday it all changed. Suddenly I was taking bookings for the Friday and Saturday. When someone rang and actually said that they need a taxi straightaway to take them to Newcastle Central station, I nearly collapsed.

Mrs Jones from Laburnum Grove which was literally around the corner from my house never knew that she was my first ever customer. If she had thought I was nervous on the journey into town she never said and from then on in was a regular customer, so I must have done something right.

And that was that. Bookings continued to be made and my diary would fill up. I enjoyed meeting lots of new people, everyone said how brave I was driving around at all hours of the night, but I didn't like to think about it, if I did and thought of all the things that could happen to me, I wouldn't have left the house.

In the first year I had secured about 250 customers; I wasn't rich, but it kept a roof over our heads and even though after the initial business card drop I hadn't done any more marketing, every week there would be more and more new customers. It was a success.

But I paid the price for it. I worked every day. Even if I only did one little run, the rest of the day I would have the mobile with me ready to leap into the taxi the minute someone needed me. I was frightened to take time off, what if someone went to a rival company and I never got them back? So I ploughed on, in all weathers I would be there. I put on snow tyres in the winter so I wasn't hampered by the frost and snow and in the summer I kept the air conditioning on so customers had a pleasurable cool journey without having the wind blow off their head because the windows were open.

I went out of my way to make sure that everyone had a pleasant journey. I kept the back of the taxi stocked with up to the minutes magazines; mostly customers wanted to chat, but for those that didn't they could happily flick through a magazine until we reached their destination. But mainly they wanted to talk. Everyone had a different story to tell, some good and some bad, they would get out of my taxi and I would feel privileged that they had allowed me to have an insight in to their own worlds. I enjoyed it very much; but it could be exhausting. Dragging myself out of bed at 4 in the morning to take someone to the airport could be a right killer, especially if I had only stumbled into bed at 2am after having a late pick up from the city centre.

When I first started rival taxi firms would drive up close behind me or they would blind me with their main beams as they approached me. But I was going nowhere and they soon got used to me, some even gave me a wave as we passed. Before I had even started trading I had gone to the local police and told them what I was doing, I asked that they might keep an eye on me; if they saw me pulled up somewhere and they thought there was any chance that I might be in trouble, could they stop, even if it was just to say hello. So far I hadn't needed them, but it was nice to know that they were there.

The taxi did have a detrimental effect on not only my personal life, but also my poor sore feet and hands. It didn't matter how much I cared for them, the winter months played havoc with them and I would ultimately have chilblains which drove me mad. The in and out of the cold lifestyle didn't suit them and I was forever having to bathe them, but sometimes I didn't get chance and I would writhe at them without even realising I was doing it, it wouldn't be until the scabs appeared did I know I had let them go too far and took action to repair them.

I had very little free time. I was a slave to my mobile and whereas I was happy enough visiting friends and family, even if they were at the other side of town, now I tended just to pop in. A quick coffee and I would be making my way home, my house the centre of my work universe now and the only place I felt I could relax between jobs.

The girls were growing up. Samantha was now working full time at Mills and Boone Funeral Director, she worked long and hard hours, but she seemed to love it. Delighted that she was now a partner in the business, she went out of her way to make sure that every service was carried out with loving care. Their business was booming. Luke had asked Samantha to marry him when she turned 21. Of course she said yes and we were all thrilled that sometime in the future the childhood sweethearts would be husband and wife. A date had been set for August 2013; that would give us all time to make arrangements for time off, it was even more difficult for Samantha, Brian and Laura than it was for me, one day for all of them to be away from the business was a very rare occurrence.

Hayley left school. She had no interest in going to work with her sister and her dad and had set her heart on becoming a midwife. She happily went off to college to do a course in Health and Social Care and met her first serious boyfriend on the bus the first morning she went. Rocco Reed was two years older than her, I actually thought his name was just a nickname when Hayley started saying 'Rocco this and Rocco that!' But it was his real name, his mam and dad were actually customers of mine, he had a younger brother called Bruno and a sister called Sissy. They were a nice family and I had no qualms about Hayley hanging out with him. She was pretty as a picture and Rocco Reed was lucky to be with her.

The rest of the family continued expanding. I lost count of the number of great nieces and nephews I had, but there always seemed to be someone in the family either pregnant or getting engaged or married. Of course I would only pop to the celebrations, if they all thought I was ignorant they never said. It was my job.

My mam and dad continued to holiday around the world, sometimes there would just be the two of them, but they liked it better when they went with one of their daughters and son-in-laws. They remained in good health and in good spirits. They worried about me, they told me often enough, but as my regular customer list grew, they relaxed a little bit. They were always bumping into my customers who they knew and they would be given rave reviews on the service they had received and who they had recommended my service to. They were proud of me.

Lynne celebrated 25 years of marriage, John managed to surprise her with an around the world cruise. She was one of my regular 'pop ins' and I missed her while she was away. I didn't see as much of Adele as I used to, but we text every day and she would be the one who would keep my mood buoyant when sometimes the job got on top of me. She was going to be a doctor's wife, no she was going to be a consultant's wife. They were doing it in the summer in Cyprus. Obviously it wasn't an occasion I could just pop to, so I had had to turn the invitation down, but Samantha was going with Luke. Adele was moving too, they had eventually found a house they both loved and would be moving into it before the wedding. I was so happy for her, after the disaster that had been her first marriage, her subsequent affair with Clive, she deserved to meet Mr Right.

As much as I spent my time with lots of customers and the time I spent 'popping' in on friends and family; and after three years of being on my own, I was lonely. Hayley was a busy little bee and I was often home alone. I didn't mind my own company; I read and watched a fair bit of telly, but I missed someone just being there when I got in late at night. Seldom able to go straight to bed, I would spend the final hour before my bed called me winding down and wishing that just now and then there was someone to share a mug of hot chocolate with and tell them about my night's events.

But I didn't go anywhere to meet anyone and even though I did have male customers, their female counterparts were usually a customer of mine too. Sometimes I would have a group of lads to bring home from the city centre, one of them would be a son of one of my customers and their mam would have given them my number because I was reliable. I couldn't afford to turn business away so I would grit my teeth and make my way into the city to bring them home. Every time I did it I vowed I would never do it again. Whether it was the novelty of having a woman driver or they did actually find me attractive, they would flirt and flirt with me and offer me all sorts of sauciness. The journey home would be a nightmare and I would count my blessing I was out of the dating game.

But that was as far as opportunity for romance went on the taxi; a bunch of 20 something's who fancied their chances.

Like in every other aspect of the taxi, I saw the best and worst of relationships. I took newlyweds to the airport, all glowing with happiness and hope for the future. I carried couples back from the city centre who although they were loves young dream when I had dropped them off four or five hours earlier, hated the very sight of each other on the way home when the alcohol had kicked in. On some occasions I had actually had to call the police when they had started really fighting when I dropped them off outside their homes. Sheepishly I would get a text a day or two later apologising for their behaviour, but the next time it would be the same again, it made me wonder why they actually wanted to go out together.

I took girls to meet their first dates, others to meet people they shouldn't even be meeting. I had widows who although they had passed their driving tests a million years ago had never driven because that was something their husbands had always done. When the husbands died they would be stuck with a car they had no idea how to drive and a mobile number for a lady taxi driver who would make sure they were looked after really well, just like their husbands had. I saw all sorts. Something's made me smile, often they made me cry.

I had a lot of thinking time. I analysed my own relationships and came to the conclusion that maybe I couldn't have done anything any differently; it was just one of those things or in my case three of those things. I tried to think that out there somewhere was a man that would be perfect for me. But the years were ticking by and there was no sign or even a chance of meeting him.

A lot of the time I was crippled with loneliness. Not that anyone would ever know, I was happy Val whenever I was with people. But when I was in the taxi on my own, or in the empty nest I called home, I struggled. I was close to a lot of my customers, I had a lot of time for them, especially the older ones. I started to accompany them on doctors and hospital appointments, they never wanted to be a bother to the family. I enjoyed their company, they reminded me of Ada and Thora and I would like to have thought that if their family couldn't look after them the way they should have, there would be someone outside the family that could.

I was shocked that so many of my customers, widowed and living on their own, actually had families. Some had children who had gone away young to university or to work and had never come home again. They would visit on their mam's birthday or mother's day and at Christmas, but they never really came home and these women hero worshipped them from a far. It was so sad. Even sadder were the ones that had family actually living on the doorstep and they had the same philosophy as the ones living miles away; birthdays, mother's day and Christmas. It was shocking.

So when they rang me to go on appointments I would subtly ask if they were going on their own. If they said they were I would ask if they would like me to stay with them. Some did, others didn't. But I'd be there if they needed me. I would wait in the waiting room or if they preferred I would go into the consultation room with them and make notes. They would then be able to let family members know exactly what was going on when the relatives rang to see how the appointments went. There was often devastating news, being with someone when they were being told that there was little hope for them, really did hit home. I would treat my ladies with the respect and empathy they deserved, if there was follow up appointments, I would offer to take them. I made sure I was there for them if they needed me. But it was a fine line. I didn't want people or especially the family thinking I was there for what I could get, it was nowhere near the truth. I cared. I just wanted to be useful. I just wanted them to know I was there. But the number of funerals I went to grew every year and each time my heart broke a little bit more.

Samantha would go mad. 'Mam, you get far too close!' She would say when she spotted me at yet another funeral. But I couldn't not pay my respects, I was close to them. They told me their life stories, the highs and the lows, loves and losses. I was involved whether I wanted to be or not. When sometimes there was only a handful of mourners, I was very glad I went.

It was hard work, the late nights and early mornings. I survived on 5 hours sleep a night, no matter what time I went to bed, between 5 and 6 hours later I would be wide awake; sleeping any longer brought on a hangover type headache. So when my eyes opened, that was that for the night. I would cat nap of course; in the bath, on the settee while I watched the latest fiasco on Jeremy Kyle. I could fall asleep for 2 minutes and wake up feeling like I had slept for hours.

And it was all such a worry. I would have one or two weeks where I worked flat out and made good money, then I would have the next three or four doing hardly anything; it was a very much hand to mouth existence. I couldn't plan and I couldn't save. I might have been good at the customer service side of the business, but the money side was a mess. There was always something unexpected to pay for; a new tyre, or new track road ends. The list went on. The money my mam and dad initially lent me remained unpaid; there just wasn't the money to be able to do it.

I seemed to be in a constant state of anxiety. Diesel prices had rocketed over the years, but I had had to hold my prices, everyone was in the same boat, money was scarce. If I put prices up people would go elsewhere, their loyalty fickle when it comes down to the pounds, shillings and pence. So I persevered.

Being out and about, the people I met and the things I saw, changed my whole outlook on life. Whereas before I had been sheltered from the nitty gritty of life, hiding in my nice house with my nice family and my nice job; I now saw things without the flowering of my rose tinted spectacles. The loneliness endured by the elderly, abandoned by their families, in many cases having had sacrificed so much to help them get a start in life; sending them off to university only for them never to come home again. I couldn't imagine the circumstances that would lead to me walking away from my mam and dad, or for that matter Samantha and Hayley leaving me; it had been bad enough when Samantha had virtually moved out when Phil and me had got married, I didn't see her every day but we stayed in touch. I couldn't get my head around the total abandonment of it all.

But for every one of them that was alone; there were others who were treat like the Queen Mother off their families. They had big strapping grandsons who thought nothing of arriving in their boy racer cars on a Sunday to take their grannie's out for lunch. Or son-in-laws who would spend hours cutting the hedges and lawns knowing that it was a bit too much for their mother-in-law's to do on their own. For every sad story there was another that filled me with hope.

Two remarkable things happened to me in the course of my journeys. The first one was, I didn't envy the youth their youth. This took me by surprise. I had always thought, if I had my chance again I would do this or do that. But I could think of nothing worse than being part of the youth of today.

I carried lots of young girls; lots of them I had watched grow up, they maybe started to travel with me at 17 or 18 and over the years I had got to know them. The pressure on them was immense. Not just academically, but socially as well. Girlfriends, boyfriends; every aspect of their lives was on constant show on social media websites. How they look, how they behaved. There wasn't a single aspect that wasn't out there for all to see; if it wasn't them posting it, it was one of their friends. The amount of girls who I had took home from a night out in the city centre hysterical because some so called friends had posted a picture of their then boyfriend wrapped around some other girl in another part of the city beggared belief. And then there would be an onslaught of texts and phone calls to the boyfriend and by the time we had made the 7 mile journey home, the boyfriend was dumped; there was no chance of a cooling off period. Everything was just so instant.

Comments; likes, it did little for young girls confidence. They were always striving to look better or nicer. Always in fear that if they didn't look good, then a picture would appear and the comments would start to flow. The girls I took into the city centre for their nights out resembled nothing of the girls I would see wandering around the town through the day; with their spray tans, extensions, false eyelashes and 3 inches of make-up, they were all clones of each other in varying forms. Where had the individuality gone?

I had tried the media websites and wasn't comfortable being part of it. My friends all loved it and would tell me off for not joining in. They all talked to each other constantly and hairdressing night was always full of did you see or have you seen who I'm friends with now? But it wasn't for me; I didn't want to know who was in a relationship with who, who was having spag bol for their tea or how many weeks it was until someone's holiday. Too much information.

It wasn't just the peer pressure for the young ones. It was their lack of opportunity. They should have been having a ball, but the opportunities were less for them instead of more. Mostly were on zero hour contracts so there was no chance of ever getting a mortgage; they wouldn't even be able to save the money for the deposit let alone secure one. I envied my elderly customers much more than my younger ones.

The older ones might not have had much growing up; well nothing really. But everyone was in the same boat. Nowadays, everyone had to have everything; I'd had 3 year olds in the taxi that had better mobile phones than the one I had to run my business off. It was so mixed up. The older ones had opportunities; maybe not university, but they had apprenticeships and job opportunity. They could walk out of a job on a Friday and start a new one the following Monday. They could progress. The younger ones were exploited, no two ways around it, there were no jobs so they stayed put and put up with it. In short they were exploited.

The older generation had morals. They met someone, fell in love and married and mainly they stayed married until death us do part. My ladies talked about their married lives; not always a picnic, but they stuck at it; leaving wasn't an option. Whereas the younger ladies jumped from boyfriend to boyfriend, sometimes overlapping and often ending up with a boyfriend one of their other friends had been with. Some just did the one night stand thing. It reminded me of when I thought I had been a one night stand with Brian, I had been mortified, but to these ladies it was second nature. I would sit in the city centre waiting for fares and I would look around me at the younger generation. It seemed that largely the girls could drink as much as the boys, they would stagger out of the pubs and clubs wearing hardly anything and I would shudder; how on earth did they make it home in one piece? One night one girl in particular caught my eye; a bonny lass she staggered in front of my car with her friend trying to flag down an available taxi. Dressed in a short kilt, a tiny top and the highest shoes I had ever seen, her skirt billowed up in the wind showing all and sundry that she was just wearing a G-string; but no as she continued her pursuit of a taxi, the front blew up to reveal that she was actually wearing no underwear. I couldn't believe it. I wanted to drag her into my taxi and give her my leggings. But then she jumped into a taxi and was gone. I was shocked to the core. What had the younger generation come to?

I was turning into a right grumpy old woman. My car seat was my soap box and I became opinionated on everything. The generation gap, price of fuel, benefits; you name it I had an opinion. But then there was the other side of my business. I had had girls in labour needing to get to the hospital as fast as possible; I'd even have two whose waters had broken whilst we had been travelling. And then I had the privilege of collecting new-borns from the hospital; I was always flattered; trusting me with such a precious cargo. I was inundated with presents at Christmas, but mainly I was humbled that my customers let me into their lives. Without asking I became part of the fabric of their lives.

The second remarkable thing that happened was I found my Faith. I didn't have an epiphany or anything. It was much more subtle. It was more to do with being thankful for who I was and what I had. Always grateful for my family and friends, my business seemed to empathise this more, even though realistically I spent less time with them than I ever had, even with all the popping. But I certainly appreciated them more. The network that kept us all together. Even my exes; well not David, but certainly Brian and to some extent Phil, who still remained a good friend; a better friend than a husband in reality.

And the seasons. And the sunrises and the sunsets, which to be honest I hadn't really took notice of before. But being up early I saw beautiful dawns and late at night I saw amazing sunsets. I watched the trees change according to the seasons and I would watch the wildlife scamper across the road in front of the taxi. Seeing a deer would bring me to tears, it was such an honour seeing these shy majestic animals. It was the moon in the sky that shone a light on the darkest of nights; and the constellation of stars that I would pretend I knew what they were, when actually I didn't have a clue.

Something was stirred in me. I couldn't think that it was just the work of evolution, it all had to mean more. It had to be God's work. And the more I thought about it, the more curious I became. In the end, on my next available Sunday, I made my way to the Parish Church where me and David had been married and I had the immediate feeling that I was home.

I didn't go to Church 'religiously', but I knew where it was when I needed it. I always felt better after I had been. My tolerance of people grew and I developed the knack of turning the other cheek. Sometimes the things I saw and heard made my blood boil, but who was I to criticise; these were my customers, the ones that paid their money that kept the roof over my head. We were all God's creatures.

But as the years rolled on, I became more and more disillusioned. I would drag my backside out of bed at 4 in the morning to take a family to the airport for their annual two week holiday; not one of them worked. Sickness benefits paid and whereas they weren't well enough to work, two weeks lazing by the pool was fine. When I had to delay a minor operation because I would need to take six weeks off work because I wouldn't be able to drive; I knew that my time 'taxi days' were coming to an end.

So I gave myself 6 months. I would be turning 50 in 6 months' time and this was no game for a middle aged woman. The car and my feet had had it. The car was costing me hand over fist and my poor feet were now beyond repair. I kept them constantly covered up, in the winter months I wore boots, but they were such a mess I kept them hidden in the summer too; they were embarrassing. My toenails were yellow so I would keep nail polish on them just in case I was ever in an accident, but they were also misshaped with constantly being squashed into boots.

I think the family all gave a huge sigh of relief I was making out roads. As much as they were proud of what I'd achieved, they still worried about me being out on the roads all of the time especially late at night. But with as many skills as I had, I had no idea what type of job I would be able to get. After all I had started Val with a Vehicle because I didn't have the Va Va Vroom to get a job before, and that was when I was younger and much more employable.

As I dithered about, not sure if I was really doing the right thing, the few customers I had mentioned it to were devastated, but said they understood, Hayley came up with the killer blow. Sitting me down at the kitchen able she told me her news, she was pregnant. You could have knocked me down with a feather, I just hadn't seen it coming. She was just about to go off and start her nursing degree at university and she had always seemed so in control of everything that had happened in her life. Her and Rocco were as close as ever, but I had always thought that she took precautions. Obviously I didn't ask her what had gone wrong; I just sat in front of her dumbfounded with throbbing feet and a flush setting the rest of my body on fire.

She seemed to be in control; she didn't want to move in or set up house with Rocco, she said they were too young and it would ruin them before they had even had a chance. No she wanted to stay with me, at least until after the baby was born. She had spoken to the University and they were happy enough for her to start her course and if she managed until just before the baby was born, then she would be able to pick up the following year if a place was available in the crèche for the baby. The only thing she didn't seem to have planned and therefore she wanted me to do, was tell her dad.

By the time I had pulled the taxi onto the drive of Mills and Boone Funeral Directors, I was wishing I hadn't agreed to tell Brian. Hayley was his baby; he still babied her even though she was a young lady. I knew for a fact that Brian wasn't keen on Rocco, not because he wasn't good enough, he was a hard working young man and doted on Hayley, even if she had been dating Prince Harry; Brian wouldn't be happy. The thought of Hayley having relationships with boys of the opposite sex was a complete no no to Brian. So the news that his little girl was pregnant was going to blow his gasket.

It was Laura that spotted me first, coming out of the office she looked really concerned to find me walking into the building. Assuring her all was well and I was more of a social visit, she said that Samantha was out and Brian was with a client. I waited; she brought me a cup of coffee and we had a bit of a catch up. But I could tell she didn't believe me, she could tell by my flushed face that this was so much more than a social call.

By the time Brian came to greet me in the waiting room; I was bright red and had the feeling I was going to burst into tears. It had been hard enough for me to get my head around the news; I couldn't think what it was going to do to Brian. So when we were sitting on our own; I just said it. As per the silence was deafening. If he thought to blame me for not being more responsible, he stopped himself. I think he knew this was as devastating for me as it was for him. Not knowing what else to say, I stood up and left. The rest was up to Hayley now. I'd done the hard part.

And for the next couple of weeks I stayed out of all of their ways. Samantha had rang, at first furious, but later more concerned. Hayley was going to be her bridesmaid in August, something I assured her that Hayley would still be able to do; after all the baby was due in early April. And then she was concerned about Hayley doing it on her on. As far as Brian and Samantha were concerned the reason why Hayley had decided to stay at home to have the baby could only mean that Rocco wasn't interested. I did try to explain that they weren't splitting up and were actually being really sensible fell on deaf ears. So I gave up.

My mam and dad took the news really well, whether it was because they were virtually walking out of the door to go on their latest jaunt to somewhere exotic or they really didn't mind, only time would tell. But they seemed fine. Everyone seemed fine. Everyone said Hayley would make a great mam and eventually a great midwife. If only I was so sure.

The one thing I did know was that running a taxi and becoming a new granny with a daughter and grandchild living in the house wasn't going to work. This had to be it. So as 2012 drew to a close and 2013 dawned, this was going to be the last New Year I would spend on the taxi. As the hotel loomed up in front of me I had made it with 5 minutes to spare. 2013…… bring it on. One daughter having a baby; the other getting married and me turning 50. This was definitely going to be my year; whether it wanted to be or not…….

January

January turned out to be a very unremarkable month. The snow came and I dug my way to the taxi, and then I did it again and again. My hands were red raw and my feet throbbed; then so did my nose and ears. It was hard work. But my customers were grateful that I managed to get them to wherever it was they wanted to go. I sat on my heated seat and continually steamed off my damp clothes. The taxi took on a smell all of its own; it just didn't get the chance to dry out.

I thanked God when I made it safely home after each journey. I wasn't scared; I knew my vehicle well so could feel even the slightest of slip on the snow. But other drivers!!! I honestly didn't know how some of them had even passed their driving test. True not everyone had experience in adverse weather conditions, but the majority fell into two distinct categories. There were the ones that still drove at 70 mph and would go racing past, or there were the ones that drove at 3 mph. Did they seriously think they could get up a hill at that speed; they would set off and they would come back down again! I had on occasions had to jump into their car and get it up to the top; otherwise I would have sat there all day. And going down hills sitting on their brakes??? So it was less about my own driving and more being alert to what was going on around me.

Hayley was blooming. At 6 months pregnant she looked radiant; pregnancy suited her. She had started University and so far was managing just fine. Rocco was forever turning up with treats for her; whether they be directly for her in the shape of chocolates or a DVD so she would put her feet up and watch it with him; or something for the baby. He had grown up and was looking forward to this baby coming as much as the rest of us were. Because we were. After the initial shock had worn off I went out and bought needles and wool and started knitting little cardigans and mitts and I never came away from the supermarket without a little something in my trolley for the baby.

Brian had got used to it too. He had huffed for a few weeks, then he had ranted for a few more 'you're throwing your life away/ you're too young!' But he got over it. After all she was his little girl and this baby would go without nothing as long as he was around. Even him and Rocco had reached some sort of truce as whereas before Brian had blatantly ignored him, he would now include him in anything he organised to do with Hayley.

Samantha was full of excitement for her forthcoming wedding. If she was put out that Hayley had beaten her in the baby race, then it didn't show and she was another one who would turn up with something for Hayley to put away for the baby. Luke and Samantha had bought a little house not far away from Mills and Boone Funeral Directors. Brian had helped them with a deposit, but they were both on good money anyway and spent all their spare time making the little two up two down a little palace.

Because she had moved all her stuff out of her bedroom at my house; well virtually everything, I had to climb in and out of the loft to put her numerous teddy's and dolls, CDs and books into storage; me and Hayley set about making her bedroom into a nursery for the new arrival.

It was a labour of love and one I relished doing. Hayley had opted for a surprise, so it was all neutral colours, but could easily be given a splash of pink or blue when the time came. By the time January was coming to an end, the nursery was ready, it looked like something out of one of the magazines Hayley was keen on spending her money on. In short it was beautiful.

And at the end of January there was some amazing news. Julie emailed. In fact she emailed us all. All there was was a little photograph of a house. Puzzling, no narrative, just a picture of a little new build house. It was Rocco who recognised it, he had been doing some work on the estate and told us that it was one of the new builds they were building where the old Co-op had been flattened. Why would Julie send us a picture of a house on that estate? Then the penny dropped. It must have dropped for the rest of them too because the phone was ringing off its hanger. Julie was coming home. Julie was coming home but this time she was staying. Somehow, obviously due to all the available technology nowadays, she had bought a house, five minutes from my mam and dad's and no doubt a 7 minute walk from my house. She had bought a house and she was coming home for good. After over 30 years she was coming back. The wanderer was returning.

February

The weather got worse and whereas usually I would be able to motor my way through it, it was beyond even me and my expert driving skills!! As quickly as a channel was cleared in the cul-de-sac, another blizzard would appear and all the hard work of me and my neighbours was covered and we would have to start all over again. My customers would ring, especially the more elderly ones, they needed milk and bread and the disappointment would be there in their voices when I told them I had had to come off the road. So where I could I would wrap myself up, traipse around to the shop and delivered minimum essentials to them where I could.

But mainly I would stay indoors, cocooned in snow. Hayley had took flight at the first sign of the bad weather and was staying with Brian; from his place she could walk into University in 15 minutes or so. So I was home alone. I wasn't lonely; my phone buzzed constantly; the girls, friends, even the exes – all concerned about how I was doing. But I was fine. I used the time to redraft my CV and even dipped my toe in the water by applying for a few jobs, I watched daytime telly, took long leisurely baths and each time the weather perked up, I was out shovelling snow.

Eighteen months earlier I had joined Geordie Go-getters – the dating website that Adele had met Peter on. I didn't take it seriously, but because I didn't do other media websites; in those weeks in the snow, I dipped in and out of it. I had spoken to a few interesting people, but there had never been anyone who had stirred my interest enough to actually go and meet. Like any other of the similar sites available; you had to sift through loads and loads of messages to even chat on-line to someone who was genuine and not just interested in one thing. I persevered; it had worked for Adele; her and Peter couldn't be happier, but it wasn't working for me. Maybe I was too long in the tooth and maybe a little bit over cynical. But at the end of the day; I think I was a little old fashioned. If there was someone out there for me, I wanted eyes across a crowded room, a slow manoeuvre towards me and then the 'where have you been all of my life?' I could dream.

I didn't like to think that I would be on my on for the rest of my life. Was it better to be with Mr not quite Right now, theoretically making him Mr Wrong, than staying on my own until Mr Right turned up? That was if such a thing even existed. It made my mind boggle, so I stopped analysing, picked up a book or my knitting and watched the car crash relationships on Jeremy Kyle.

The weather perked up so I went back off to work. Business was slow, no one quite trusted the break in the weather so they didn't want to go too far in case they got caught out. But I made countless trips with customers to the supermarket where they bought bags and bags of food 'just in case.' I popped to see the girls and my mam and dad and even managed to squeeze in a supper with Lynne. Then my customers that had stocked their cupboards and freezers to the hilt had been proved right. The heavens opened and inch upon inch of snow fell. I was once again alone.

The up side of this was that on Valentine's Day morning, the day of my 50th birthday; there was no fuss. The roads remained blocked and there was no cars moving in or off the estate. The telephone rang constantly wishing me a happy birthday and well-wishers saying how sorry they were that they couldn't see me in person, but that was fine. I really really didn't mind. There would be fuss later; when the roads re-opened and we could all get together, but for that day, my 50th birthday – I was alone and it was brilliant.

With the chances of me having to work at all that day were slim; I had Baileys in my coffee, every cup of coffee. I took my latest book in the bath with me and spent a good hour letting water out and refilling it; bliss. And best of all I spent the whole day in my dressing gown. It was the best birthday I had had in a long time. I knew everyone was thinking about me; I had had the phone calls and the texts to prove it, but for that one day; it was my day and I did exactly what I wanted. With my frozen meal for one and into bed by 10 with my book, a rare luxury with having been running the taxi for so long; it finished the day off to a T!

But of course the weather did improve and the family arrived, each bearing cards and gifts and I enjoyed each and every one of them. My day had passed and somehow receiving the fuss on a day that wasn't my birthday made it more achievable. I didn't like being the centre of attention, maybe I should always have my birthday on a day that it wasn't actually on. The whole family were going for a meal on the last Sunday of the month; obviously in honour of my 50th, but I was picking Julie up from the airport late on the Friday night. It was a double celebration, something else I could manage. I didn't mind sharing at all.

So on the last Friday night in February; me, my mam and dad and Janet made our way up to Newcastle Airport. A veteran at flight arrival information now; I delayed the family exodus because Julie's flight was running two hour late, but after only an hour my mam and dad rang and said they didn't mind paying the airport parking charges, they wanted to go straightaway. My dad wanted to watch her flight come in. I didn't have the heart to tell them that they wouldn't be able to see anything, it wasn't like they were in the departure lounge! So off we went. And the four of us sat in the little Greggs café and sipped on hot chocolates and ate muffins waiting for the prodigal daughter to arrive home. We took it in turns to go and check the flight status on the arrivals board. After three more hours there it was flight KL971 from Amsterdam was approaching. We were all up and out of our seats; the viewing gallery was long gone so we made our way out of the terminal and as the plane approached we waved frantically, hoping that by some chance not only would Julie have a window seat, but she would be able to see us all in the dark of the night.

But she was home and for the next 45 minutes we craned our necks around the revolving door as it automatically opened to expose a weary passenger. And then it was her. Older, thinner but unmistakably Julie came sauntering through. The tears we cried. The others had all seen her in the intervening years, but I had only managed to have Skype conversations with her. To have her standing there in front of me, home at last, took my breath away. I sent a silent prayer up to my God for not only bringing her home, but for keeping her safe all of these years that she had lived on foreign soil.

It was a happy family that made the 30 minute journey back to my mam and dad's; where there was a little surprise in store for us all. Unable to settle themselves Carol and Avril were there waiting for us. A pot of tea was brewed ready and Avril produced some chocolate cake she had managed to rustle up while her and Carol had kept their vigil. No sleep was had that night. There was just too much to talk about, too much to catch up on; gaps to be filled and plans for the future made.

By the time we arrived at the restaurant the following Sunday lunchtime; it was if the James sisters had never been apart. The whole family were there. All my sisters and their husbands, their kids and their partners and the kid's kids. Usually I would have felt quite conscious that I didn't have someone with me, but I had Julie; she was my plus one. I made up for the fact she had never been married; I wasn't even sure if there had ever been a boyfriend; or girlfriend for that matter, it was something we never talked about. But she certainly didn't let me forget that she couldn't marry because I had used up the allocated quota for the James family. It was a good job I could laugh.

The afternoon was wonderful, even when the waiters came over with a cake and everyone sang happy Birthday to me, I didn't mind. I felt content. It wasn't until I saw Samantha talking to a tall fair haired boy did a shadow cross the afternoon. He looked very familiar, but as I sat stirring my second cup of delicious coffee I couldn't figure out where I knew him from. When his head went back and he laughed I had it. David. It wasn't David though, it was one of his boys. Glued to my seat in panic; I couldn't decide whether to go over and introduce myself or just pretend I hadn't seen him. Samantha caught my eye and beckoned me over. 'Mam, this is Toby!' He was so like his dad, it was unsettling. Not the lads fault I smiled my biggest smile and said 'Hi Toby, I've heard so much about you from Samantha!' How cliché. But what else could I say. He was the image of David, in fact so much like him it was disconcerting. I chatted away for a few more minutes and then made my excuses and went to the ladies.

I was fighting back tears. Why after all of the years? Because David had hurt me, badly. The lad out there was proof that David had left me for someone else. I stood looking in the mirror. I was 50 year old and had failed in every relationship I had ever had. The image staring back at me didn't look 50. Granted it didn't look 30 either mind; but I wasn't bad looking, I hid my grey well, thanks to Lynne and my eyes still sparkled. I might have been down in the men stakes, but I wasn't out.

Samantha came into the toilets. 'Oh mam, I'm so sorry, I didn't mean to upset you. I just thought that after all these years you wouldn't mind so much. And me and the boys are so close and a big part of my life; I wanted you to meet Toby when you had chance. I didn't mean to ruin your day!'

She hadn't. It was just a fright. I assured her it was fine and it was only because I hadn't been expecting to meet him at all, least that afternoon. Taking the chance, while the opportunity was there, I said. 'Do you see David?' She did, apparently not often when she was little, she was a bit of a bone of contention to the new wife. But over the years, when David realised how close her and the boys were, he would include her in outings and stuff too. Samantha said that she never wanted to hurt me, so had always just kept these trips to herself. Now that she was older, David and her had a much rounder relationship. She saw him once a month or so, they would do lunch or she would go over to his house. She said it was Brian she had asked to give her away when she got married and she said that David understood why she had done this. But in her own words. 'Me and David are sweet!'

So now I knew. My beautiful older daughter had known her dad all along. I sighed with relief, it was so much better than her not knowing him at all. If I should have been angry that she had never said anything, I wasn't. They had done what they thought was best. She was a lucky young woman, she had two dads. Well three if you included her granddad who still doted on her and she him.

Making my way home later that night, I felt even more content than I had in the restaurant earlier in the day. Granny Ada always used to say that things had a way of sorting themselves out. Maybe she was right!

March

There's a phrase 'March comes in like a lion and goes out like a lamb!' Reverse that phrase completely and that will be true for my March.

The weather had turned exceptionally mild. The daffodils and crocuses in the garden were standing proud and ready to burst into bloom in the March sunshine. All around me there were signs that spring had actually sprung and I felt as if I was bursting with hope.

Hope for what I wasn't sure. Hope for the new baby, for Samantha and Luke and their future together. Hope that someone would read my CV one day and realise that they couldn't run their business without me. Hope that maybe one day, I could share my thoughts with someone who would want to hear them. It was all hope; but hope made me feel good.

I went off to Church, it was Lent so I had decided that I was giving up chocolate; quite a difficult task since it had become my pick-me-up when I needed an energy boost on the taxi. An apple just didn't have the same kick. I enjoyed the Lent period at Church, because it lead to my favourite part in the Christian calendar, Easter.

A time of new beginnings. I didn't understand the whole concept of Easter, but I did know that God had sacrificed his only son in order to save us all. Being a parent myself I thought that this had been an almighty gesture. One that wasn't taken seriously enough in today's day and age, but one I myself truly appreciated.

So I ploughed on with the taxi, a smile on my face and all the while applied for a multitude of jobs. Hope in tact; I had every faith that the right job would come along at exactly the right time. The six months I had given myself had been and gone, but was always under the philosophy that things happened for a reason and at that time, I was meant to be on the taxi.

But I started looking for signs. I was constantly counting cars or looking for magpies; nothing escaped my radar of looking for the right combination of signs. But there was no job, no knight in shining armour coming for me. The hope I had at the start of the month started to fade towards the end.

When the Vicar rang my mobile one afternoon in the last week of March I wasn't fazed. He was a customer; despite being a male, he was one of the many men in my area who had become good customers over the years. I knew I was safe if I knew where they belonged and who with. So thinking that he wanted to book me to take him to the train station or airport, I answered it with my usual chirpy greeting. Apologising in case he had heard wrong and saying that he wasn't usually one to listen to Church gossip, he wondered if I was looking for a job. I told him he had heard right and intrigued as to what he was going to say; I mumbled a quick explanation why I was on the lookout for employment. When I eventually gave him a chance to tell me the reason for his call he said that he had received an email about a job that was going within the Diocese. It was a secretarial job working for the Bishop. A little more than part-time hours he wondered if it would be of any interest to me.

Of course, I stammered back to him, I would be very interested. I gave him my email address and he promised to forward me the information with regard to applying and said that he would happily recommend me for the position if I wanted him to. I was delighted and promised I would get straight on to it as soon as I got home.

It was a turn up for the books. I printed off the relevant information and spent the next couple of days making sure that my application was perfect. I might not even warrant an interview but I was going to give it a damn good try. I sent a copy off to the Vicar and the original off to the Bishop's office along with a silent prayer that this was the job I had been made to wait for. Good money, regular hours and a certain je ne se qua about working for a Bishop.

The following morning I was up early taking one of my regular customers to work. I sometimes liked to go around in a circle when I did jobs rather than travel the same road twice. Never mind, I had dropped my customer off and the road leading back home was a bit of a short cut through country lanes. The mornings were still quite dark, but at 7am dawn was just breaking so although I still had my headlights on, it wasn't quite pitch black dark. Turning around a bend I could see shadows on the road up ahead. I couldn't quite make out what it was, so I slowed down to a crawl and approached the object.

As I drew near the shadows took shape; there were two of them and they both turned their heads and looked directly at me. I pulled the taxi to a stop. They were deer. Two of them, both doe. They stood stock still in the middle of the road and continued to stare at me. I shuddered and little goose pimples sprang out all over my body. They looked so familiar; but how could they? The staring continued for a few more minutes, me at them and them at me. It couldn't be! In unison they turned their heads away, lifted them high into the air, dropped them down in a kind of bow and then took great big leaps over the hedge at the side of the road and into the trees and away. I didn't know if I believed in reincarnation, I didn't particularly know much about it. But in the dawn of that Thursday morning on the 28th day of March, I believe that those two female deer were my grannies Ada and Thora. I had seen my grannies' eyes in the eyes of those two beautiful female deer. They were there for a reason; they had come to tell me everything was going to be alright.

Because they had no sooner leapt the hedge when my mobile started ringing. Hayley!! Her waters had broken and the baby was on its way. I could hardly drive home for the tears. For the deer; for my grannies; for Hayley and the baby; for me. I was going to very shortly be a granny myself.

By the time I pulled up at home the familiar burning had started in my feet. Hayley on the other hand was as cool as a cucumber; she had rang the hospital and they had told her they would be ready for her when she arrived, then she had called Rocco and then her dad and then her big sister. Everyone knew what was happening and where they had to be and when. There only seemed to be me that was flapping. I remembered my grannies and tried to stay calm as I bundled Hayley into the taxi and then ran back into the house to collect the assortment of stuff she had left by the door for the hospital only the night before.

Rocco and Brian were waiting at the entrance for us when we arrived. Sensible as ever, Hayley had pre-arranged for Brian to pick Rocco and Samantha up on his way, so there were only two cars to worry about parking instead of four. It was still quite early so we all managed to get parked in the designated area that served the maternity unit at the back of the main hospital.

Having agreed to be one of Hayley's birthing partners, I was now filled with dread at the prospect. Watching your own child going through agony was something I wasn't relishing, I had the feeling I would be useless. So when Samantha suggested that maybe she should go with her to start with; I didn't object.

With nowhere else to go, Brian and me headed for the cafeteria for a much needed cup of coffee. I had jobs booked in that I would need to have carried out by one of the other local firms, so while Brian went to the counter I quickly re-booked all my jobs out and sent messages or rang the customers and told them what was happening. Lots and lots of good lucks later, I made my way to a deathly pale Brian.

I smiled at him; this was a totally alien situation for us both. I jokingly said that he did actually look like death warmed up, but it only produced a thin smile. That was his little girl in there going through hell and for once there was nothing Brian could do to make it better for her.

As we sipped our coffees we chatted. He had kindly bought us both chocolate brownies; I devoured mine, I didn't have the heart to tell him I had given chocolate up for Lent and under the circumstances I was sure that God would forgive me for succumbing to a medicinal chocolate pick me up.

Brian told me business was good; Laura was well; Samantha was a natural and his dad and Sally were both in good health. He didn't have much more to say beyond that. He didn't really do much beyond work. I told him about the job working for the Bishop – Brian said he had met him once or twice and seemed like a very nice man. I told him news about the family – Brian said he had seen my mam and dad; Julie; Janet; Carol and Avril (when I thought to myself??) I told him bits of news about the taxi. And when I actually ran out of conversation I told him about my deer!!

This did pique his interest. He seemed to have lots of funny little stories that he had been told about messages from beyond the grave. He was just about to start going into detail when my mobile beeped. Samantha. We had to make our way back down to the delivery suite. Surely it wasn't time for me to go and do my bit already?? The chocolate brownie started to stir in my tummy and my feet started to itch. I had to trot beside Brian just to keep up with him as he took long strides to the lift and then I sort of cantered to the delivery room where Hayley had disappeared into just over an hour earlier.

There was no one around. The midwife who had buzzed us into the unit was nowhere to be seen. Unsure what we should do we sort of wandered up and down the corridor in different directions in the hope that someone would hear us and come out and tell us what was going on. The chocolate brownie was creeping up my throat and I thought I was actually going to be sick, when a door opened and Samantha was standing. With her dad on one side and me on the other, she had a puzzled look on her face. What was wrong? Had something happened? I really was going to be sick!

'It's a girl. She is beautiful and they are both doing great. Come and see her!!' I was stunned; Hayley wasn't even having contractions when we went up for coffee, it was her first baby! Surely it should have taken hours?? But no, Samantha said it was a little girl. I was a grandma; I had a granddaughter.

Quietly me and Brian followed Samantha into the delivery suite. As sure as eggs were eggs, there was Hayley sitting up in bed, Rocco at her side and in her arms was a tiny bundle. She was so small, but even before I got to the bed I could see she had a mass of thick black hair.

Hayley looked shattered, but she had the glow only someone who was a new mammy had. Rocco looked so less the cool lad I had come to know and love, he looked like an emotional wreck. 'Mam, dad meet your first granddaughter. Theodora Reed, these are your grandparents!'

I was fit to burst. At a couple of weeks early she had weighed in at 6lb 9ozs, small but perfect. I cried and cried. So did Brian. We managed to each get a little cuddle before Rocco's mam and dad arrived, if we thought we were emotional wrecks we had nothing on Rocco's parents! When the midwife came to say that they were taking Hayley and baby up onto the ward, we all took our leave promising to return later in the day. There were only fathers allowed on the maternity ward outside of visiting hours so one by one we kissed Hayley, Rocco and the new arrival and left the new little family to be taken upstairs where they would remain for the rest of their stay.

Brian wanted to drive me home, but I said I would be fine; I wanted to call and see my mam and dad. Samantha went with her dad, so I made the journey out of the city centre alone. My first journey as a grandmother. It had all happened so quickly, one minute I was eating chocolate brownies the next I had my granddaughter in my arms. I thanked God as loudly as I could for her safe arrival and for keeping Hayley safe and so the prayers went on. I thank God for everything.

Pulling up outside my mam and dad's I sat for a few minutes pulling myself together. They would be so excited when I told them the news. Thoughts of the deer sprang into my head. It was Thora and Ada I was certain of it; they had come to warn me what was happening and to let me know all would be well. Seeing them filled me with hope again. And so I thanked them. In the privacy of my taxi I shouted it as loud as I could. Thank you Thora and Ada!!!! Thora and Ada; Thora and Ada. Theadora!!! My new granddaughter's name was made up of Thora and Ada's. I couldn't stop crying. I had Theadora and I had hope!!!!

230

April

Theadora's arrival brought with it an abundance of everything. People, gifts, money and above everything else love. Before she even got home from hospital; she was Teddy, the name suited her; she was just so cute.

As soon as she got home from the hospital, the house had a steady stream of visitors, each brought gifts or money; I didn't have enough vases for the flowers or ledges for the cards. Rocco all but moved in, it didn't faze him changing her nappy or getting up to feed her numerous times in the middle of the night. I tried to work, but it was too difficult with all the people coming and going, so I booked myself a week off and enjoyed the festivities.

It was nice seeing everyone; I had been popping for far too long. Brian and Samantha called every day and my mam and dad were backwards and forwards. As were my sisters, Hayley's cousins, friends and her Auntie Laura, Granddad and Grandma. It was a time for catch ups, some long overdue.

But I had to go back to work. There had been no invitations for interview, but I kept up the search. There had to be something. The holiday season was starting and the diary started to fill up with bookings to and from the airport. The taxi was picking up, but my heart wasn't in it anymore. I would kick myself when I had to forgo bathing or feeding Teddy because I had to go out on a job. It was just so frustrating, I wanted to do more for them.

Not that they needed my help, the three of them seemed to be managing fine. Hayley didn't show any signs of having the blues, in fact if anything she was ecstatic, motherhood suited her and the first time they took

Teddy out in her pram, Hayley and Rocco couldn't look any more proud of themselves. I prayed that it would last. They were still so young.

Samantha was finalising the arrangements for her wedding. Everything was virtually done, it was just the little things, like me finding an outfit as quickly as possible and Hayley having her final fitting in a couple of months' time. But mostly she was ready. We were all off to Blackpool for her hen party in July. Why Blackpool? I had no idea, maybe she had loved it when she was 18 and we had gone for my 40th, but of all the places we could have gone to, she had chose to go to Blackpool. Luke had more sense he was off to Benidorm; at least he was guaranteed a bit of sunshine. Somehow Samantha had talked Brian into going, more to keep an eye on Rocco she had said, but the thought of Brian in his Florida print shirt on a stag do in Benidorm made me smile.

So it was a bit of a busy April. New baby, taxi and Samantha turning up at all hours with little baskets filled with 'maybe' outfits for me on her IPad. I had an idea what I wanted, but it was falling on deaf ears with Samantha. In the end I rang Adele and asked her if she fancied a day's shopping, after all she was mother of the groom and I didn't want us turning up in similar outfits. But mainly I wanted someone my own age and a friend to be with me to actually tell me if my bum looked big!

Julie seemed to be settling back well, her house was nearly ready, in the meantime she enjoyed being at my mam and dads. She had missed out on so much in the thirty years she had been away, being a globetrotter had its' setbacks. She was certainly making up for it now, she called to see me regularly and didn't mind that she would have to sit and twiddle her thumbs while I went on jobs. She was excited about putting down roots and made me laugh telling me stories about how the builders had taken to hiding from her when they saw her coming onto the site to chase a completion date.

She had certainly lived the life. Even though she had lived the life of a nomad, travelling and working around the world, then doing it again and no doubt again, Julie had been very astute and had managed to build herself quite a tidy nest egg for her rainy day. She said this was mainly due to some sound advice she had had from a fellow traveller who she had met years earlier, she had bought into stocks and shares. Not all of her investment had yielded, she had even had one or two biggish losses, but the majority had and all her wheeling and dealing was enabling her to buy a new house cash and to give her a steady income for the rest of her days, providing she didn't live too lavishly. I was impressed. I did often wonder how she was paying for the house, I had struggled to get a mortgage when I bought my house and I had been living and working in the country all of my life.

Mystery over; I had a very clever sister. When she eventually got the keys for her house we were all there to help. It was a labour of love for us all. Packing boxes arrived full of Julie's life on foreign soils, every picture or ornament or rug had a story behind it. Instead of taking a couple of days to get her settled in it took us a week; there were just so many stories to be told.

Easter at Church, I managed to fit in as many services as I could. It was still my favourite time, for some reason the sadness of the crucifixion really got to me. In the taxi I would listen to customers saying what they were buying their children for Easter or how many Easter eggs they had got on Easter Sunday morning and it would make me mad, not for the fact that my customers didn't really know what Easter was about, but because it was just another commercial exercise for the retailers. Hypocritical, I know, after all I was working too and having to charge the standard hiked up fare that the council stipulated for plying my trade on a bank holiday.

It was the same at Christmas. Everyone was trying to outdo each other. It was like the true meaning of Christmas had disappeared entirely, it was all just too commercialised. Christmas would start in the taxi in September when the kids went back to school and the mam's would rush off down to the Metro Centre to make a start on the hundreds of pounds they would spend on each of their children; it wasn't that that got to me, it was the shops scaremongering parents into buying things that early just in case they ran out of this year's big thing. No one wanted their child to not get what they had asked for off Santa Claus and be disappointed on Christmas morning. And from September it would run all the way through to Christmas Eve, which by that time my nerves would be shot and I would park the taxi up outside my little Church at 11.30pm and go and Worship at Midnight Mass. I just needed to strip it back; it was the season of goodwill; I saw it everywhere, people were just that little bit kinder to each other. But I needed to have the comfort of the Nativity to remind me what it really is all about.

Teddy made her first public appearance with me on Easter Sunday. I was the proudest, if not most nervous Granny ever when I took her with me to Church. There were a lot of my customers there and they had heard so much about Theadora and seen little pictures of her on my mobile phone, that they were straight across to see her, all oohing and arghing. When the Vicar blessed her, I wanted to cry. My pocket was full of little bits of money people had given Teddy when they met her. Some traditions made it through time and Teddy's little bank account was £43 richer thanks to the tradition of crossing the baby's palm with silver.

And then on the last day of April, I got a surprise. I had been invited for an interview; by the Bishop no less. I read and re-read the email. I printed it off, read it again and I panicked. There was a list of all the documents I would need to take, a copy of the interview format and some sample questions and there was a page about the protocol of the interview and what happened if I made it successfully through the first interview stage. As happy as I was that I had actually got someone to see me face to face, I was terrified. It had been a long time since I was interviewed, in fact I had never really been interviewed properly before. Sitting in the taxi later that day, I could feel the old familiar throb in my feet; 'here I go again!' I thought. 'And thank God Lent is over!' I went on to myself; reaching over and grabbing a mini chocolate egg out of the docket and cramming it into my mouth.

May

By the time interview day came, I was wound up like a coil. I had tried on so many outfits and checked and re-checked my paperwork to make sure that I had everything, it was bordering on OCD. The address I had was for the city centre, I had initially thought I would be going to the Cathedral, but my A A Route Planner showed that the office was actually in Font Street and nowhere near the Cathedral. I set off far too early for my interview, at least an hour too early, but I hated tardiness and even with all my experience of getting to destinations on time; I didn't want to take a chance of bumping into road works or something and being late.

So I knew exactly where the office was that I needed to be. But I was far too early, my feet were already nipping in my stilettos, so spotting a coffee shop opposite; I made my way over and took a seat. I didn't often have a chance to just sit and sip coffee anymore; so I fully intended not to sit and wind myself up in fear and nerves, so instead I sat looking out of the window, watching the world go by and tried to think of nothing. It worked, I felt visibly relaxed as I stood to go across the road and into whatever lay in store for me beyond the little blue door.

And I decided I was just going to be myself. Taxi driving wasn't the same as being a Personal Assistant, but they did have similar qualities and I would concentrate on those, my work within the Community and my administration and book-keeping background.

One and a half hours later, I opened the little blue door and exited on to the street. I felt good, I had done my best. I needed a caffeine injection so headed back across the road to the café I had been to earlier, where I could sit and analyise my interview in peace before I made the journey home.

I decided that I hadn't made too bad a job of it, I had answered all of their questions, giving accounts where need be and I think they understood that even though Val with a Vehicle – Va Va Vroom was a success, the reasons why I wanted to give it up made sense. I did hope that I didn't come across too big for my boots, because I really wasn't. I worked hard and sometimes had to dig deep to appease customers. It was how I earned a living and kept a roof over my head. I just hoped I had done enough. They said that if I was successful, they would call and ask me to go back and have a further interview with Bishop Jack.

I really liked the café. I liked to think that if I did get the job I would be a regular there. The prices weren't too city centre prices, the coffee was good and there was a nice atmosphere. All the walls were covered in artwork produced by local painters; some of the places I recognised, all of them were for sale. The price for some of the pieces was staggering; it made me wish that I was more artistic and had concentrated a little bit more on my painting by numbers when I was little.

Back home; the euphoria I felt when I left my interview started to fade as the telephone call didn't materialise and the days rolled on. The taxi was busy, I was up and down to the airport every day, sometimes two or three times, but at £20 a pop, I wasn't complaining. My heart really wasn't in it though, every journey felt like work which was something it had never done before. I had tried not to build my hopes up about the Bishop's job, but I had. In my head I was working in the little office behind the blue door and eating my lunch in the arty café cross the street.

If my customers noticed that I wasn't my usual enthusiastic self, they didn't say. They probably thought it was because I had a new baby living with me and I was having disturbed sleeps. They were right, my sleeps were disturbed, but not because of Teddy, more like because I had to get up early to take customers to the airport. It seemed that every flight out of Newcastle to Spain was leaving before 8 in the morning.

Teddy was doing great. Every day she grew a little more and became more alert. Hayley was managing just fine and although Rocco was still around all of the time, he didn't stay every night because of his work commitments. Every few nights, Hayley and Teddy would go and stay with Brian. It wasn't always convenient for Brian to come over, so Hayley had got in the habit of staying at least one night a week with him and Laura, that way all that side of the family could see Teddy without intruding on me. At first I hated the nights when they weren't there, but like everything else, I got used to it and would do a huge tidy up, catch up on the endless piles of washing and end up with a stint of therapeutic ironing.

I liked them being there. It was hard work with the taxi but we were coping. Hayley had set her heart on returning to University at the end of September. She had already been in and had a meeting with her tutors and had a look around the crèche. Happy that Teddy would be well cared for while she attended lessons, she had committed herself to some coursework which would keep her on track for her return into the second year.

'Us sisters' had a meal at Julie's new house together. It was the first time we had all sat around the table together in a very long time. Bless her, Julie had even arranged to do it on a Tuesday night, normally my quietest night of the week and one where me and the Va Va Vroom wouldn't be missed.

It was a lovely night. For once I wasn't driving; I had taken the 7 minute walk there and I just had to drop Rocco a text and he would come and collect me. With no early morning jobs, I enjoyed a couple of glasses of wine in good company. We laughed a lot. Julie had made some beautiful dishes; the names of which I had no idea, but they were spicy and each one of them had a tale behind it. It was good to have her so near to us all again.

The next big thing we were all doing together was Samantha's hen party in Blackpool, which by the end of the night I was really looking forward to. Rocco arrived to pick me up, us all up. Before we left he took a photo of us all on my mobile. It wasn't until I had a look at it the next day did I realise that me Julie and Janet looked like triplets again. All three of us wearing black tops and had similar hair colours and styles. Over the past couple of months, living back in a less sunny climate Julie's leather look skin had started to fade and you had to look quite closely at the photograph to make out which one of us was who.

The rest of the month was made up mainly of work. With still no news about a job, I tried to settle into the taxi the best I could. I tried to console myself with no news was good news, but hope was fading and I tried not to think that this was as good as it was going to get for me.

I was lucky, I had nice customers who cared for me. They were so grateful that I was there for them. But I was weary and just a little bit jaded. I needed time off in the coming months and I always felt like I was letting my customers down by not being there for them when they needed me. I tried to change my philosophy about the taxi, would I be able to spend as much time with Teddy if I had a normal job? Probably not. So I smiled, put my head down and my backside up and just got on with it. Yes I was lucky. There were worse jobs I could be doing!!!

June

June was a party month. At the beginning Luke took Brian and Rocco along with various other members of his family and friends off to Benidorm for the weekend. The thought of Brian in Benidorm still made me smirk; I hoped he was going to be ok.

I was busy with work and in between I either looked after Teddy or pottered around in the garden. I was alright; I might have been unemployable but it wasn't as if I was living on the breadline like last time. More shocking was that Julie had got herself a part time job. I didn't even know she was looking, but she had started going into the new café that had opened in the High Street and when they said they were looking for someone to operate the barista; she applied and got it. Seems she really was a jack of all trades. And it was somewhere else for me to pop!!

When I answered my mobile to a Mrs Winn I was flummoxed. Thinking that it was someone wanting to book a taxi, it took a while for me to digest what she was actually saying. Mrs Winn was from the Bishops office. She was apologising for the delay in getting back to me, but there had been some people off with a sickness bug and the appointment selection had had to be put back until they were fully staffed. Anyway the long and the short of it was that I had been shortlisted and therefore invited to an informal interview with Bishop Jack. I was flabbergasted. After all of these weeks, the only thing I had been expecting was a rejection letter. My hands shook as I wrote my interview date and time down. Again apologising for the short notice; my interview was two days away; Mrs Winn rang off saying she was looking forward to seeing me on Thursday.

I wanted to cry. I had no idea how many other candidates were meeting The Bishop, but I didn't care. I had been shortlisted and that was my chance to show the Bishop that I was the woman for him.

Two days later sitting in the little café over the road from the office; I wasn't so confident. Even though it was June I had had to wear tights and boots with my suit; my feet were up like puddings; just like they always did when I stressed. I tried to keep in my mind-set that it was just an interview and if I was meant to get the job then I would; but I was in knots.

But it wasn't so bad. It was more of a chat really. Bishop Jack wasn't as old as I had thought he was, maybe 60. He himself had a new granddaughter so we were on common ground straightaway. He asked me about the taxi, which I could obviously chat for hours about but I was wary of trying not to blow my own trumpet and then he asked me about my office experience. It all seemed to go well. His last question was more general about my Vicar, it was obvious that a word had been put in his ear about me and as I left the office I felt a spark of hope. Maybe I might just have done enough.

It would be a waiting game again though. They would be in touch as soon as a decision had been made. But they didn't say how. Letter? Email? Phone call? Why hadn't I just asked? Back in the café over the road, I sipped on a hot chocolate and once again analysed the interview. If it was on personality then I think me and Bishop Jack had got on quite well. If it was about administration experience, then maybe I had been out of the job market just a little bit too long.

I felt calmer now. There was nothing I could do. It was in the lap of the God's; literally. I would make a concerted effort not to look for signs, I wanted the disappointment to come from the Bishop himself, not the birds in the garden or a Ford Focus and an Audi A4 in the wrong colour.

The café once again was lovely. It would be a shame if I didn't get to come in for my lunch regularly, I doubted that I would be in the city much in the future otherwise. The paintings were still on the walls. Some had been here the last time I had been in for my first interview, others were new. The originals must have either been sold or returned to their owners to be taken elsewhere to be sold.

A picture in the corner caught my eye. Getting out of my seat I went to have a closer look. It was a woodland glade in winter, snow was on the ground and the trees were all bare. Standing in the middle of the glade were two deer standing next to each other. Both had their heads turned looking straight towards me. I knew them. They were doe deer. The artist had captured them completely. They were my deer. It was Thora and Ada; Theadora. The tears were rolling down my face, I didn't care if people saw. The artist had seen them too. There was no doubt in my mind that these were the deer I had seen on the morning that Teddy had been born. I couldn't take my eyes off the picture. I turned over the tag so I could see how much the picture cost. £249. I was gutted. There was no way I could justify spending that amount of money on a picture; I hadn't spent that much on my wedding outfit as Mother of the Bride.

In the days that followed I thought about the picture a lot. Every time I thought about the job, the picture would pop back into my head. But I couldn't justify buying myself such an extravagance, the taxi was busy but it wasn't always like that and I had to bank the good weeks to cover the bad.

When Mrs Winn rang again my brain found it difficult to digest what she was saying when she wasn't wanting to book a taxi. When I did hear what she was saying I didn't take it in. She must have thought I was an idiot. She was offering me the job. I had got the job. I couldn't speak, I was mumbling but I must have said something coherent because she said that she was delighted I had accepted and would forward all the information I needed to me by email. I had the job.

I rang everyone. Friends, family, exes!!! This was it, I was changing my life. As bad as I felt about leaving my customers; this was the right thing to do. I was going to get the regular hours and the regular income. I was going to get my life back. I didn't have a start date, but surely I only had a matter of weeks left on taxi; I could do weeks, it was the thought of years that I couldn't do.

I was just so excited. And proud of myself; I had managed to pull it out of the bag, when really I shouldn't have had a chance. When the email arrived the next day, I scoured it for the start date; Monday 1st July 2013. It was just over two weeks away. I had it in black and white. I was going to be PA to the Bishop from 1st July. There was so much to do. The taxi to wind down, new clothes to be bought and a hen party in Blackpool to attend.

But I did it. I didn't think that giving up the taxi would be as emotional as it was. I cried with customers, I cried when I was on my own and when I had the signage removed I cried some more. I sold the mobile number and the goodwill to the local firm who helped me out when I had too many jobs or I needed to take some time off. I didn't get a fortune, there was no guarantee that my customers would move over to them, but there was enough to pay the bills until I had my first salary at the end of July, to pay for my weekend in Blackpool and to add some new pieces to my work wear wardrobe from five years previously.

And in Blackpool we had a ball. As well as my sisters and Adele, Lynne and Jayne came. I didn't see as much of Jayne as I used to, mainly because of the lack of time I had with running the taxi, but we text and would have long chats on the phone every now and then. She still worked for the solicitors, was still single and very happy with her life. She never seemed to age, standing chatting with Samantha and her friends, she could have been the same age. A regular in the pubs of Newcastle she knew some of Samantha's friends and was as happy in their company as she was with us. So it was a right mixed bag that took to the pubs of Blackpool, very much like we had done ten years earlier when we had gone for my 40th.

Blackpool held no ghosts for me. It was where me and Phil had met, but I couldn't even be sure if I knew where the nightclub was! And to be honest, I had no regrets about my ill-fated third marriage. We hadn't really known each other before we moved in together, the age gap that didn't seem to matter did matter, it mattered a lot and instead of gaining a husband I had gained a spoilt child. But we had remained friends; Phil was always one of the first people I gave news to; he was living with someone now, from what I could make out she was older than him. I suppose she would have to be, his mam had done a real job on him and he would need someone who would be able to step into her shoes and look after him in the way he was accustomed to. No regrets though.

Brian turned out to be a better friend than husband. I knew he would be there for me if I needed him, not just for money but for emotional support too. He would be there for the girls if God forbid I couldn't be, all his girls. He was a great dad to Samantha as well as Hayley and he was now a doting granddad. He was a good man. Even Rocco had come back from Benidorm with stories of Brian and his generosity; he seemed to have let his hair down and enjoyed himself. So all in all I had no regrets about marrying Brian either. David was a subject I didn't think about too much, he didn't deserve my time.

Poor Samantha, her job really did come back to haunt her! Instead of wearing the customary white veil and L plates, was dressed as a corpse bride. She looked amazing, her friends had done a grand job on her and when fellow revellers asked why she was dressed so, her friends were quick to tell them that the tall beautiful girl was actually an undertaker by trade.

We had a ball. If Hayley was nervous that Laura was looking after Teddy for the weekend, she didn't show it. She had her first proper night out since she had got pregnant, but still managed to party until 6 in the morning. Me, my sisters and friends all called it a night at about 1am. Instead of heading back to the bed and breakfast we found our way into a little café and drank coffee, ate bacon sandwiches and chatted. It was a nice ending to a lovely weekend. By the time we staggered back towards our beds, the sun was starting to rise, it was 4am and whereas I had seen sunrises often, the rest didn't so much. We sat on the wall outside the bed and breakfast and watched the beginning of what was to be a beautiful sunny June day. In my mind there was only one person who could have painted such a stunning morning….

July

The first day of July was the first day of the rest of my life. Of course I was far too early, I think I must have been born early. So I parked up and made my way around to the office with the blue door hoping that I wouldn't be the first one to arrive. My stomach was in knots, I was so nervous, but I knew of old that in no time I would feel like I had worked there all of my life. It was just a first day thing. Luckily Mrs Winn was already there and working away on her PC when I arrived. She seemed genuinely delighted to see me and wasted no time in getting into the office procedures and the duties expected of me.

Mrs Winn's job was a little vague to me, she seemed to be the Bishop's private secretary, whereas I was his PA. My desk was opposite hers and for the first few weeks my work was fed from her. It was okay, surprisingly the office was really busy. The Bishop would come in from time to time, he seemed to do a lot of his work from his private residence and would come into the office laden with Dictaphone tapes for me to transcribe. There was a lot more variety to the job than I had envisaged and the four days I was in post would fly by.

With the luxury of having three days off every week I had an abundance of energy, I would plough through the piles of correspondence on my desk and then help Mrs Winn with anything she needed doing. Mrs Winn or Rosie as she insisted I called her had been given the mammoth task of archiving Church information. Churches were being sold off all of the time, but the paperwork relating to the Church had to be kept for all eternity; one of our jobs was to register all the information; reference and then seal it away. It was sad, each Church had so much history, but a part of the job I loved. Each Church told a story. The Diocese was huge and whereas one Church might be rural and its congregation was mainly made up of farmers, another would be city centre based and have a completely different congregation.

I loved the history of them all and treat each Church that would be sealed up in a box and placed in a dusty vault with respect. I catalogued as much information as I could, scanned documents and wrote narratives about the Church just in case one day someone came along and wanted to know something about it.

I liked working with Rosie. Firstly thinking she was a bit strict and a bit old fashioned, I had been wrong. She was just dedicated to the job she had done for the past 20 years. She told me stories of the previous Bishop's and she told me how, like me she found the decline of the Church's population a tragedy. Living a five minute walk away, she didn't drive; she was a widow and her children had long flown the nest. Her job was her life. So even after just a couple of weeks we had grown close. She liked to hear all about my family; especially little Teddy. She had grandchildren of her own but they were in Canada and she didn't see them very often, thoughts of my taxi customers went through my head. But Rosie had a sister close by and a lovely sister-in-law by all accounts and she also had a huge network of friends. Having lost her husband five years earlier to cancer, she was happy in her widowhood and had no intention of meeting anyone else. She insisted she was a bit long in the tooth, but she was a fine looking woman and when I told her that 62 was the new 42, she just laughed.

So by the end of July I was in a good place. I really did enjoy my job, had made a new friend in Rosie and couldn't really say that I missed the taxi at all. It was funny, whereas I would travel around town in the taxi all and sundry would wave, now that it was stripped down, no one recognised me; I would lift my hand to wave to someone only for them to stare at me as if they had never seen me before in their lives. In the car I was invisible.

My first wages were paid into my account on the last working day of the month. It was strange having a salary again. I was paying emergency tax until all the information from the taxi was sorted, but it was still more than I had hoped.

Leaving work on the Thursday afternoon I made my way over to the little café across the street. I hadn't been in since I started work, the previous thoughts I had had of having leisurely lunches hadn't happened. If I wasn't having a sandwich at my desk, I was running to Boots or Mothercare to pick something up for Hayley. So this was the first chance I had really had to go in and have a coffee. That wasn't my real mission though. When I got the job I had made a promise to myself that when I got paid I would have one big extravagance; I would buy the painting. If it was still there on payday then it was meant for me; in my head I thought that the artist had painted it especially for me, they had to have done. Why else would it be hanging in a café across the road from where I had got myself a new job, a job that was also preordained by some force bigger than me? I had sent off hundreds of applications, but there had only been one that had asked me to go for an interview. Rosie said that she knew from my CV that I would get the job, even before she had even met me. She said there had been lots to choose from, but mine somehow stood out. Meant to be!

So even though I had taken a chance by not coming to buy the picture earlier; I had the strangest feeling that it would be there waiting for me. And it was. The hairs went up on the back of my neck when I saw it and the tears pricked at my eyes. My deer of hope! Delighted to have sold the picture and no doubt clapping her hands because she had made herself a bit of commission, she wrapped the picture up in bubble wrap while I drank a complimentary cup of coffee. All the while she chatted about the artist, a local man, he specialised in woodlands and she said his work was very popular. She said his name was James Bradley! The flush started in my feet and roared up to my face. It was all the proof I needed that this was really meant to be. My grandmothers; Ada James and Thora Bradley......

250

August

The picture took pride of place in my living room, nobody understood why I had bought it and Hayley thought that it looked out of place against all the other quite modern prints and photographs I had on my wall. But I loved it. Brian was the only one who saw what I saw in it and was even more amazed when I told him who the artist was. I didn't even bother trying to tell my tale to everyone else; they all thought I was quirky enough.

August was all about the wedding. Samantha was like a bear with a sore head, she would wind herself up into such a state about place settings and wedding favours that she would actually be sick. I helped as much as I could, but she was on a mission, every suggestion I came up with was wrong, so in the end, I just did as I was told and kept my mouth shut.

The night before the wedding Samantha came home to stay for the first time in a long time. It was a proper girly night. Me; Samantha; Hayley and Teddy. Now that there was nothing Samantha could do even if something did go wrong, she was more herself and more relaxed.

We all bathed Teddy together; she had her first tooth and smiled continuously so she could show it off. Unluckily for Laura, she had spotted it first and in the old tradition that the person who finds a baby's first ever tooth has to buy a present, there was now a lovely new baby walker in the nursery ready for Teddy when she was ready for it.

After we all cooed and nursed and the girls tucked Teddy up in bed, I made some supper, opened a bottle of white wine and set the dining room table for the three of us. It was a nice night. As always happened when something major was going to happen I someone's life; we chatted and reminisced. Holidays, Phil, Samantha and her job, Hayley and

Teddy. Though tempted as we were to open a second bottle of white; at ten o'clock we called it a night and made off to our beds, well me and Samantha were sharing, but an early night was at least being attempted seeing as Lynne was coming at 7am to do our hairs. Thinking I would never sleep; I was flat out as soon as my head hit the pillow and so was Samantha.

With a chaotic morning behind us, I sat at the front of of the Church with my mam and dad nursing Teddy. I didn't feel nervous, I hadn't had time, by the time Lynne had hurriedly left to get herself ready, one of Samantha's friends had turned up to do our make-up and so it went on. It wasn't until Brian arrived did I get a chance to have five minutes to myself while I pulled on my dress and put on my hat. I was pleased with the look, I had been right to take Adele with me, the dress was classy and elegant in a very fashionable pale green; without it being mummsy. The addition of almost perfecting matching hat and shoes finished it off to a T. The approving wolf whistle off Brian as I walked down the stairs was all the praise I needed; ex-husband or not, he was still a bloke. And of course I repaid the compliment, he looked very dapper in his morning suit, he always wore a suit so well.

Now as I sat at the front of the Church, I took the opportunity to take in the congregation. The whole family were there; I loved it when we all got dressed up and today everyone seemed to have gone the extra mile; there were hats everywhere. Adele looked stunning in her fuchsia pink two piece suit, on her head she had on the biggest fascinator I had ever seen, poor Peter kept getting jabbed with the feather as her head went backwards and forwards talking to various family members. Avril came bounding down to the front and taking a restless Teddy off me, took her seat in the pew behind.

Luke looked terrified. There was no chance of Samantha not turning up, but unlike his bride to be, he wasn't used to being in the limelight and I could see he was chewing away on his bottom lip.

The organ fired up and we all stood and turned to watch Samantha and Brian make their entrance. And there they were; my beautiful girls. Samantha first holding on to her step-father's arm; she was stunning and as I watched her slowly make her way down the aisle, the tears started. And then there was Hayley; one of the three bridesmaids, it was hard to believe that she had only had a baby six months earlier. Her dress was figure hugging and she wore it beautifully. I was so lucky.

The service went by in a bit of a blur. My eyes were constantly welling up with tears, it was just so lovely to watch the two childhood sweethearts commit to each other for the rest of their lives. I didn't feel cynical about them; every newly-wed thinks that theirs will be the marriage that withstands the test of time, I just thought that somehow they had it.

The vows were made, hymns were sung and before I knew it I was holding on to Luke's dad's arm and walking up the aisle behind the bride and groom, bridesmaids and ushers. I beamed at everyone, those I knew and those I didn't. I was just so proud.

I spotted Samantha's half-brothers first, they were sat with their girlfriends or wives at the back of the Church. I had seen Sandra and Tony nearer the front of the Church; Sandra was another with a huge floppy hat on so I couldn't miss her. But I didn't notice the tall middle aged man with Simon and Toby until I was almost level with him. David. Samantha's dad was in the Church. I hadn't seen him on the guest list and I frantically wracked my brain to the place settings I had poured hours over with Samantha; he wasn't on that, I would have remembered. My face burned, I don't think my feet had had chance to take in that he was actually there or they would have been causing a rumpus too. I resisted the temptation to stop and stare at him and continued to put one foot in front of the other and make it out of the Church.

It was a flurry of confetti and endless photographs outside the Church. The weather had been kind and the sun was shining brightly, no one was in a hurry to go anywhere and I huddled in the bosom of my family and friends; safe that if it actually had been David, he wouldn't sought me out with so many of my sisters there.

But the crowd started to make their way to the reception and as we filed out of the Churchyard towards the waiting cars, Samantha shouted me over to where the photographer was snapping away taking less formal photographs. I hadn't had chance to say congratulations, so with Teddy in my arms I went over and gave her a huge hug. 'My dad is here!' She said blushing. 'It's okay Sam, I spotted him in Church, don't worry about it, it's your day!' And then there he was standing in front of me. I was speechless. I didn't know what to say and I don't think he did either. When the photographer rounded the three of us up for an impromptu snap, Hayley quickly took Teddy out of my arms and me Samantha, David and Luke, smiled into the camera.

He hadn't said a word to me. He kissed Samantha on the cheek and whispered something into her ear, made his way out of the Churchyard and was gone. He wouldn't be coming to the wedding breakfast, but he had come to watch his only daughter get married, even if it was her stepdad that walked her down the aisle. For the first time in almost 30 years; I had a flicker of respect for David Craig.

And the rest of the day was wonderful. The food, the speeches, the company. Everything was perfect. I tried to put thoughts of David to the back of my mind, but people had seen him and continually asked me how I felt. Even Brian; he said that Samantha had asked if it would be ok if David came to the Church, he didn't mind on the condition that she didn't tell me. I should have been annoyed with them for not saying anything, but they were right; I wouldn't have been able to fit into my stilettos I would have been so wound up with nerves. It was all right, I forgave them.

A few drinks in the afternoon and by the time dancing started at the evening reception I was one of the first up on the dance floor. It was so good the whole family being together and of course it was an added bonus that me and the new mother in-law had been friends for a long time, it made it all feel extra special.

It was while I was sitting with Adele, that a man talking to Peter caught my eye. I hadn't seen him before and was obviously part of Peter's circle of friends and had come along for the evening reception. He was about my age, maybe a bit older, dark and from what I could make out under the disco lights, was built like a rugby player. I didn't get chance to ask Adele about him, a tipsy Brian came over and grabbed me and Adele and before I knew what was happening the three of us were in the middle of the dance floor doing our own middle aged version of the Macarena.

Half a dozen dances later, when the slow numbers came on, I made my way back over to where my mam and dad were sitting. I was impressed, it was almost midnight and my mam and dad were still going strong, but the night was coming to an end and I could tell that they were itching to get home and have themselves a nice cup of tea. So collecting their assortment of coats and bags; I walked with Julie to the hotel foyer and helped them into a waiting taxi, promising to have a walk around and see them the following day. It was while I was returning back into the function room, that I came face to face with Mr Rugby Player.

On his way out as I went back in; our eyes locked. Less eyes across a crowded room and more in a doorway, the effect was just the same. For that instant I was lost. The almost long forgotten somersaults were back in my stomach and the flush that earlier in the day had escaped my feet and went straight to my face, was back where it belonged starting at the bottom and making its way up.

But we were both in the memento of walking and for either of us to stop would cause a commotion in the doorway; Julie was hot on my heels and I could feel her hand in the small of my back propelling me forward and in an instance, we were passed each other and he was gone. The slow records had come to an end, everyone was starting to get ready to go home and I was so swept up in thank you's and good byes; I didn't have chance to look for Mr Rugby player again.

As me, Hayley and Rocco made our way home in the taxi I thought about the man. I had never seen him before, probably wouldn't again, but he had made an impact. He was the first man who had caught my attention in a very long time. No doubt there would be a Mrs Rugby player somewhere in the background, maybe she had even been there tonight, that was my luck all over. So for the second time that day I pushed a man who had shook my world for a few minutes to the back of my mind. It was funny, seeing David at the Church earlier in the day seemed like a lifetime ago as I made my way home. An earthquake at the time, but the aftershocks weren't that bad. He was Samantha's dad and that's all he was. And that was the end of that.

September

It was nice to have a little bit normality in my life. After the wedding Samantha and Luke had jetted off to Lanzarote for a fortnight and Hayley spent the time preparing to go back to university. It was a quiet time, the nights were starting to eek in as autumn approached and I spent the evenings after work tidying up the garden and generally enjoying some me time. The previous months had been so chaotic what with the new job, hen party and then the wedding; it was lovely just to do nothing.

I had settled into work really well, September was the last month of my probationary period and I was hoping that Rosie would be happy enough with me and my work to make my contract permanent at the end of the month. I had grown to love the job; surprisingly there was a lot of hustle and bustle. The Bishop was always going up and down to London for services and meetings; the poor man spent more times on trains than he did sitting in his office. His job was so much more intense than going around in his robes carrying his crook. He was forever in meetings, with his own priests, other Bishops or with local councils wrangling over red tape. But he always remained cheerful, he was very much a man who's glass was half full and the more I got to know him the more I admired him.

I managed to have a couple of weekends away with Julie too. It was funny to think that even though she had been to every corner of the world, she didn't really know anywhere on her own doorstep. When she asked if I would like to have a couple of nights away in Edinburgh with her and a fortnight later in York; I had no hesitation. We were the only two single sisters so it made sense that she asked me before the others, but it was an open invitation and after the two of us had had such a lovely time in Edinburgh, the other three managed to make time to come to York with us for the second weekend.

It was nice getting to know Julie, she had had such a colourful life. She thought the same about me. I suppose three ex-husbands does constitute colourful by anyone's standards! But Julie had lived in some of the most beautiful places in the world. She still had friends everywhere and it appeared that she hadn't always been living in these places by herself. Nicola and Julie had parted ways not long after they had left England. By then Julie had met her 'investment banker' who had so wisely told her what to do with her money when it became clear that she wouldn't be going home and working for a British pension anytime in the near future.

He had been an American, bored with his lifestyle he had taken to the open road just like Julie had. He had been 20 years older than her, but she said he had been her soul mate. Because he had upped and abandoned his family back in the State; she didn't think we would approve of him, so had kept him very much in the background when she made her weekly calls home. They had been together roaming the world for 15 years and stayed together in Italy for a further 4 years where she had nursed him when he had been diagnosed with cancer which ultimately taken him from her after almost 20 years together. How hadn't I known this? My sister had had a long term partner for longer than I had any one of my husbands and yet there had been no talk of him.

All she could say as it was one of those things; he had been older and married and the secret became so embedded that there was no opportunity to bring him out into the open with her family. I asked if Janet and Graham had met them when they came out to see her and got married, but no; he had taken himself away for the time they were there. No one had known. Poor Julie; he had been her soul mate and we didn't know. She had photographs she said, she would show me the next time I went around and she promised that one by one she would tel everyone. It was too late to meet him now, but I was pleased that she hadn't been alone, pleased that she had known what it was like to be loved. Clifford. Clifford Fitzwilliam. I wish I had known him.

By the end of September the long nights of daylight were really shortening, but the garden was ready for the winter. I certainly wouldn't miss the taxi in the winter, in fact I didn't miss the taxi at all. It had been such a big part of my life that I thought when I dragged myself out of bed for work at 6.30am; I would miss the chance just to potter in a morning like I used to if I didn't have any jobs. But I didn't. I could get a lie in on Friday's, Saturday's and Sunday's if I wanted, so the early start to get into the city was no hardship.

And my feet were in tip top condition. The girls had bought me a foot spa for my birthday and a couple of times a week I would sit with my feet soaking in it and Teddy bouncing on my knee. So with the onset of winter, there was no sign of the usual red blotches that indicated that my chilblains were back and I vowed to keep them that way. For the first time in their fifty years, my feet weren't my Achilles' heel.

October

The month started off really well. The weather still hadn't turned and it was good news all around at work. In my probationary meeting with Rosie she didn't just offer me a permanent contract, but full time hours and a pay review after a further 6 months. I was over the moon and Rosie and Bishop Jack seemed to be delighted with me too. My life was so much easier to manage with a regular salary and set working hours. I was happy enough to work the extra day, it even had the added bonus of further 5 days annual leave.

Hayley started back at University. It was hard work for her. The course only equated to 4 full days, but she had to be up early to get Teddy ready for crèche and she would go to bed late, preferring to do her course work when Teddy was tucked up in bed. I helped as much as I could. Teddy was sleeping through the night and Rocco would come and spend a couple of nights a week with us so he could bath her and take some of the pressure off Hayley. I did more of the practical stuff; washing, ironing, packing Teddy's bag for the following day.

Teddy had settled into the University crèche well, she would come home, have her tea, bath, supper and then bed. She was a happy baby and the transition for her and Hayley into University life didn't seem to be having any adverse effect on them, if anything interacting with her children was bringing Teddy on leaps and bounds.

Samantha and Luke were settling into married life. They both worked so hard and Samantha was often on call, but she loved her job and by all accounts was excelling at it. Brian called often to see Hayley and Teddy, the younger girl certainly had her granddad wrapped around her little finger and he rarely turned up without a little something for his granddaughter.

When Lynne rang one night and asked if I fancied a drink around at her house, I wasn't fazed. Now that I didn't pop in and out, I often had the girls over or went to one of their houses, usually for supper and a bottle of wine. I should have been fazed, she usually said ring Adele and Jayne and the sisters. But she had specifically asked me!

Arriving at her house, I was shocked how tired she looked. All her kids had gone now, there was just her and John, but she looked like she hadn't slept for a week and all at once the alarm bells were ringing. Surely things hadn't gone wrong with her and John, they had been together forever and they had seemed as together as always at the wedding. And it wasn't one of the kids; she would have told me if anything was wrong with one of them over the phone; just like she always had.

So when she had opened the wine and poured us a glass each, I didn't have a clue what she was going to say. But I wasn't prepared for what she did say. She had breast cancer. I sat on her settee with my mouth open, no! She looked tired but not ill, surely it couldn't be right, and if she had cancer she would look really ill. But she did, she had had the diagnosis a week earlier. She was going into hospital two days later to have both her breasts removed. I cried, I couldn't help it, I didn't want to, I wanted to be strong for her, but I couldn't. She was my oldest friend and I didn't even know she had found a lump.

She hadn't. She had found lots of lumps. At first she had thought they were nothing, just part of going through the menopause, she said after all her boobs had had some hammer, she had breastfed all of her children. But a mammogram had clarified that there was indeed something there and a biopsy had confirmed that they were cancerous. Both breasts had to go, then chemo and more than likely radiotherapy. The prognosis was good she said, women survived breast cancer every day and if all went well then she could have some reconstruction work done.

She was just so brave. I wasn't sure I would be a chipper, but she said that the family were being amazing and John although scared witless was taking a long break from work to look after her. I didn't know what to say, I was so devastated and scared. I wanted to help, but didn't know what to do. She assured me just being there with her now was all I needed to do. Just be there when she needed me. She jokingly said I was going to have to find myself another hairdresser for the time being, a small price to pay under the circumstances, but this brought on more crying; off me of course.

Lynne was talking wigs, but I couldn't hear her. I just wanted to wrap her up in cotton wool and keep her safe. I couldn't even think about how she was feeling and what she was about to go through. I didn't want to go home, I just wanted to stay with her, and I wanted to make it go away. Why Lynne?? She had never smoked, she didn't even drink very much. She had always been there for me and I was going to be there for her too. I clung on to her so hard as I was leaving she said I was hurting her, but I didn't know what to say, there was nothing I could say. 'Keep in touch. Take care.' There were no adequate words. 'I love you!' I sobbed as I walked out of the door and into a waiting, shocked Rocco's car.

November

Seven weeks after Lynne had her operation, she passed away peacefully at home. We had been friends for almost 50 years. It had all happened so fast, her breasts had been removed but the cancer had spread quickly and it was in her lymph nodes, liver and kidneys. The chemo did little to help and it was Lynne's decision to stop the treatment and die with dignity.

She said she was putting her house in order, brave and stupid in equal measures, she made sure that she spent time with everyone who was important to her before it became too difficult for her to do. They could control the pain, but not the cancer and with ceasefire in the battle; the cancer advanced at a rapid rate.

My faith was shaken. Why would God do this to Lynne? She was one of the good ones? She had never hurt anyone, she had been a good wife and mother, and it made no sense to me. I was angry. And I felt helpless.

I would go around and see her after work, usually I would just stay for half an hour, there were other people she needed to spend time with and I didn't want to out stay my welcome. Then I would go home and make corned beef pies and stews for me to take with me the following night so at least I knew John and the boys had something to eat.

When one night I went and she was in bed, I knew she wouldn't come out of her bed again. At first she was quite chipper, she was well rested and full of chat, but within days her medication was having to be upped and she spent longer and longer periods sleeping. She was fading away before our very eyes.

And then one day I got a call off John; she had gone early that morning. She was 51 years old. Rosie told me to go home, I was no use to her. But I didn't go home, I went to the Cathedral. I sat and sat, I didn't find any comfort. The only thing that happened was my hands, feet and nose grew cold.

I still didn't go home. Another detour. This time it was Mills and Boone Funeral Directors; I needed to see Samantha or Brian. But I found Laura. She already knew about Lynne, of course she would, they were always going to be Lynne's choice of undertakers, they even had her funeral wishes already logged and ready to use; all Lynne's choice of course. As delicately as she could Laura told me that Samantha and Brian were at Lynne's now meeting John and bringing Lynne back with them.

She took me into the main house, into the kitchen and made me a strong cup of coffee. And we talked. Of all the people in the world I could talk to, it was my ex-sister-in-law. I had never really spoke to her that much when I was married to Brian, I had always found her aloof and a little bit stuck up. But sitting at her kitchen table, she really came into her own.

Of course, death was something she dealt with every day. Bereavement was their business and they did it well. But she talked sense. She told me how she had struggled when she had first started in the family business, especially if the deceased were young; babies, children. She said she found it hard to know what to say to the bereaved families, but she had learned. Death was as much a part of life as birth was; if we were lucky we would make it into our dotage, but often life wasn't that kind and dealing with a young couple whose child had died in its cot, or a toddler who had had leukaemia or a teenager killed in a car crash when he wasn't even the one driving.

Laura had seen it all. As much as it hurt, it was the circle of life and it would come to us all. She said we had to make the best of each day; live it as if it was our last. Be kinder to the people we loved and even people we didn't. We never got over loosing people; but it got easier. Time was a healer; a clique yes, but true. We had to believe that one day we would see those we had lost, but in the meantime we had to take comfort in the things around us that reminded us of them. A song on the radio, a smell, something someone says that your loved one used to. And if you had faith then you kept Praying for them. Just because you couldn't physically see them, it didn't mean that they weren't around us.

She was amazing. Laura Mills was a dark horse. I had always thought her cold, but I had misjudged her; she was a salve on my open wounds. She excused herself when her mobile rang and walked into the other room. Returning she said it had been Samantha; they were on her way back. I didn't want to be there when they brought Lynne in. So I did something I hadn't done often. I cuddled Laura; thanking her for helping me make a little bit sense of it all.

Later, in my living room I looked at my picture. Laura was right. Ada and Thora had passed years ago, but somehow from beyond the grave they had got a message to me. They had given me hope. I liked to think that wherever it was that Lynne was, she was at peace; that her pain was gone and that one day she would get a sign to me to let me know that all was well with her. I was going to miss her so much.

Samantha once again conducted a funeral of someone she loved. Always having known her as Auntie Lynne, it was Samantha that had gone and sat on Lynne's bed and noted down her requirements for her funeral. The first was that there was to be no flowers; Lynne said it was a waste of good money and the money we would spend on flowers should go to a good cause of our own choice; whether it be a cancer charity, the RSPCA or the Monster Raving Loony Party; but there was definitely not to be any flowers. So following the hearse in our cars; the coffin was bare of flowers and Lynne's wish number one was ticked off the list.

The second was that there was to be no Church. Never one to have attended Church in the first place she didn't want to be seen as a hypocrite, so here we all were on our way into the Crem. Samantha walked in front of the hearse the whole way; just as she had done for her great-granny years earlier. This time she was wearing a beautiful amethyst suit with a top hat and veil. Another of Lynne's request; no black attire.

Eva Cassidy's Over the Rainbow played as Lynne made her final journey into the Crem's small chapel. There was standing room only as many of her family, friends and customers came to pay their respects. John was to do a reading; Lynne had been schooling him in it for weeks, but doing it in the comfort of your own home is completely different to do it in front of a chapel full of people with your deceased wife's coffin lying next to you.

But he did it. He did it beautifully; though his voice caught a couple of times, he made it to the end. As he read; the curtain drew around the coffin and Lynne was gone. It was all that simple. As we filed out of the Chapel 'I Had the time of My Life' from Dirty Dancing played out. I broke down completely. I couldn't remember the amount of times me and Lynne had held hands and danced to it. Another tick on Lynne's list. To make Val lose it altogether!

I was just so sad. The wake had been a lively affair, another of Lynne's requests, I stayed a couple of hours and then made my excuses and left promising John I would keep in touch. I would, but it would probably be by text. Social etiquette didn't particularly allow single women to be friends with newly widowed men. John was old fashioned and I knew without a doubt that he would be embarrassed if I turned up at the house. But a text every now and then wouldn't hurt; just to see if he was ok, it was the very least I could do for Lynne.

So I threw myself into work, grateful that Rosie piled more and more work on me. At night I would lie in my bed and read through my texts off Lynne; I couldn't bear to delete them off the phone. One day they would disappear as new texts pushed them further and further down the list, but for the minute they were there and I made the most of them.

Winter had arrived with vengeance and the wind and rain suited my mood. It was dark in a morning and dark by the time I left work. I tried to stay bright for Teddy; she was a joy to be around and we had developed a lovely relationship, we had fun and whereas when the girls were little there was always something that needed to be done; when I was with Teddy it could all wait.

I met up with Laura a few times. She had dropped me a few texts on the run up to Lynne's funeral checking I was okay. After the funeral I had invited her out to lunch as a thank you and somehow after all of the years of knowing each other but not really knowing each other, we had struck up a great friendship.

I found her to be really intelligent, sensitive and loving. She adored the girls and was fond of both Luke and Rocco who she said she always beat on Fifa on her Xbox. Laura had an Xbox?? I really didn't know her at all. She confided in me that she was sad that it looked like she would always be a spinster, outside of men at work she didn't really meet anyone and said that the men she had met over the years had ran a mile when they found out she was an undertaker! But she was happy with her lot and said that her and Brian got along well. It was funny. But we didn't talk much about Brian, he was our common denominator but he was a bit of a no no subject, not that I minded, there were other things to talk about apart from Brian Mills.

270

December

Christmas felt different for me this year. For a start mine hadn't started in September like it used to on the taxi. I didn't have a single thing organised and I still wasn't sure who was going where and who with. The sadness was still hanging on me, I missed Lynne so much. Even though I didn't see her every day, I knew where she was and vice-versa. Now there was just a void where she had been, as selfish as it was, I wished she had stayed around longer.

Work was extra busy. Christmas brought with it a whole array of problems, extra meetings, extra services the Bishop needed to attend. But it was jolly in the office, not garish, there was an air of expectancy as if something special was going to happen. I found it contagious and by the end of the first week in December, I found myself popping out on a lunchtime to do my Christmas shopping.

Because this would be the first Christmas I had totally been off for years, both the girls were having lunch with me on Christmas Day, along with Rocco and Luke. Then Hayley and Rocco were going to Brian's in the afternoon, Samantha and Luke to Adele's and I was going to Avril's, where my mam dad and Julie would all be. It sounded like a perfect day and I shopped until I dropped on the run up.

Obviously I bought too much of everything. Food, drink and instead of the usual rush into the shops for whatever presents I could lay my hands on, this time I had the whole of the city at my disposal, the time to shop and the money to do it. This year I put some thought into my gifts. I bought what people needed and less what they would have wanted.

I wasn't sign watching; I had nothing to watch signs for. I had a job I loved and any thought that I might harbour about meeting Mr Right just didn't seem to be that important any more. If it was meant to be it would happen. In the meantime I was taking Laura's advice on board and living each day as if it was my last. I cherished the time I had with my family and made a concerted effort to spend time with friends. Life was short, too short in some cases. But life was for living and if anyone was going to give me a kick up the backside and tell me that; it was Lynne.

And she did. A week before Christmas I had topped up the water dish for the birds in the garden and put out fat balls and nuts. I was standing drinking coffee and watching out of the kitchen window, waiting for the influx of winter birds to land and devour the tit bits, when I heard a tap tap tapping.

I couldn't see the little bird at first, but the tap tap tapping continued. There was a little robin sitting on the kitchen window sill. The hairs on my neck stood to attention and my feet, snuggly and warm in my slippers, started to burn. The tapping continued and I inched my way over until I could see what it was tapping at. It was tapping at me. I looked at it closely, it looked familiar. How?? It was just a robin. But instead of having one big red mark on its breast; it had two. Two very distinct red breasts, but it was its eyes; they were big and brown. They looked like Lynne's eyes and without realising it the tears were running down my face.

Once again someone from beyond the grave had got through to me.

The heat was burning through my body, the tapping had stopped but the little bird with the two red breasts was staring at me. Confident because there was an inch of glass between us, it continued to stare, safe in the knowledge that I couldn't hurt it from inside the house. I was overwhelmed. I mouthed the words 'I love you!' The bird did a little bob with its head and then took flight. It was her; I knew I wouldn't tell anyone about the robin with the two red breasts, but I knew. And once again I was filled with hope. Hope for what I wasn't sure, but I knew whatever I was going to face in the future, I had the strength to be able to deal with it. There was something out there for us, when we thought that was it and we were dead and buried, there was something else for us. I knew because I had now had it twice, three times if you counted the grannies separately. I was blessed and somehow my wavering faith was restored.

So by the time Christmas morning came, I was in a much better place. Hayley, Teddy and me were up early but we had agreed that we wouldn't start on the piles and piles of presents until Rocco, Samantha and Luke were there. The two of us pottered around the kitchen getting lunch prepared, while Teddy sat in her highchair and chattered away to us in her baby gibber. By 11 everything was prepared and all three of us were in our glad rags and raring to go by the time the rest of them arrived.

Then it was bedlam; there were presents and paper everywhere. Teddy had enough new toys for her to play with something different every day of the year. Everyone was delighted with their gifts off me and as usual I was spoilt rotten with perfume, books and clothes. There was one present left under the tree; I couldn't believe we had missed it. Reaching out for it, it was addressed to me. 'To mam, love Samantha and Luke xx' I was intrigued, they had already bought me so much. But I ripped off the paper and found another gift box, I hoped it wasn't one of those presents that had layer and layer and layers; I needed to go and baste the turkey.

But it wasn't. Opening the lid of the gift box I was confused. There was a pair of little blue booties!!! Surely this must have been Teddy's present, but she had been out of booties for ages now, these were a new-born's size. I looked at Samantha. She was grinning from ear to ear. 'Oh my God – You're pregnant!' I screamed. 'Yes mam, I'm 21 weeks!!!' No!!!! How hadn't I seen it??? I made her stand up and show me her tummy, she was huge! But then there had been so much going on and if I hadn't been looking for it then I wouldn't have seen it. I was crying – again! She said that they had known for about 12 weeks, but with Lynne being poorly they didn't want to say anything. Hayley had known but she had been sworn to secrecy; then they decided that because they had left it so long, they may as well wait until after they had found out what it was and make a Christmas gift of it.

I couldn't stop crying. I was going to have a grandson. I already had a beautiful granddaughter and now I was getting a grandson, it was too much. The tears wouldn't stop and because I was crying, Teddy joined in and we all laughed.

And that was the start of a wonderful Christmas. Lunch was a success and afterwards when we all left for our next destinations, we were brimming with cheer and in my case Pinot Grigio. Samantha's news was met with cheers at Avril's and it was a very merry me that dragged myself into bed in the early hours of Boxing Day morning. Only to have to get back out of bed when the room started spinning to stumble my way into the bathroom where I sat hugging the seat for a very long time.

The rest of Christmas was much more sedate. Julie had invited me for lunch on Boxing Day and the usual 7 minute walk to her house took me more like 15 because I was feeling so fragile. But one Bloody Mary later and I was sipping on a glass of white wine; I was turning into a roaring old sop. There was just the two of us for lunch, my mam and dad had decided they were just going to stay home and put their feet up, but I had a feeling that they wanted to stay in and watch their new Sky package that we had clubbed together to get them for Christmas. I had spoken to them and they were fine and hoped we all had a good time. 'All?' I thought there was just going to be the two of us!

But after a leisurely lunch, Avril and Alan; Janet and Graham; and Carol and Ian arrived. Trivial pursuit in hand the rest of the day was filled with a never ending game of Trivial Pursuit mainly due to the fact that we were playing in pairs and we spent more time bickering about the answers than we did to actually playing it. And of course there was a fair amount of alcohol consumed again.

Another night where it was after midnight before I climbed into my bed, I couldn't remember a time when I had enjoyed Christmas so much. Especially now I wasn't continuously clock watching and having to pop out to do jobs. I was glad I had no plans for the next day; a lie in was on the cards and this time there was no spinning room or toilet I wanted to cuddle; just a long dreamless sleep.

The rest of the Christmas break I didn't do much. I looked after Teddy so Hayley and Rocco could have a rare night out together, I had a meal at Samantha and Luke's and of course I went to see my mam and dad quite a bit. Somehow, Lynne dying had made their mortality all the more important to me. They were both heading towards 80 years old now, and I wanted to spend as much quality time with them as I could. The rest of my spare time was spent reading and taking long baths.

When Adele rang to ask what I was doing on New Year's Eve I really hadn't planned to do anything. She apologised for the short notice; Peter had originally been working, but he had been called in to work Christmas Day and Boxing Day so he was off for the New Year and had decided that they wanted to honour the New Year with a get together for their family and friends. She said it was going to be quite an informal affair, she was asking my sisters, Jayne and of course Samantha and Hayley. Did I actually have a choice? So I agreed and promised I'd be there for 8 on the dot.

In the end it was just me and Julie going. Hayley and Rocco were making the most of me being out of the house and Samantha was on call so didn't want to go and then be a party pooper in case she needed to go. Carol; Ian; Janet; Graham; Avril and Alan had booked a table at an Italians; me and Julie had both been invited but thought it a bit too coupley and declined the offer.

So it was just me and Julie who our designated driver Rocco dropped off at Adele's at 8 o'clock. For it just being an informal affair, there was a lot of people there and I was pleased that I had chosen to put a new little black dress on. The house was tinkling everywhere with fairy lights and there was a delicious smell coming from the kitchen. Adele greeted us like she hadn't seen us for ten years and I could tell straightaway that she was nervous, there were a lot of Peter's friends and colleagues there and many of them were very well to do. But if the decoration of the house was anything to go by, Adele was going to do a grand job.

Jayne followed us in, I hadn't seen her since Lynne's funeral and I hadn't had a chance to tell her the good news about the forthcoming arrival. So drinks in hand, the three of us found some space in the corner and for the next hour had a good old catch up. By the time Adele announced that the food was served; my head was spinning a bit and I knew I had already had a little bit too much to drink!

There were so many people there, no wonder Adele was flapping. But the food was good and everyone seemed to be having a good time. I was so pleased Julie and Jayne were with me. I might be the Bishop's PA, but I would have been out of my league if I had been on my own.

Two hours later, I didn't feel the same. The drink had flowed and whereas before all the guests were a little uptight, now they were animals. The settees had been pushed back and now everyone was dancing on the makeshift dance floor. I laughed; how the mighty had fallen.

Julie and Jayne had gone in search of more food and I was standing at the edge of the room, lost in my own thoughts. It had been a bit of a year. I had said that 2013 was going to be my year and to a certain extent it had been. I was a grandma; I had given up the taxi and had myself a really good job working with some exceptionally nice people. Julie was home; and to be honest I don't know how I had lived all these years without her being just around the corner from me.

But I had lost Lynne. The hole that she left in my life was irreplaceable and I wouldn't even try to fill it, even with my new friendship with Laura; she was making a space for herself in my life. Every day I searched the garden for 'robin two breast' but she hadn't been back, not when I had been looking for her anyway. But she had given me hope and she was right to! Like Laura had told me the day Lynne died, birth and death were the only sure things in life. Teddy was my hope for the future, just as my grandson would when he arrived next year. My girls and my grandchildren.

My New Year resolution was going to be right out of Forrest Gump 'Life is a box of chocolates; you never know what you're going to get!' It worked for him, look what he had achieved. I smiled to myself, maybe it will be easier if I look at the glass as half full.

It was ten to midnight. The posh partygoers were throwing some shapes on the dance floor, or attempting to. I left the room in search of Julie and Jayne, I didn't want to be in a room of strangers when the bells chimed. In the kitchen, they were talking to Peter and some tall man standing with his back towards me. I recognised the other man immediately, even from behind I would know him anywhere. Mr Rugby Player!!

Adele was beside me, a tray of champagne ready to toast in the New Year. Handing the tray to me she asked if I would take it into the living room and she would follow with another tray. I could hardly walk.

Somersaults and dead legs along with the burning body didn't bode well for carrying Adele's best crystal glasses tottering on a tray. But I did as I was told, the music had been turned off and Adele was shouting for everyone to gather in the living room for the countdown.

I had handed the last glass of champagne out just as the countdown began. I scoured the room for Julie and Jayne and could see them in the doorway. Squeezing my way past the guests gathering around the silent television, the countdown was at 3 before I actually got to them. No chance of my number association this year then. Grabbing Julie's hand, I pushed myself in next to her just as the cheering began.

'Happy New Year ……..' Everyone was hugging and kissing. Before I knew what was going on we were all holding hands and singing our very own rendition of Auld Lang Syne. I wanted to cry, just as I always did when the old year went out and the new one came in. The new one that brought us all hope.

2014, what would the year bring. A new baby in the family for sure, but what else? The box of chocolates was back in my head. It would bring whatever it wanted to, it was bigger than I was. I kissed Jayne and Julie again; the music boomed and just as I was about to go and throw some shapes of my own on the dance floor, someone touched my arm. Mr Rugby Player.

He was saying something, but the music was so loud I couldn't make out what he was saying. I shrugged my shoulders and nodded my head out towards the hallway. He smiled before he turned away; this time it was a crowded room, but once again we were standing in a doorway. But the burning was there and the somersaults and as I made to follow him, the dead heavy legs!! He certainly had an effect on me.

Out in the hallway, the music wasn't quite as loud, this time when he spoke I could hear him. 'Aren't you Samantha's mum?' He said with a faint Irish accent. Swoon, swoon. 'Yes, I am. I thought I recognised you from the wedding!' I said sounding much more confident than I was, my legs no longer felt heavy, they had actually turned to stone. "I thought I recognised you too. I was only at the evening reception, I wasn't able to get to the wedding breakfast. You looked very beautiful. I mean you look very beautiful now as well!' He actually had the decency to blush. 'Thank you! And might I say you have a very fetching accent!' It was obviously the champagne that was doing the talking. 'I work at the hospital with Peter, different department, but we've been friends for a long time. I've only been up here about six months!' He went on. 'So how are you finding it? Do you like Newcastle?' I asked, when all I really wanted to ask was was there a Mrs Rugby Player?

Yes he liked Newcastle. He lived in Gosforth. No didn't get out much. No there was no Mrs Rugby Player! Just a very ex one. The conversation flowed. Still unable to move even if I had wanted to, the flush had started to recede and I felt a little bit more normal.

Adele came bounding up, two glasses of champagne in hand for us. 'Oh, that's great, I meant to introduce you two at the wedding, but I see you've managed to do it yourself!' She said laughing. 'Actually!' Mr Rugby Player went on. 'We haven't formally been introduced. Adele was loving it. 'This is Valerie, Val, not only is she the mother of my daughter-in-law; a very expectant daughter-in-law, just in case I hadn't told you! But Val is also one of my oldest and best friends. Val, this is Robert. He is one of Peter's oldest friends and now works at the hospital with him. Robert is also a consultant; in chiropody! That's feet just in case you didn't know!' She said laughing, that all knowing laugh that people had when it came to my feet. Oh my God, I thought to myself, he's a foot doctor!! He was saying something, but I was so busy thinking about my feet and the foot doctor I didn't hear what he said. 'Sorry, I didn't catch that, what did you say?' I asked. 'I said, no one calls me Robert, apart from my mother!' He was laughing. What he said next made my feet swell, my body overheat and my concrete legs turn to jelly! 'Call me Bob; Bobby. Bob Hope…………………….'

A Note From the Author

I hope that you enjoyed reading Show Me A Sign as much as I liked writing it.

It's something different. I am superstitious myself and always look for signs and indications!

And if you did like it; please spread the word; it is so difficult getting books out to the masses when you do it all yourself.

But I have a head full of stories so check out the ones already written and keep an eye out for news ones.

Love Gill xxx

Printed in Great Britain
by Amazon